# LOTTO

# LOTTO

## JOE McDONALD

LOTTO
Published by Ovation Books
P.O. Box 80107
Austin, TX 78758

For more information about our books, please write to us, call 512.478.2028, or visit our website at www.ovationbooks.net.

Distributed to the trade by National Book Network, Inc.

Copyright© 2009 by Joe McDonald

Publisher's Cataloging-in-Publication
*(Provided by Quality Books, Inc.)*

McDonald, Joe, 1931-
    Lotto / Joe McDonald.
    p. cm.
    LCCN 2008924694
    ISBN-13: 978-0-9814534-3-9
    ISBN-10: 0-9814534-3-0

    1. Swindlers and swindling--Fiction. 2. Lawyers--Fiction. 3. Lottery winners--Fiction. 4. Middle-aged men--Fiction. 5. Suspense fiction. 6. Psychological fiction.  I. Title.

PS3613.C38715L68 2009          813'.6
                QBI08-600116

Cover concept design by Kristy Buchanan

10 9 8 7 6 5 4 3 2 1

# REMEMBERING GLORIETTA

# ACKNOWLEDGMENTS

I would like to thank the following for their contributions to this book. Whether modest or substantial, their help is sincerely appreciated:

Christina Lee Boyer, Kenn Davis, Hal Ebbighausen, Royce Ferguson, Idian Reiss Flores, William Greenleaf, Ryan Hamilton, Kym Jones, Luis at Boquete Highlands, Beverly McDonald, Laju Nankani, Carol Orlock and the WUC Creative Writing Group, Phil Rach, Christie Salzman, The Seattle Police West Precinct and Harbor Patrol Unit, Isais Segundo, Robin Anne Tolbert and Mary Zakos

# PROLOGUE

The dark sea lay silky and quiet. Needle points of light from the houses up on the bluff a mile away flickered in the distance like little stars. The boat sat silent and still. Yellow shafts of light from inside the cabin fell onto the water, spreading away from the boat like a broken halo.

The explosion, like the instant brilliance of a strobe, flashed incandescence across the water onto the bluff and the silvery boat masts in the marina. The sound, with a strength and will of its own, rumbled and rolled through the marina like a harsh wind and echoed off the bluff. Resting gulls fluttered up from their perches.

The blast shattered the boat's salon door, flinging the debris out into the aft cockpit. The cabin windows were blown away. Shards of glass scattered across the water, and bits of curtain fabric drifted for a moment in the night air. The blackness that filled in behind the blinding flash of the explosion swallowed the ambient light from the city. Then a softer glow puffed from the boat's interior. In seconds the blaze spread from the salon into the forward stateroom.

A beach party of beer-drinking teens, alerted by the blast, watched as the fire took over the boat and cast a pleasant, weaving light on the surrounding water. A homeowner up on the bluff called the Coast Guard. Soon their helicopter hovered overhead, scanning the dying vessel and looking for survivors. There were none to be seen.

From Pier 54, eight miles away, the Seattle fireboat raced to the scene. It arrived as the still-burning hulk settled sternward and slipped away, yearning for the bottom and an end to its fiery torture. The firemen scanned their spotlights over the odd chunks of cabin debris. "Whoever was aboard went down with the ship," one of them said.

# CHAPTER 1

The two bourbon bracers he'd had at the Nite Lite took the sour edge off things. For several months, that had been his regular stop on the way home from work. Two drinks weren't enough to forget his troubles, but enough that he could look past them for a while. The rut he was in at work, his bitchy wife, and his failed marriage—they'd still be there tomorrow. The Nite Lite lounge would be there too.

Mike drained his glass and, for a second, thought about having another. Instead, he slapped a couple of bills on the bar and gave the bartender a wave. "Tomorrow," he said as he slid off his stool.

Two other men, regulars like Mike, were leaving too. Earlier they all had shared a few sport stories. Mike followed them out the door. Outside, one turned back to him. "Hey, man, it's a nice evening for a stroll down to Ivar's for some clams. Wanna join us?"

Mike smiled. "Thanks, guys. Maybe some other time."

"Sure."

Mike watched them amble off. One block to the south, the street angled off a bit. Just a slight change in direction, but enough that in a minute or so the two men would be out of his line of sight. Maybe that's what he needed: a change in direction. *The way I'm headed now is for losers.* He turned and headed for his car. It was parked in a lot on Virginia Street, three blocks away. Traffic had thinned out now, and he'd have an easy drive home.

As he stepped around the corner, he saw them about halfway down the block. A woman in tight jeans and a Mariners shirt was backed up against a parked sedan. She was shielding her ears with her hands as the guy shouted into her face. Maybe she said something then—Mike couldn't tell—but the guy started slapping her head, a real he-man, using both hands. Her glasses flipped off onto the sidewalk.

They didn't seem to notice as he approached, and he was just a few steps away. His steps slowed; he couldn't just walk by. As he fumbled with his cell phone, he wondered how promptly the police responded to trouble in that part of town.

The woman was the first to spot him. Her Orphan Annie eyes darted from Mike to her abuser.

The guy apparently picked up on it. He snapped around, silent for a moment, his squinty eyes sizing Mike up. "What are you lookin' at, asshole?" he said. Then he noticed the cell phone in Mike's left hand. Before Mike could punch up a number, the guy stepped over, grabbed the front of Mike's jacket, and pulled him close for a head butt.

The sudden move tipped Mike off balance, and the butt grazed his cheek. Before the guy's next move, Mike pumped a quick right fist up into his belly. The man wheezed as he lost his air. He let go of the jacket and stood there, awestruck, as if it were impossible that anyone would dare hit him. Mike was surprised himself. He couldn't believe he had done that, hit the guy like that. Juiced up with adrenalin, he powered off his right foot and put his weight behind a solid shot, again into the guy's midsection. That one doubled him up. The man backed away, moaning and cradling his hands to his stomach.

Still clutching the phone, his fingers trembling, Mike turned to the woman. "You want I should call the police? Take you home or something?" His voice quivered from the excitement.

She stared back, dazed by the sudden action. Then, catching her breath, she pushed away from the car and came rushing at Mike with both arms flailing. He couldn't believe it. He raised his hands to ward off her wild swings and began backing away. "Lady, what the hell are you doing?" Damn. He sure didn't expect this. "I just saved your ass, for God's sake." She kept at it, shrieking some sort of curse in sour, beery gasps.

2

Her boyfriend recovered, came up from behind, and slammed a roundhouse right to the side of Mike's head. He dropped to his knees then pitched forward, barely catching himself with his hands. Little sparks of light flashed across his vision. Boyfriend wasn't finished, though. He swung a clumsy kick aimed for Mike's gut that missed, but hit his left thigh. Then the woman got into it, making little jabs with her foot.

The sudden whoop of a police siren froze the action. A uniformed cop bounced out of the passenger seat of the cruiser and came around the front of the parked sedan.

"Hold it right there." He motioned as if he were going to draw his gun. In the next second, his partner came around from the rear.

"Okay, you two," the first officer said. "Step back toward the building there."

The guy shuffled back into the lee of a dusty storefront, massaging his right hand. The woman hesitated, as if unsure if she wanted to stand near anybody.

Mike's head cleared a bit, and he struggled to his feet.

"You okay, sir?" the officer asked. His nametag read "Davis."

"I don't know." Mike touched his right ear to see if it was still there. "Yeah, I guess so."

Davis moved over to where the guy was standing. "Okay, let's begin with identification." The woman looked puzzled. "Yes, you too, ma'am."

The bully explained that they were married and gave Davis his driver's license. The second cop took it and returned to the patrol car to run a records check.

Davis then asked, "All right, what's going on here?"

"Well, uh, my wife here and I were having a little argument." He pointed to Mike. "This guy comes along and butts in. I asked him to leave us to handle our affairs without his interference, and he hits me. Just like that—bam. Boy, I was hurtin'. Then he slams me again. Harder this time. I thought he was gonna kill me." He turned and gave his wife a look. "Ain't that right, honey?"

She flicked a glance at Davis and then mumbled, "Yeah...that's pretty much what happened."

Mike started to interrupt. Officer Davis held up his hand. "Just one minute, sir." Mike blinked and touched his ear again.

The husband went on. "Then he started in on my wife."

Davis glanced at the woman, who slid her gaze away to avoid his eyes.

"You're telling me that this man over here was so upset seeing you innocently arguing with your wife that he started beating the two of you up?"

The guy nodded in earnest, eyes flicking between the cops.

"Well, it didn't look that way when we drove up. You had this man on the ground and were kicking him."

"Well, yeah. I finally got a punch in and decked him. But I was afraid he'd get up and…" His voice faded, and he winced as if it hurt to talk.

"Uh-huh." Davis grimaced, expressing his doubt. He turned to Mike. "Any of that sound right to you?"

"No. The liar there was slapping the hell out of this woman as I was coming down the sidewalk here." Davis's eyes widened at that and focused on the woman. Mike went on and gave his account of the action. "Then shithead here hits me from behind and down I went. You came along just in time."

Davis stepped over and examined the woman for signs of physical abuse. The woman's face was a little puffy, but that seemed a result of lifestyle.

Davis's partner returned then and advised that there weren't any outstanding warrants for either of the couple. Davis told them to get in their car and leave. The parked sedan was theirs.

As he headed to his car, the husband edged close to Mike and muttered, "I'm not through with you, pussy kisser."

Davis heard the threat and started to say something, but then let it drop. He noted Mike's name and address and asked, "Think you should see a doctor?"

"No. I'm okay. Car's in a lot down the street."

"If you wish to press charges, a copy of our report will be at the records section downtown. I can tell you, though, that it wouldn't be worth the trouble." He paused, noticing Mike's deep breathing. "You sure you're okay?"

4

"Yeah. Just trying to settle down. I, uh, have never been involved in anything like this. Mixed it up…hit anybody."

"Yes, well, you might be a little more cautious next time. Courage is a great thing, but it's usually best to leave matters like this to the police."

Mike gave a wry smile. "Yes, I intended to."

"Well, if you're sure you're okay, we'll be on our way, then." Davis shook his head. "You just got a taste of what we face sometimes in domestic spats. Neither party is on your side."

They shook hands. Davis and his partner got into their cruiser. Mike watched them pull away and head down the street. He wondered if he should take the bully's threat seriously. He went this way to his car almost every workday evening. But that guy didn't know that. To hell with him. Then he thought about his car in the lot a few blocks away. He was already late for dinner, if Janet had even bothered to fix it. He turned and retraced his steps to a stool at the Nite Lite.

# CHAPTER 2

A little after eight, Mike pulled into the driveway and parked up close to the door on his side of the garage. He couldn't put the car inside because his mother's things were stored there. After she died, he'd rented a truck and brought them over from her assisted-living apartment. At first he intended to sell the nicer things to an auction house then give the rest away. Subconsciously, though, he may have foreseen his own future needs for some extra furniture.

He sat for a few moments, listening to the car engine *tink* as it cooled down. He rubbed the sore spot on his left thigh, felt his swollen ear, and considered the greeting that waited inside. "In full control," he said as he heaved himself out of the car and headed for the house.

He tottered for a step or two, then straightened his posture to an exaggerated erectness. He frowned, wondering why he should care what Janet thought. Their marriage was over. It would be official in a few weeks. He went through the garage and entered the house by the side door.

In the kitchen he noticed the smell of soy sauce and overcooked vegetables. Janet had already eaten. Her dirty dishes sat in the sink under the slow drip from the mixer spout that he was supposed to fix. Pantyhose were sitting in sudsy water in the other basin. Mike nodded. She was probably soaking Larry's cum out of the crotch.

7

He rinsed Janet's dishes and started to put them in the washer when he saw it hadn't been emptied from yesterday. Starting with the bottom rack, he emptied the machine and put everything away.

Sound from the master bedroom TV drifted into the room. "You back there?" he called. There was no answer. He was pretty sure she heard him, though. He sauntered down the hall and leaned against the bedroom door frame—her bedroom, now. He slept in the den. The spare bedroom was for guests. "We're keeping that room nice," Janet had said. He really didn't care. The den had a comfortable futon and a widescreen TV.

She was undressing. "I'm going to shower," she said in a vapid voice. He knew that meant he was invited to leave. "Tough day at the office, huh?"

She ignored his question. "There's some takeout in the fridge."

He didn't move as she slipped out of her bra, bewitched by the easy sway of her breasts.

"Well?" she demanded, her thumbs hooked in the waistband of her panties. "You gonna just stand there? Why don't you go fix a drink. Looks like you could use it. Just half in the bag. Finish the job."

"Good idea," he said, ignoring the sarcasm. He wasn't in any hurry, though. He wondered if he should tell her about the evening's dustup, then decided not to.

Janet stepped out of her panties and dropped her underthings in the hamper. Her figure was as good at thirty-five as it had been at twenty, maybe better. She patted her tummy, still firm and flat. She stood there for a moment as if to say, "Take a good look, loser. None of this is for you. Not anymore."

Wasn't it a bit strange? The love they once shared had completely ebbed away but, for him at least, the lust had not. He guessed that was a male thing.

"I'm listing the house," she said finally, noticing his look, his eyes a little droopy.

He perked up. "When?"

"Next week." She pulled a robe out of the closet.

"Will we agree on the price, or is that just up to you?"

"I think it will go for three twenty-five. I'll list at three fifty."

He thought that was reasonable. "Okay."

They had bought the house the day after their second anniversary. Janet had wanted a ranch-style home with a view. Several Seattle neighborhoods had expansive, in some cases territorial, views, but a territorial view commanded a territorial price. They settled on a 1950s, three bedroom, two bath rambler in West Seattle. Their view was a narrow glimpse of Elliott bay. The previous owner had updated the kitchen and installed inexpensive paneling in the third bedroom, which became their TV den. Mike was happy with their choice. They were handy to a neighborhood shopping area and close to the bus line. But Janet had never been satisfied. "I want to sell the house" and "I want a divorce" had almost been spoken on the same breath.

"That gives you this weekend to clear out the garage and basement," she said, pulling him out of his musings.

"Whoa now, Janet. I'll need a little more time than that. I thought I'd have a garage sale. Most of Mother's stuff is pretty good, worth some money. And I can't use all of it. Could you hold off on the listing for a few days?"

"No, Mike, and you're not having any damned garage sale. I'm not going to wait while you screw around with something like that. You can get off your sweet ass, rent a truck, and get that junk out of here. Take it to Goodwill." She stood there, holding the robe along her hip, not hiding anything. "And you better find an apartment, too. Have you even started looking?"

"Not exactly."

She knew what that meant. "Uh-huh. Well, the house will show better if we're not in here messing it up."

"So, you moving out, too, then?"

"Not right away."

"Oh…"

"But don't worry about it," she snapped.

He shrugged.

She noticed the side of his face. "You fall asleep on the sidewalk?"

"What do you mean?"

"Your cheek's a little swollen. Looks bruised."

He stepped over to the sink counter and checked himself in the mirror. "Must be allergic to something."

"Yes, common sense and ambition. It's a family trait. I should have seen that when I met your parents." She smirked. "Real winners."

Mike closed his eyes and set his jaw, thinking of a retort, then decided against it. "Yes, my folks were just ordinary people, not rich, but they had a good marriage…better than what we've done with ours."

Janet rolled her eyes to the ceiling. His compliant response obviously disappointed her. He got the feeling she liked it better when he snapped back. It stoked her enmity, kept the heat up—maybe edged out regrets and guilt.

"Yeah, well, we've reached the end of that sad trail. Now it's time for you to find a place and clear out your stuff." She paused, then added, "It's in your best interest too, you know. A neat house gets a better price."

Mike wrinkled his nose at the thought of moving. "The house isn't going to sell that fast."

"So we should just dawdle? That's your problem, Mike. You seem satisfied just poking along, going no place."

Mike shrugged. He considered slipping in a crack about her relationship with her boss, Larry, the key to her so-called real estate career.

As if her point needed reinforcement, she went on. "The market's peaking in this area, and we don't want to miss it, whether you're in the mood or not." She softened her look, and he thought for a moment that she might ease up. She turned toward the bathroom. "Now will you please get out? Go find your friend, Early Times."

Mike first met Janet at an outdoor campaign party for one of the local state senators, a popular Democrat with a lot of attractive young friends. Mike had been invited by his friend Ron, who had said, "Meet my hip friends. You might get lucky."

Janet was one of the standouts. As the party moved along, after the speeches, pledge forms, and volunteer sign-up sheets, Mike noticed Janet standing alone. A rare moment. He approached and introduced himself. He asked if he could get her a drink.

"Sure," she said. "A chardonnay, if there's any left."

He returned with two plastic cups of Mountain White. "This was all they had." Janet shrugged. They found a spot to sit and began with small talk. She later told him she was impressed by his easygoing manner, which bordered on pensive. He was a bit different from her other male friends. Mike was good-looking, had a nice build, a cool sense of humor and—almost to her disappointment—he made no overtures.

Two weeks later she called him at work. She had two tickets to the Repertory Theater and asked him if he would like to go. Mike was quite surprised. He didn't think he had made much of an impression or that she would have any interest. "Sure. That sounds great."

The line went silent for a few seconds, as if Janet was not sure how to continue. Finally she explained. "Well, I've been dating this guy off and on and…" He could almost hear her shrug. "Anyway, let's just say he's not in the picture right now. So if you don't mind…a last minute invitation."

"Not at all. I'm honored you thought of me."

The play was a delight and put the audience in a buoyant mood. Conversations sparkled at the intermission break. Janet spotted three girlfriends and introduced Mike. As they were returning to their seats he asked, "Did I pass?"

"I'll know tomorrow," she said.

After the play Mike suggested drinks at a neighborhood bar.

"Okay," Janet said. "Or we could go to my place. I have a nice Pinot Gris in the fridge."

Twenty minutes later their clothes were scattered on the living room carpet. They barely touched the wine. And three months after that they exchanged rings at the Shoreline Covenant Church.

The first four years together were remarkable, rousing, bewildering, and sometimes volatile. Perhaps the relationship burned through its initial energy too quickly for it to last. Like a spring flower with a brief season, the marriage bloomed and then, as if naturally fated, it slowly lost its beauty.

Mike didn't have an answer for the gradual withering, other than bringing in more money. And Janet was impatient to redecorate. "Carpet's not right for our décor," she said. "And the drapes look like something Lenin would choose." She had gone over swatches and samples with a decorator. Several items, including a sofa, had been selected. A promotion was due, and Mike was sure he would get it. The increase in pay would please them both. He counted on it. They both did. When the promotions were announced, though, he was not on the list.

Janet wasn't very sympathetic. "Shit. Now I have to tell these people to hold off on my redecorating plans."

After five months of off-and-on bitching over Mike's stalled career, Janet decided to get a job. She had been a steno in her father's engineering office before they married. She could have gone back to that, but she saw herself taking on a larger challenge: real estate sales.

"My friend, Frieda, is doing very well in a John L. Scott office," she had said. "And there's Larry Weston, with his own firm. He handled some deals for my dad. I met him once or twice. He might remember me. Just drive people around and show them houses. Hell, anybody can do that."

Mike agreed that a job might be good for her. The sense of accomplishment from work might make her feel better about herself and possibly toward him as well. He realized, though, that she wasn't doing it for self-satisfaction. She was doing it for money. She was doing it because he didn't earn enough to please her.

■ ◻ ■

Weston did remember Janet and happily offered her a desk and a good deal of his personal attention. Real estate sales wasn't quite as easy as she'd imagined, though, and commission income was slow at the beginning. But Weston did help, as he had promised. He sent a few listings her way and offered to assist with closings.

Mike had suggested that whatever she earned should be hers exclusively. None would go toward household expenses.

12

"You don't think my income will amount to much. Is that it?" she snapped.

"Not at all," he lied. "I'm sure you will have remarkable success."

"Well, fine. I'll just hold you to your offer, then."

The activity, challenges, and social contacts related to her new occupation softened Janet's disposition, at least for a while. She devoted more attention to her personal appearance and began jazzing up her wardrobe. She was a beautiful woman anyway, but now she was eye-poppingly glamorous.

It baffled Mike that as Janet's career blossomed, she became increasingly cool and indifferent, at least toward him. She was either too tired or too distracted for intimacies. Mike was offended and got grouchy as his advances were routinely denied. Perhaps her job was too stressful. The thought didn't compensate him, though. He began making occasional stops at the Nite Lite.

■□■

Not long after his marriage started to head south, Mike got a call from his mother. His father, who had a history of heart problems, was in the hospital and wasn't expected to recover.

When Mike arrived, he found his mother sitting at her husband's bedside, almost as pale as death herself. His father was sedated, but would surface for moments, mutter something, and then fade out again. Each time, Mrs. Collins leaned in close. "We're here, John. We're right here." It was clear how much her husband's appearance distressed her. She made faltering little pats on his arm or shoulder, as if that might dissolve the grisly set on his face. Two hours dragged by without any change. Soon Mrs. Collins, a frail woman anyway, was exhausted from the stress.

"You need a break, Mom. Why don't you get a coffee or something in the cafeteria. I'll be here."

She nodded, her face drawn by despondency. "Okay. Come and get me if he…" She didn't finish.

"Yes, I will."

Minutes after she left, John Collins roused. He opened his rheumy eyes, looked around, and noticed Mike. He squinted as if struggling to comprehend the situation. Then his lips edged up a bit at the corners to form a weak smile. "Tim…You came. My God…it's worth dying to see you, Son." His voice was low and gravely. He winced from the effort, then found his wan smile again.

"No, it's Mike, Dad."

His father didn't understand. "Mike? No, I haven't seen Mike…" His lids lowered, and it seemed he would drift off again.

Mike started to correct him again, and then felt there was no use to it. Maybe the delusion would ease dying. Tim wasn't coming back, but his father would never accept that—obviously not even in death. Mike felt an overwhelming pang of sadness, not at his father's imminent death, but at their pathetic and senselessly broken relationship. Feelings that he had repressed for years were now burning in his mind again. His eyes watered then, and a tear slid down his cheek.

Mr. Collins roused then as if in counterpoint to Mike's unspoken plaint. "Tim, will you look after your mother? She will need you now."

"Yes, Dad, I will."

"Good." His eyes closed, and he didn't speak again.

Mike went to fetch his mother.

■□■

After his father's death, Mike had urged his mother to sell the family home and move to an apartment, or better yet, a retirement home. His mother had been rather frail for years, and Mike felt living alone, with the house to care for, would be too much for her, even with his regular help. "You won't have so much housework, and it would be a chance to make some new friends."

She wouldn't have it. "I've lived here over half my life," she said. "My soul is in these walls."

For nearly a year, with Mike's help, she managed. Shortly after her sixty-ninth birthday, though, she began having "spells," little blackouts that her doctor confirmed were transient ischemic attacks. Mike insisted then that she move in with them. "We have plenty of room, and you should have someone around for company."

They gave her the guest bedroom and shuffled most of her furnishings to the basement and garage. Janet didn't say much at first. It soon was evident, though, that neither woman was happy with the arrangement. The air thickened under thinly veiled antagonism. Mike tried to conciliate, but had no luck. Janet became increasingly resentful while his mother became dour and whiny. Two unhappy women under the same roof was too much. It was decided that Mrs. Collins should move to an assisted-living facility.

"You're moving the wrong woman," his mother said as she and Mike were packing her things.

Mike nodded. "Yes, Janet has been difficult these past weeks." He considered his remark for a second. "Well, longer than that, actually. But I haven't been all that considerate, either. She's had disappointments—mainly in me—that I didn't respond well to."

His mother looked as if she had doubts.

Mike shrugged and went on. "I should be more attentive, I guess. More understanding. More like dad was with you. Maybe if I perked her up with some unexpected kindness…maybe that would help."

His mother rolled her eyes. "Dream on."

■□■

The next day, remembering his comment, Mike thought he'd drop by and take Janet to lunch, someplace special. He was there at noon. He introduced himself to Darlene, the receptionist, who seemed quite fascinated that he was there. "Oh my," she said. "Your wife just left. I think she's having lunch with Mr. Weston. They seem to do that on Wednesdays."

"Oh…thanks."

That evening, Mike was barely in the door when Janet let loose. "You checking up on me, Mike?" She was sitting at the kitchen table finishing her dinner. A Tony Roma's takeout box sat next to her plate.

"You mean at the office today?"

"Yes. Darlene, the nosy slut, said you were looking for me."

"That's right." He blinked. "Jesus, Janet, I thought I'd take you to Serafina for lunch, bit of a treat. I wasn't checking up on you."

"Yeah? Well, call first from now on. I don't like surprises."

"Oh…sure." He lifted the lid of the takeout box. Except for a few rib bones, it was empty.

■□■

The following Wednesday, at 11:30, Mike pulled into the lot across the street. He could see Janet's car parked alongside Weston's building. At a quarter to twelve, she came out, got in her car, and headed north. She looked great. Mike pulled out into traffic and lolled along about a half a block back. A few blocks up, Janet turned into a Safeway lot and parked. As he was sliding into a spot at the McDonald's next door, he saw her lock up and get in a white Cadillac. Probably Larry Weston's.

While Janet and Larry had lunch at a nearby Thai place, Mike went back to McDonald's for a Big Mac to go. Forty minutes later, he followed them to an older motel on Aurora Avenue.

■□■

Eight months later, depressed, morose, and lulled to apathy by her purposeless existence, Mrs. Collins lost her will to live. On the morning of her seventieth birthday, Mike's mother quietly found eternal sleep.

The funeral service was limited to a few old friends and a cousin's family from Wenatchee. Put in an uncharacteristically sentimental mood, and inspired by two morning pick-me-ups, Mike limped through the eulogy. When he returned to his seat, Janet set her jaw and nudged him. "Wallow in guilt if you like, but don't put any blame on me." He gave her a sour look, which she returned with flinty eyes. He knew, finally, that there was no hope for their marriage. It gave him a sense of relief.

# CHAPTER 3

The next day at work, though they may have noticed, none of his coworkers asked about the bruise by Mike's ear. He was glad. Les, the bartender, hadn't mentioned it either. Mike swirled the last of the bourbon and chips of ice in his glass and thought about having another. The crowd was light that night. There were just four other customers in the bar. Mike liked it that way. He had gotten to know Les, and when it was quiet, as it was, they could chat, Les polishing glassware and Mike sipping Early Times.

The Nite Lite was a working man's bar. Office girls and stockbrokers went to the trendy places, and that was fine with Mike. He got a generous pour at 1980 prices. The furniture and fixtures came from the eighties too, except for the curved bar—that took you back to the fifties. Ten loose stools were pulled up to its well-worn elbow pad. Little ceramic souvenirs gathered dust up above the liquor bottles on the back bar. A previous owner had collected some. Others were donated by patrons. There was a hula girl from Honolulu, a buffalo from South Dakota, a six-inch Statue of Liberty, a boy posed to pee in an ashtray, and a myriad of mementos from all parts of the country. Four small tables, deuces, sat against the opposite wall, and if the bartender was working alone, the patrons there would fetch their own drinks.

"Ready for another?" Les asked. He knew the answer.

"I believe I am." Mike slid his glass across the bar.

Les reached back for the bourbon. "Your wife ever complain about the hours you keep, Mike?"

The question prompted a lifeless smile. "She has, Les. She says she wishes I wasn't around so much."

"Oh." Les gave a nod and a perplexed smile as he poured. Then he moved down the bar to serve two of the other customers. He rang up their order and came back to resume shining the glassware. "You know, in my thirteen years behind the bar here, talkin' to customers, getting to know some, I've never had a guy tell me about his happy marriage. Now, I'm not saying that everybody that comes in has a bad one; it's just that the good ones I don't hear about."

"Well, guys who spend time in here, the boozers, they wouldn't sit and soak this stuff up if they were happy, would they, Les?"

"No, maybe not. But whether they are happy or not, I'm glad for their business."

"Way I look at it," Mike said, "some drink because they're unhappy, and some are unhappy because they drink. I haven't decided which for me. Probably both." He took a swallow. "Anyway, things will soon be changing. The wife filed for divorce a while back." Mike pulled in a full breath of the bar's filtered air. "Which is fine with me. We don't get along anymore, and she's making enough now I won't get stuck with alimony." A big swallow finished his drink. He tapped his glass for another. Les grabbed the Early Times from the back bar and poured an extra half ounce into Mike's glass.

Mike's eyes popped and he smiled. "Now that's a generous drink."

"That's a stockholder dividend."

"I'm a stockholder?"

"What I call some of my regulars, and you're the lucky one today."

Mike swirled the amber liquid in his glass. "Speaking of luck, anybody win Wednesday's Lotto?"

"One winning ticket. Some lucky guy hit it for twenty-three mil."

"Any money on your ticket?"

"Haven't checked."

"Let's find out. Got a paper?"

Les moved down to the end of the bar and picked up the rear-ranged pages of the morning *Seattle P-I.* He rummaged through the loose sheets till he found section B. The lottery numbers were on page two. Meanwhile Mike took a five-dollar ticket out of his wallet and laid it on the bar. "What's the first number?"

"Thirteen."

"I got a thirteen."

"Nineteen."

"Okay."

"Not me." Les looked at the next four numbers. "Looks like I have a three-dollar ticket, though."

"What are the last four numbers?"

"Twenty-seven, twenty-eight, thirty-six, and forty-two."

"Wait a minute…twenty-seven and twenty-eight?" Mike was smiling now.

"Yeah."

"Thirty-six?" His eyes widened.

"Yeah, and forty-two."

Mike blinked at his ticket. "Jesus, I think I have the winner."

"No!"

"Yeah. I can't believe this. Read 'em back to me again."

Les did. He read the numbers twice again before they believed it. Mike couldn't take his eyes off his ticket. "Am I dreaming this? That last bourbon put me on a trip?"

Les laughed. "You just became a damn millionaire."

Mike shook his head, still trying to believe it was true. He was afraid the numbers would change right before his eyes or that the paper had them wrong.

"Maybe your wife will be a little easier to get along with now. Think so?"

Mike wondered about that. His smile faded. "No…this is money I hope she never sees."

"You gonna hold the ticket till after the divorce?"

"I guess so. Probably should check with an attorney, though. Make sure she can't come back afterward for half."

"Good idea. You have a lawyer handling the divorce? He'd probably know."

"I haven't hired one yet. May not have to—there's not much to argue over. But if I do, I don't think I'd tell him about this anyway."

Les hunched his shoulders as if he couldn't see why. Then he noticed a new customer coming to the bar and moved down to take his order. Mike sat in a daze, forgetting his drink. When Les returned, Mike asked, "Know any shysters?"

Les chuckled and thought for a second. "Well, not personally. Mandy, next door in the pool parlor, had an attorney handle an injury case for her. Said he was pretty sharp. He might be okay. You could ask her."

On his way out, Mike stopped in to see Mandy. "Feinberg's the guy's name," she said. "Norman Feinberg. He's in the Smith Tower." She wrote it down on a cocktail napkin.

"Thanks. I'll give him a try."

# CHAPTER 4

Norm Feinberg's office was on the sixth floor of the Smith Tower. He shared space with Bernard Levine, another attorney. In addition to the rent, they shared a receptionist steno, Mary Ellen Bromley. Mary Ellen capably handled the work of both attorneys. She was fast on the keyboard, understood legal terminology, and easily maneuvered through their legal forms database. She was soft spoken, and Norm imagined if he ever met a small-town librarian, she'd be a Mary Ellen. Her looks were pleasant, but not striking. Working in her favor, though, she had a nice, narrow waist, well-shaped legs, and the supple skin of a woman in her mid-twenties. She was a little light on top, though, and avoided blouses or sweaters that defined her bustline. Norm wondered if she saw that as a personal inadequacy. She seemed shy toward men and was reserved, he thought, toward him. Why? He felt he was still in pretty fair shape; he had a slight paunch, maybe, but so what? He disregarded his reddish hair that was thinning on top, his modest height, or the wince his face took on when he wasn't smiling, as if he were thinking of a bad tooth.

The outer office reception area was furnished in a tasteful, understated way that spoke of efficiency rather than opulence. A trim, modern-styled leather couch, side table, and chair were set on one side of the reception area. A low table in front of the couch rested on an authentic Persian rug. The highlight of the room was a large oil painting—a marine scene—that hung on the wall behind the couch. Mary Ellen's workstation, a desk, computer, and credenza, faced it from across the room. The partners' private offices faced west with a nice view of Elliott Bay.

While he waited for Michael Collins, his 11:30 appointment, Norm fretted over the brokerage statement he had received in the morning mail. His IRA account, after a series of bad decisions and desperate trades, had plummeted to eighty-three thousand and change. It wasn't a surprise. He had known pretty well what to expect after the last conversation with his "full service" broker. But there it was, all spelled out, blow by blow. It was three pages of pain. Three pages with all the entries in the debit column. Greed and bad advice had eliminated his early retirement plans. He passed disconsolate eyes over the file folders on his desk. "I'll be screwing with this crap till I'm seventy."

His telephone jingled. "Mr. Collins is here, Mr. Feinberg," Mary Ellen said.

Feinberg opened his office door, forced a smile, and came out to meet Mike. "I'm Norman Feinberg," he said and offered his hand. They shook. "How can I help you?"

"Some legal advice," Collins said.

Norm nodded. "I can probably handle that." He led Collins into his office and motioned to one of his guest chairs. Norm had a large teak desk that was outsized for the room, but was needed, covered, as it was, with a scatter of papers and disordered client folders. Shelves of law books occupied one side wall. A filing cabinet, safe, and framed certificates on the other side wall put the room out of balance. The second guest chair sat in a corner piled with more folders. Two large windows took up the space behind his desk. Personal photos of people on and around boats were tacked to the wall on each side. The clutter almost gave the space a cozy feeling.

Collins settled himself while Norm closed the office door.

"Well, to begin, I'm the lucky winner of the recent Lotto jackpot." Collins said this as if it were almost an everyday thing.

The revelation stunned Norm. "What? You just won the lottery? Good lord, that's twenty million dollars." Norm moved behind his desk but remained standing, fascinated by Collins's incredible fortune.

"Twenty-three, actually." Collins nodded. "Nice, huh? But I'll take it in a lump sum, so it would be half of that."

"And now you want to set up a trust or something?" He seated himself up tight to the desk, attentive.

"No, not a trust." Collins leaned forward in the chair. "Here's the deal. I'm getting a divorce. The marriage just hasn't worked, so we're ending it. Neither of us are contesting it or anything like that, and the division of property shouldn't be a problem either."

Norm started taking some notes, writing them on a legal pad. "How long have you been married?"

"Seven years."

"You have an attorney representing you in the divorce?"

"Well…I have one in mind. But I don't want him involved in this."

Norm was a little surprised he hadn't hired a divorce attorney. "Okay. So what do you want me to do?"

"I'm wondering how I can keep the winnings out of my wife's hands. I don't care about the house or any of our other stuff, but I sure as hell don't intend to share the Lotto money. So if I wait till after the divorce is final to cash the ticket, could she do anything about it?"

Norm struggled to keep a neutral expression. *This clumsy bastard blindly falls into riches while I invest my way into poverty, and now the greedy jerk wants to cheat his wife.* He began tapping his pen on the notepad, as if ticking off the possible answers to Collins's question. It was a pretense. He knew at once how to resolve Collins's problem.

"You bought the ticket with community funds, I would imagine. You don't have separate property, do you?"

"No, everything is community. But I bought the ticket with my own spending money."

"That doesn't matter. The income, from which your spending money derives, is community income. Your wife would be entitled to half since the winning ticket was purchased before the final decree."

"If she found out that I won."

"It's pretty likely that she would. The papers announce the winners, and in your case, they would probably want an interview." Norm pursed his lips as an exclamation point to his comment. He adjusted his glasses again. Then a bizarre thought came to him. What if the bozo was somehow cheated himself?

"What if she signed a release?" Collins asked. "A waiver or something when we finalize everything and agrees that she has no claim to any other assets?"

"Well, first, she might be suspicious and refuse. But even if she did sign it, such a document wouldn't hold up. She could claim that the jackpot was a hidden asset and she is entitled to half. And she'd be right."

"Damn."

"Eleven million is a lot of cash. Wouldn't you be happy enough with half?"

"You'd think so, but our relationship has gotten so bad. She's become a real bitch. Fucking her boss and letting me know it." He let out a long sigh. "Jesus."

Norm's eyes popped at that. "I see." He began tapping his pen on his notepad again. "Well, there is something we can do here that should solve your problem." He paused, waiting for Collins to react.

"What's that?"

"We form a corporation. You would be the major owner. I would have a minority interest. My name would be shown as the winner on behalf of the corporation." He watched Collins's face.

"So I share the money with you."

Feinberg could see he didn't care for that. "My part would be my fee. The rest would be yours, and your wife would never know. Unless, of course, you went on a wild spending spree. You'd have to be careful about that. No Ferrari or yachts."

"A corporation?"

"Yes."

"And though I am the principal owner, the state wouldn't know?"

"Well, the Lottery Commission wouldn't. IRS will, of course, when the tax returns are filed, but you'll be filing separately after your divorce."

"Well, I guess that's what I want to do, then."

Norm smiled as he considered the temptation that had been advancing in his mind. It gave him a rush. "Fine. I will start the paperwork, then." He made a few notes on his pad.

"Will you need me to sign anything?"

"Not yet."

"Okay. I'll be out of town for a few days. The company is sending me to Denver. But if that delays anything, I could reschedule."

Perfect. "No, that won't be problem. When do you expect to get back?"

"Next Monday. Will the corporation be ready by then?"

"Oh my, no, Mr. Collins. It will take three or four weeks just to get the tax ID number."

"That long, huh?"

"That seems to be the norm. Are you in a rush?"

"No, I guess not. Just anxious."

"Well, if you want to keep this from your wife, it will take a bit of time. You'll just have to be patient." Collins nodded. Norm leaned back in his chair as if to confirm that the plan was settled. Then he said, "By the way. Where do you keep the ticket? I trust it's in a very secure place."

"I've got it with me. In my wallet."

Norm affected horror. "Oh my God, Mr. Collins. You could get mugged, have a car wreck, your wife could go through your wallet, perhaps innocently, and then see it."

"I suppose I could hide it at home, someplace she'd never look."

"Just as bad. Imagine a house fire—there goes your twenty-three million. No, I have a much better idea." He turned his chair to the side and pointed to a wall safe. "See this? It's on an alarm system that notifies ADT if there is a burglary attempt or a fire. Safer than a bank vault. Let's see your ticket."

Slowly, Collins got his wallet, opened it, and removed the ticket.

Norm noticed his reluctance; he expected it. "Now, here is how I handle matters like this." He took an envelope from his desk's top drawer, then sorted through a loose collection of receipts. "We'll put the ticket in this." He handed Collins the envelope. "Now I'll give you a receipt which identifies the envelope as your property." He wrote Collins's name on the receipt with the notation *envelope ~ ~ -MC-1* and handed it to him. Collins nodded, hunched his shoulders as if a little unsure, then put the ticket in the envelope and slid it across Norm's desk.

"Good," Norm said. "We don't have to worry about losing this now." He moved over to his safe, placed the envelope inside, and closed the door.

Collins looked at his watch. "Okay, if that's it, then I guess I'll be on my way." He paused for a second. "Now when should I expect to hear from you?"

"Like I mentioned, it takes the IRS at least three to four weeks to issue a tax number, sometimes longer. And you need that to collect the winnings."

Collins looked at his watch again. "I've got to get going. My lunch break's almost over. Oh, do you need any money today?"

"No, we can settle that later." An easy smile crossed Norm's face. He followed Collins out of his office. "I'll call when the paperwork is finished."

Collins retrieved his cap from the reception area table.

"Looks like you're a Mariners fan," Norm said.

Collins looked down at the cap. "Oh, not really. This was my brother's. We used to go to some of the games together. After he died I started wearing it." He shrugged and smiled. "Just became a habit, I guess."

Norm stood in the doorway and watched his ticket south move down the hall to the elevator.

Back in his office, he took the notepad he had been using and added some instructions for Mary Ellen. He tore off the top sheet and took it to her desk. "Mary Ellen, no rush on this, but when you can, prepare a simple will here for Mr. Collins. My notes give the details. Then set up a new client file for him and an invoice for three hundred dollars."

"I'll do it this afternoon. Should I mail the invoice today, then?"

"No, just put it in the file with the will. I'll take care of it all later."

Norm stood at his window, watching the street below. The scheme he had just set in motion excited him. But did he have the nerve to see it through? He hated considering questions like that. They impugned his virility. He needed to be bold. This was his chance to break out of the ego-destroying rut he was in. His decision gave him a feeling of renewal. "This is better than inflating my hours," he said aloud. "Much better."

# CHAPTER 5

On Wednesday mornings, Janet had floor duty at the agency. She would take phone call inquiries and handle the drop-ins. Most of those contacts never panned out, but the newer agents were required to take their turn. It gave her time to work on a direct-mail program that she hoped would develop some listings. Wednesday was also the day that she and Larry met for lunch and a nooner.

At 11:45, she turned her Chevy Citation into the Safeway lot on Greenwood and took a spot in the back row. Five minutes later, Larry pulled alongside in his Cadillac Concourse. He looked over and gave her a wink. Janet checked her hair in the mirror, slid out, and locked her car. Larry reached over and popped the passenger door for her.

It was almost a routine by now, no shyness or pretense. They were going to have lunch and screw. She sat close and put her hand on his thigh and left it there as he backed out. Over a glass of wine and a salad, Larry rattled on about some big deal he was closing and then chitchatted about the office and her progress, which had been good, though mostly due to the unusually strong market. Her commissions finally matched her husband's salary. She felt independent and superior.

Initially, Larry was hesitant to mention Mike's name or refer to him in any way. Janet, though, had no sensitivity about her sorry marriage. She commented freely about her loser husband and was completely free of any misgivings regarding her affair with Larry.

"So, how's Mike doing these days?" he asked.

"Talking big again. Says he's set for a promotion. The same old bullshit."

"Still drinking?"

"Oh, sure. I think he's cut back some, though." She shook her head. "But I really don't care. It's almost better for me when he's loaded. Doesn't get ideas."

"What do you mean?"

"Couple weeks ago, he started in about our sex life. I told him that it had died way back. He said he was sorry he missed the funeral."

Larry chuckled. "I could tell my wife the same thing."

Janet gave a wry smile.

They were both quiet during the short drive to the motel. Janet wondered where their relationship was headed, if anywhere. To the altar? No, she didn't think so. She wasn't really in love, but that didn't matter. Life with Larry would be okay. The money would be good. Eventually he would probably cheat on her too. Tigers don't lose their stripes, or something like that.

They used an older motel on Aurora. Larry parked by a rear unit. Janet waited in the car while he went to the motel office and arranged for the room. In a minute he was back with a key that was ringed to a green plastic tag with a big number twelve on it.

Janet sniffed as they entered the room. "Do they have any non-smoking rooms here?"

Larry chuckled. "That's what this is supposed to be."

"Really? What must the smoking rooms be like, then?"

"Sleeping in an ashtray, probably." Larry watched her open a window. "You want to leave?"

"No. It's okay. The air will help. I guess I'm overly sensitive."

"Mike smoke?"

"No. Oh, he tried cigars once. Bought a cutter and some guys at work gave him a nice pocket lighter. It didn't last long, though. Said he was beginning to smell like dried shit."

Janet slipped out of her St. John suit jacket and hung it in the small closet. Larry opened a pint of Smirnoff and sloshed a heavy shot over Sprite and ice. Janet took a chair by the nightstand and waited for her drink. Her first swallow bit; most of the liquor was floating on the top. "Whoa," she said, shaking her head. "That'll warm you up."

Larry smiled. "That's the idea." He sprawled in the room's other chair, pushed off his slip-ons, and loosened his tie. There was a ritual they followed. Neither one acted too anxious, trying to be cool. Larry sweetened their drinks and moved up behind Janet's chair. He stood there for a moment, took a sip of his highball, and began to lightly massage her shoulders and neck. Janet lowered her lids, smiled softly. She knew what would come next. Larry was pretty good at this stuff. He set his glass aside and used both hands on her neck, her shoulders, then down to her breasts.

# CHAPTER 6

When Norm returned from lunch, he saw that Mary Ellen had finished the Collins will. She had three copies and the file folder lying on his desk. Without bothering to read any of it, he folded one copy and placed it in an envelope. He wrote Collins's name and account number on the outside, then placed it in his safe, sliding it next to the lottery ticket. "Now to business," he said and clapped his hands together with a smile.

Norm logged on to the Internet and began a search for an offshore bank. He scanned through several sites offering private numbered accounts, but was dismayed to see that most took up to two weeks to approve new customers. Further, they required a copy of his passport, driver's license, credit card, and a current utility bill to verify his residence. He kept his passport at home. He could sneak it and a phone bill out of the house without Maxine's notice. That would be easy. But two weeks to wait for an account, that wasn't good. He was afraid he wouldn't have that much time. He had told Collins that it would be three weeks or so to set up the corporation, but would he get antsy and want his ticket back? Could Norm stall him for three weeks, or more?

Then he came to Equity Development's Web site. They could establish an account with the Barrington Bank in four or five days, it said. He e-mailed a request for their application. Next he searched the net for a Zurich bond broker. Most, he noticed, limited their business to specialties outside his interest. Finally, though, he selected a retail dealer and sent a message requesting information in connection with opening an account.

On his way back from lunch, he stopped at the IRS office and picked up a request form for an employer ID number. The clerk said if he sent it by mail, it would take about thirty days to get a tax number. But if he called their processing office, as a courtesy, he could get it over the phone. She gave him an 800 number. Quite pleased with his progress, he buzzed Mary Ellen. "Would you bring me the Toops file?" He thought for a moment. "And Paul Rosen."

"Are you sure you mean Mr. Rosen, Mr. Feinberg? He's been dead for over two years."

"Yes, I know. Just bring me his file, please."

Mary Ellen found the files and brought them in to him. "Are they reopening Mr. Rosen's estate? I thought that was all settled."

"Not to worry, Mary Ellen." He took the files and said thanks, but she didn't leave. She stood there, as if awaiting further instructions. He noticed that she was wearing a new sweater, a nice one, formfitting— must have been a gift. It was a bit tight, snug around her little tits.

"Will there be anything else, Mr. Feinberg? I was wondering if I could leave a little early today."

"No. Nothing else for now." He considered the afternoon schedule he was planning for himself. "Stay till four, okay? I'll be going out for a while. If I'm not back, turn on the answering machine." A carnal thought gave Norm a thin smile. The excitement of the day had made him horny. *Oh, yes, there is something else. Bend forward over my desk for a few minutes, Mary Ellen. I have something I'd like to slip into that little nest you have down there.* Mary Ellen blinked as if she could read his thoughts and scurried back to her desk.

Rosen's file, which included a copy of his estate tax return, gave the deceased's old address and his Social Security number. Norm copied it down. Toops had been one of Norm's deadbeat accounts. He still owed Norm money for work done on a DUI charge. He added Toops's address and Social Security number to his note, and after a moment of consideration, entered it on the IRS form as the corporate president. Using Rosen might be too risky.

Over the telephone, he passed along the info the IRS needed and was given an ID number for "Money Street Corporation." He was told to send in the form, completed and signed. He said he would.

Norm then closed the door to his private office. Mary Ellen didn't need to hear the next call, and it would be best that she didn't. He found the Seattle office for Washington's Lottery in the phone book and dialed their number. "Hi, my name is Wilson, and I have a small question for you," he said. "My cousin has won one of your drawings."

"Last Wednesday's Lotto jackpot?"

"Oh my, no. But she will get several hundred dollars, maybe more, I guess. Anyway, she has a little trouble getting around, and since she's setting up a new bank account anyway, she thought she'd go to the same bank that you use."

"She's opening a new bank account just to handle a couple hundred dollars?"

"Well, no." Couldn't she just give him the damn bank name? Twit. "She has to do that anyway. What bank does the lottery use for its payouts? It's not a secret, is it?" he said with a Shelly Berman whine.

"Not at all, sir. Lotto checks are drawn on Bank of America."

"Okay. Thanks. Good-bye."

He called Toops. On the fourth ring, Buddy answered rather tentatively. "Hello."

Norm wasn't sure he recognized the voice. "Is this Buddy?"

"Yeah, who's this?"

"Norm Feinberg."

"Oh…hi, Norm. Uh, what's on your mind?"

"Buddy, I've just had a real stroke of luck. Some big bucks. But I need your help. Be a very nice cut in it for you." Norm swiveled his chair around to face the window. He liked to watch the action on the street below.

"Oh, yeah?" Toops asked, a touch suspicious.

"Yeah. And we need to move on it right away. You're not too busy this afternoon, are you?" The dumb bastard was never busy.

"Well, no. Uh, what kind of money are we talking about?"

"Let's just say seven figures for your share."

"Seven figures? You mean like a million? You shittin' me?"

"Not at all." He turned back to his desk. "Look, I'm in my office right now, but I can get to your place by three or so."

"Okay. I'll be here."

"And sober, I hope."

"Oh, hey, Norm, you don't have to worry about that. I'm even working again."

"Really?"

"Yeah. Well, part-time."

Figured. "That's fine. I'll see you soon." He cradled the phone and picked up the folder he was using for his notes and the IRS form. He told Mary Ellen he was leaving, maybe for the day. "Be sure and turn on the answering machine when you leave," he said. She nodded that she would.

This was exciting stuff. Norm felt he had never been so alive, so intense. Dealing with flakes, losers, welfare cheats, and whiny litigants who were really the victims of their own bad decisions and stupidity had become a soul-eating grind. Stealing twenty-three million, now that was really something. You could be proud doing that.

Buddy lived on Thirtieth Avenue East, near Thomas. It was an older neighborhood that, because of its convenient location, was attracting young, middle-class buyers who were gentrifying the area. A mix of nicely renovated homes sat among several that still reflected years of neglect. Norm had been there once before, and Toops's place was one of the sorrier ones.

Buddy and his sister had inherited the house from their mother. His sister, who lived in Renton, went along with Buddy staying there, though he had done little to keep it up. As an occasionally employed wino, Buddy couldn't seem to find time for yard work, much less painting or cleaning windows.

Probably concerned for their own property values, the neighbors on either side kept Buddy's front yard up. They cut the grass and set their sprinklers to keep it green. Buddy seemed to accept it as his due. "Us Nam vets deserve a helping hand now and then," he would say. Buddy had been in the army for two years. The nearest he came to Vietnam, though, was Fort Hood, Texas.

Norm turned onto Buddy's street and began looking for a place to park. "Jesus, do these people ever move any of these wrecks?" Finally, a block away, he found a spot. Two young black boys watched him squeeze in up to the curb. He noticed them. He'd probably find his hood ornament and wheel covers gone when he returned. Maybe they'd sell them back to him. He waved. "Hi there, boys."

Toops was relaxing with his neighbor, a good-looking woman, midtwenties. They were sitting on her covered porch nursing beers. Was Buddy trying to coax her into something?

Buddy waved him over. "Hey, Norm. Come meet my neighbor." Norm cut across Buddy's freshly mowed lawn. "This is Lorene White, lives here next door," he said, tilting his head toward her house. "And this," he said, talking directly to Lorene, "is Norman Feinberg, my attorney." Saying it seemed to inflate him a little. He straightened up in his chair for a second then stood up, extending his small, soft hand for Norm to shake. Buddy was small all over at just 5'5" and 135 pounds. His face tapered to a narrow chin, which he sometimes graced with a goatee. One eye would sometimes wander independently of the other. One felt his mind was wandering as well.

"Like a beer, Norm?" Smart guy, offering Norm one of Lorene's beers.

Lorene had a pleasant face: nicely proportioned, pretty, but not ravishingly beautiful. Her raven hair was pulled back in a bun, exposing turquoise ear studs. Her complexion had a soft caramel tone, like Halle Berry. It was her figure, though, that froze Norm's gaze. Dressed as she was in shorts and a skimpy halter top, he was mesmerized by the deliciousness of it.

"Nice to meet you, Mr. Feinberg," she said.

Norm bounced his gaze from Lorene to Buddy then back to Lorene. "Yes. Nice meeting you too, Ms. White." Norm reached toward her and they shook hands. He noticed she wasn't wearing any rings. "You live here, just yourself, Lorene?"

She smiled. "For a couple more weeks, I am. This is my uncle's place. He and my aunt are in Afghanistan. He's on a job over there."

"Nice that they have someone to watch their place."

"Nice for me too. Gave me a place to live while I went to school."

Norm wondered what school that might be. "You go to the U?"

"Yes. Just finished."

Buddy leaned forward, looking impatient. "So what's the deal, Norm? How we gettin' all this money?"

Norm winced. Buddy, the dumb shit, was ready to blab and show off in front of Lorene. "Well, I got my car just down the street. Haven't had lunch yet," he lied. "Let's go to Starbucks. I can tell you about it there." He turned to Lorene. "Very pleasant meeting you, Lorene." He stumbled a bit as he backed away, his eyes on her titillating body.

■□■

They settled in a quiet corner with two double lattes. Norm sipped his drink pleasurably as if they had no other reason for being there. Buddy took one sip and then slid most of the drink down his throat as if he was dousing a fire.

Norm noticed, "Uh…you want another?"

"Nope. One's plenty for me." Buddy studied his nearly empty glass. "Guess I'm not a fancy coffee fan. Tastes like melted ice cream. Too bad they don't serve beer in here." He sighed and glanced around as though he might spy one sitting on the next table over.

Norm rolled his eyes and decided not to comment. "That neighbor of yours, she's pretty nice. Where's she from?"

"Panama."

Norm blinked as if Buddy's answer touched a nerve. "Oh…" He sipped his latte. "Wouldn't it have been easier for her to go to school down there?"

"I suppose. Said the U was better, though. Better reputation."

"So she gonna stay here or go back to Panama?"

"I think she plans to go back once her uncle returns." Buddy's attention was on two young women who had just entered. He watched them move up to the order counter.

Norm studied his latte. "Panama…huh. Well."

"This what we came here for, Norm?"

"What?"

"To talk about my neighbor. You got some interest there?"

"Don't I wish. Afraid I'm a little too old or she's a little too young for something like that, though."

"She's twenty-seven, which to me is just perfect."

"Twenty-seven and she's just finishing college?"

"Yeah. She had to work a few years to save for tuition. Her parents didn't have the money for a school up here."

Norm nodded and made a smile, barely moving his lips. He finished his latte and gave Buddy a steady look. "Okay, here's the deal." Buddy straightened up in his chair. They were finally getting to it. "I'm the lucky Lotto winner."

Buddy's eyes gaped. "Jesus, the big jackpot ticket?"

"Yes."

The two young women had their espressos now and moved to a table. Norm had to wait for a response as Buddy watched the girls settle themselves, getting a good look at leg. He turned back. "So where do I come in?" he asked.

"I'm getting a divorce. It's a sad story. My wife's been cheating on the side, and I've had enough of it."

Buddy's jaw dropped, and Norm spied the hint of a droll smile. His client liked hearing juicy stuff like that.

"Anyway, I don't want her to learn about it and then get half. To keep her from finding out, I want to set up a corporation and have the winnings paid to it instead of to me personally. You and I will be the owner stockholders. For helping me out, you will get a share."

Buddy locked onto Norm's eyes. It was obvious he had some doubts. "You're shittin' me, aren't you, Norm?"

"No. Why would you say that?"

Buddy tilted his cup side to side and watched the last of his drink slosh back and forth. "Well, Norm, if we have a corporation, won't your name be on record too?"

"Not with the lottery people. The IRS would see it, though, when we file our tax returns."

"Uh-huh." Buddy was uncertain. "So what's my share gonna be?"

"I was thinking ten percent."

"Ten percent? Gee, I'm savin' you from giving half to your wife."

Norm gave Buddy a hard, steady look. "That's true, Buddy. But there's a lot of guys out there—and I know several—that would be more than happy with a million dollars as their share of this deal." Then he started to get up as if he were going to leave. "I'll give you a ride back to your place."

"Hey, hey, hold on there, Norm. I didn't mean to get greedy here." Buddy was a little flustered. "You're right, ten percent would be fine. Yeah, that'd be just fine." He patted the table with the palm of his hand as if to clinch the agreement.

Playing it really cool, Norm opened his file folder and pointed to the IRS form. "Sign here," he said and handed Buddy a pen.

Buddy glanced over the form for a moment and then signed it.

■□■

Bank of America had a branch on East Madison, not too far from Starbucks. Norm pulled in to their lot and snagged the last open parking space. The New Accounts desk was just off to the right of the door. A pleasant-looking young man was there working with his computer. Norm moved up close. "I'd like to open a new account for a corporation we've just set up. We do that with you?" he asked.

The banker smiled. "Yes, sir." He stood and handed Norm and Buddy one of his business cards. It read "Business Banking Specialist." "My name is Jeff Nelson, and you are?"

Before Buddy could say anything, Norm spoke up, "I'm Norm Van Brocklin." Buddy blinked at that and tossed a quick glance Norm's way. "And this is the corporate president, Buddy Toops."

Toops didn't look like a corporate president to Jeff, it was obvious, but he extended his hand and they shook. Jeff pointed to his two guest chairs. "Have a seat there, and we'll do the deed." He smiled as if he had said something cute. "Van Brocklin? That name seems to ring a bell." Jeff rubbed his chin. "Politics, maybe?"

Norm shook his head. "No, I don't think so."

Jeff fished an account application and a signature card out of his desk drawer. "Okay, here's what we need for a corporate account. First, your federal tax number."

Norm broke in. "Got it right here." He flashed a tilted smile.

"Good," Jeff said. "Then a copy of your articles of incorporation."

The smile faded. "They're being prepared, but do you need them now?" he asked with asperity.

Jeff leaned forward as if to imply rigidity. Maybe the Van Brocklin tone was a little much. "Yes, to open an account, we do. Do you have a Washington business license?"

"No."

"You'll need to get one. You planned to do that, didn't you?"

Norm sighed. "This is just a dummy corporation. It will hold cash, but not actually engage in any business activities. I didn't think we needed a UBI number to open a bank account." He tried to mask the bulk of his annoyance.

"Yeah, we have to have it. A banking requirement." Jeff softened his tone, almost apologetically.

It was not going as easily as Norm had imagined. He closed his eyes and tilted his head back for a second. "You need all that just to let us do business with you?"

"I'm afraid so," Jeff said.

"Wonderful." Norm turned to Buddy and handed him the bank's signature card. "Sign at the little *X* there."

"Will you be on the account as well, Mr. Van Brocklin?"

"No, just Buddy here." Norm could see that seemed to perplex Nelson. "I just help with the legal work."

"Hmm." Nelson nodded a bit doubtfully.

Norm trudged on. "All right, if I bring this stuff in tomorrow, you're not going to tell me then that you need something else, are you?" Norm had jotted down the requirements that Jeff had given him. Buddy started to fidget. Norm noticed and sighed.

"No, what you have listed there should do it," Jeff said.

"Uh-huh. You know, it's simpler to get married now than to open a damn bank account."

"But a lot more risky," Jeff said.

# CHAPTER 7

The next morning, Norm went to city hall, where he completed an application for a master business license and was given a unified business identifier number. Before he left the office, he gave Mary Ellen a set of preprinted corporate articles with notations for filling in the blanks. She was to have two copies ready when he returned. Surprisingly, there was just a short wait at the licensing department. Norm thought that was a good sign. He paid the fee and headed back to his office. More luck, he found an open spot in the loading zone outside his building's entrance. He hurried upstairs for the articles of incorporation.

"Should I set up a client account for this Money Street Corporation?" Mary Ellen asked.

"We'll get to that later, Mary Ellen. I'm parked in the load zone down there, and if I don't hurry, I'll get a damn ticket." With that, he grabbed the corporate forms and rushed out the door, intending to get Buddy. He wondered if Buddy would even be out of bed at that hour, 10:30. Then it occurred to him he didn't really need Buddy right now. The signature card had already been signed. Better to leave Buddy at home. He headed straight for the bank.

■□■

While Norm waited on Barrington Bank, the days dragged, as if the atmosphere had thickened and slowed everything down. His focus was scattered. Files sat on his desk, the workups half complete. Mary Ellen became a nuisance at times, questioning his instructions and nagging about the docket schedule. And at home, he was either distracted or edgy with his wife, Maxine. His mood swung from the excitement of his bold step toward riches to a nagging ambiguity about the scandalous path he was taking to get there. Should he feel shame for the way he was going to do this?

Then there was Buddy. He called every day. "When are we going to cash the ticket?" he would ask. He'd whine while Norm lied about bureaucratic delays holding up the corporate license.

"Buddy, I'm just as anxious as you are, for God's sake. You think I'm dragging my feet on this?"

"Uh…well no, Norm…of course not. I just thought that—"

Norm raised the level of his voice. "I'll call you as soon as I get the tax number. Okay?"

"Sure. Fine. I didn't mean to upset you, Norm."

"Right."

Mike took his usual seat at the bar. Les spotted him, smiled, and came over. "Well, haven't seen you for a few days. You out buying a yacht?"

Mike chuckled. "No. The company sent me to Denver for a class on some new equipment. Just got back last night."

Les poured an Early Times over ice and set it on the bar.

"Ahh, just what I need," Mike said. He gave Les a little salute with his glass and took half down in his first swallow.

Les nodded. "You see that attorney that Mandy told you about?"

"Yeah, guy named Feinberg. Saw him a week or so ago."

"Any help?" Les started loading glasses into the washer.

"Yes. He's setting up a corporation. It'll be the winner. Though I'm the major owner, my name won't be shown on the claim form."

"A corporation, huh?" Les finished with the glasses and reached for a fresh bar towel. He began slowly wiping drink rings from the bar.

Mike lifted his glass to give him clearance. "Yeah. That's what he said they do in cases like mine."

"How many other stockholders?"

"Two, I suppose. The lawyer will be one of them."

Two customers from one of the little tables were leaving. They waved. Les nodded. "Thanks guys," he said and turned back to Mike. "Then he gets a cut?"

"It'll be his fee. He said we can work out how much later."

"He said you could work it out later? That seems odd. You still carrying the ticket?"

"No. It's in Feinberg's safe."

"You trust it with him, huh?"

"Well…" Mike had to think about that for a moment. "Yeah. He pointed out how much safer it would be there. Gave me a receipt."

Les refolded the towel and set it by the rinse sink. "Just so he doesn't go cash it himself."

"Jesus, Les, you think he'd have the balls to do that? I've got the receipt, and you'd back up my story if it came to a dispute over ownership."

"Yeah, guess you're right." Two customers signaled they were ready for another round. Les started to move down the bar then turned to Mike. "Unless he leaves town. With eleven million, he might be tempted and take off."

Mike had already considered that possibility but had concluded that it was unlikely. It would be too difficult for Feinberg to dispose of his practice and other assets in time to abscond with the Lotto money. And if he had a family, what would he do with them? He wouldn't just abandon everything. Where would he go? There'd be a trail.

◼◻◼

Mike had told Janet that he had hired Warren Gates as his attorney regarding the divorce, though he had not actually called him yet.

He even wondered if he needed an attorney. Neither he nor Janet was contesting anything, at least not yet. Outside of the house, there wasn't much to divide. He had a vested interest in his company's 401(k) account, but he didn't think she would go after that. And since she was making a nice income in real estate, there wouldn't be alimony. She wouldn't expect that, would she? No. With the prospect of big money, he was anxious to get right to it and settle matters. Hell, he would be easier to deal with. There was no need to quibble, but he shouldn't be reckless either. He called Gates's office and made an appointment.

Later that day, after considering his conversation with Les, Mike decided to call Feinberg. Just to check on his progress.

The lottery winnings fully occupied his mind. It was hard to think of anything else. He felt like celebrating, but oddly, he had been drinking less. For a reason that surprised him a little, he felt the need to exercise a measure of control. He imagined getting plastered and blabbing his good fortune to Janet or someone else who allowed it to get back to her. Was this what having a lot of money was like? It was changing him.

# CHAPTER 8

Each morning, like a diarrhetic man rushing for the lavatory, Norm would pop out of the elevator and quickstep down the hall to his office. Once inside, still wearing his London Fog, he would fire up his PC and check his e-mail. If Mary Ellen was in, he'd barely acknowledge her.

"Hmph," he'd mutter as he scrolled through his messages. Six days after faxing his application, the account confirmation arrived from Barrington Bank. Finally—thank God. He had begun to imagine Collins bursting in and demanding his ticket. Since he had his private offshore account, he could resume his nefarious scheme. It would be a busy day.

His first stop was at Key Bank, which had a branch on Madison Avenue. For several years, Norm had kept an account there unknown to his wife, Maxine. He used it for little personal expenses and adventures that he didn't want her aware of. He found a place to park a half block away.

"I'd like to close out my account," he told the teller. She checked his current balance, and he completed a withdrawal slip. He took the funds, $18,715, in cash. With the wad of bills stuffed in his briefcase, he headed for auto row on Aurora Avenue North. He eased past a GM dealer, then a Lincoln-Mercury store. A little farther along, he noticed that Town and Country Jeep seemed to have the largest inventory, with a display of new and used cars in shiny rows from the sidewalk back to and beyond their showroom.

He pulled around the corner on 143rd Street and parked. The main lot was divided. New cars were situated directly in front of the showroom. Adjoining to the south, with full exposure to the street, they had an array of better-quality used vehicles. All were priced beyond what Norm intended to spend.

He moved to the rear row. There were some nice-looking cars there too. Some didn't have a price sticker. Those that did were still out of his range. As Norm moved from car to car, a salesman stepped out of the showroom and came his way.

"Yes, sir," he said, smiling. "What can I help you with today?" He extended his hand. "I'm Willard Smith."

After a pause Norm answered, "Buddy Toops." He gave Smith a perfunctory smile and a weak handshake.

"Nice meeting you, Mr. Toops. In the market for a car today?"

"Well, yes, I'm looking for a used car." The salesman held his smile, and Norm added, "For around three thousand."

The smile faded a little. "Hmm." Smith's tone hinted at the difficulty of such a purchase. "And what are you driving now, Mr. Toops?"

"Does that matter?" Norm replied brusquely. His fuse was short. He always tightened up around salespeople.

"Not entirely, but it does give me an idea of your taste and needs in a vehicle."

"Uh-huh. Well, I just want something reliable. I don't care about the style or make, but three thousand dollars is my limit."

"I see, well, that really limits your choice. Reliability can be a problem in that price range. But if cash is a problem, Mr. Toops, we have excellent financing here. With any credit at all, we could fit you into one of these." He waved his arm like he was blessing his inventory. "Something you'd be much happier with." He smiled again.

"I'm sure. But I don't want financing. This will be a cash deal." Norm paused. "So what have you got?"

"Well, let's see what we have in back. Follow me."

The back lot held trade-ins that, because of wear, appearance, or both, the dealership preferred not to sell retail. Eighteen cars, a mix of makes and models, were lined up in two rows. Norm could see why these cars weren't displayed out front. If they could talk, he thought, they might say, "Leave me be." He spotted a maroon Buick LeSabre with a clean body, no dents or cracked glass, although the front tires were worn. "What do you want for this one?"

"Thirty-two fifty," Smith said without blinking.

"I'll give you twenty-seven fifty, if it runs."

"Sold. I'll get the keys."

Right away Norm knew he could have gotten it for less. Shit.

Smith came back with a key, and they went for a short drive. The interior had a mildew smell, and the engine ran rough until it warmed up. They pulled back into the sales lot. "Okay, I guess it will do. How about new tires?"

"Tossed in? Same price?"

"Yeah." Norm walked around to the rear of the car and checked the tires back there.

Smith followed him. "No. Be another one hundred thirty dollars."

"Huh." Norm thought of offering eighty dollars then changed his mind. "Guess I'll stay with what's on there, then."

Smith led Norm to the showroom and over to one of the sales desks. "Take a seat," he said. "I'll get the title." In a few seconds, he was back with the title, a registration form, and a second set of keys.

Norm began to count out the cash, laying it carefully on the edge of Smith's desk. He stopped at $2,750.

Smith noticed. "You need to add for sales tax and license," he said. "It comes to thirty thirty-five all together."

Norm frowned. "How about three thousand even?"

Smith thought for a moment. "Okay," he said.

Norm added $250 to the stack.

"Now we'll need your driver's license and your insurance card."

"What for? I'm paying cash," Norm said, a little surprised.

"I can see that. But it's a state law, Mr. Toops. I can't sell a car without evidence that you are a licensed and insured driver."

"Oh, I didn't know that. Mmm. Well." He wondered what to tell Smith. *I can't show you my DL, Willard, because I'm using someone else's name.* "Well, I'll have to arrange for the insurance, then, and come back." He started to retrieve the money.

"Hey," Smith said with his big smile again. "We can handle that right here. Put the coverage you want in force right now. Just one short form, and you can leave in your Buick. No problem at all." Smith pulled an insurance application out of a side drawer.

"Yeah, well, I'd prefer to deal with my regular agent on this." Norm had the cash in his hand and started putting it back in his case.

"Uh-huh." Smith's smile became a bit dry. "Well, let's call your agent. I'm sure he can bind coverage over the phone. Save you a trip." He pushed the telephone toward Norm. "You know his number, or you want me to look it up?"

"Yeah," Norm said weakly. "I think I better go to his office, though. Discuss prices and so forth. You know, make sure of the details." He could see that Smith wasn't buying any of it. "I'll do that and be back later," he said, cringing a little as if his shoes were too tight.

"Well, however you want to handle it, Mr. Toops, is fine, no problem. Now here's what you'll need for your insurance man. Just take a second here." From the Buick's title, Smith copied the make, model, and VIN onto a sheet of memo paper. Then he handed the paper to Norm. "There's one other thing I should tell you before you leave."

"Yeah?" Norm said hesitantly.

Smith pointed to his chair, but Norm stayed standing. "But first, that Buick is the car you want, isn't it? You haven't changed your mind about it?" Smith locked onto Norm's eyes. "Should we look at some other cars?"

"Uh, no. No, we don't need to do that."

"Good. Now what I want you to know is we don't keep those cars for retail, the ones you saw up there on our back lot. We wholesale them out. We do it in batches to the local pot lots."

"Pot lots?"

"Used car dealers that specialize in older, cheaper vehicles."

Norm nodded.

"Now the cars you saw up there, including the Buick, they'll be going out tomorrow morning. The buyers will be here a little later today making their selections. The Buick, being one of the better-looking cars, will go for sure. Since that's the car you want, we need to close on the money now and hold it for you while you arrange the insurance." Norm's eyes widened. Smith noticed as he started to fill out the seller's report. "What's your address, Mr. Toops? The address you want on the title."

Norm was flustered. Smith had him in a corner. He hated demeaning himself with transparent lies. He hated it, so he told some more. "Well, I, uh, I'll just take that chance. And, uh, thanks for your help here."

Smith made a sour smile and watched Norm leave the showroom and stride hurriedly up the street.

Norm returned to his car and drove to the Haller Lake QFC store. They had a few little tables and chairs up in a front corner of the store where one could sit with a cup of their special coffees. It was kind of a mini Starbucks with lower prices.

He bought a paper and began scanning the used car ads. He was pretty certain that a private party wouldn't give a damn about insurance or licenses. He circled three likely ads. There was no answer to his first call; then he noticed it said call after six. The twit should have stayed home today. He might have sold the car. The second ad's owner was home and lived nearby.

Fifteen minutes later, Norm found his house. The guy was selling a '95 Plymouth. It looked as good as the Buick he tried to buy from Willard. They settled the deal at $2,900. The seller was surprised, but pleased, to get cash—no chance of a bad check. He signed off on the title and advised that Norm should be sure and register the sale within fifteen days. Norm said he would do it right away. He meant it too. He wanted the records to show that Buddy Toops was the proud new owner. Pleased with himself, he headed for Buddy's place.

As if blessed, he found a spot to park right in front. He looked to see if Lorene was around, maybe having a beer on the porch or something. She wasn't, though. Too bad. He would like to see her again. He bounced up the steps to Buddy's front door and rang the bell. The house was quiet. He rang again. Then he noticed the nearest front window curtain eased aside a few inches. A figure, he couldn't tell who, stood behind it. The curtain was then released, and Buddy came to the door in his underwear.

"Well, hey, Norm, what's up? We going for our money?"

"Not right away, but I do have a little present for you."

"Oh yeah?"

"Yeah. Take a look." He pointed to the car.

"Look at what?"

"The car, dummy. The Plymouth. I bought it for you."

"You bought me a used car?" Buddy was nonplussed.

"Yes!"

"Well, that's nice, but why?" Buddy wrinkled his brow and squinted, obviously puzzled by Norm's surprise "gift."

Norm could read his thoughts. "I know what you're thinking. Why a used car when you'll soon have cash for something better, right?"

"Well, yeah."

"Okay. I've got this cousin, lives in the north end. He's in a desperate way for cash. He called to see if I'd give him a loan. I said I didn't think that would be a good idea. So then he asked if I could use a car or knew of anybody else that might be interested. I figured you should have a car, even if it's just for a few days until you find something better. It will be handy while we wind up our deal. I won't have to chauffer you around. But mostly I was helping my cousin."

Buddy seemed mildly amused by Norm's story. "Uh-huh."

Norm wondered if he was that transparent. "Yeah. So I bought it. Not a bad car either. Come on, put some clothes on and we'll take it down to the DMV and get it registered."

"Okay. Registered to me, huh?" he asked skeptically.

"Yes, of course."

"And I'm supposed to pay you back when we split the money?"

"Hell no. This is just a gift, a little extra for you."

It seemed a little strange to the DMV clerk: Norm doing the paperwork and paying the fee for the new owner, who just stood and watched.

Buddy noticed the wad of cash. "You cash the Lotto ticket?"

"Not yet. Got it right here. That's where we are going next, my friend."

Buddy beamed.

■□■

At the lottery office, Norm strode up to their teller window, waving Collins's winning ticket. An attractive woman came up at once to help. "I think there's some money on this one," he said.

Kym Jones, the clerk, took the ticket and scanned it through her terminal. "Oh my goodness," she exclaimed. Then she turned to the two other employees there. "We've got a big winner here. The jackpot ticket." They came up to the window, smiling and offering their congratulations. Norm smiled in return, and Buddy shuffled with nervous energy, as if he had to go to the bathroom. Kym opened the door to the interior office area. "Come on back. We have a couple forms to fill out. Are you the lucky winner?" she asked Norm since he was holding the ticket.

"No," he explained. "Money Street Corporation is the ticket owner, and Mr. Toops, here, is the president."

"Are you their attorney?"

"Well, yes."

"You can take the proceeds in your name and distribute them to the shareholders. That's how the single-purpose corporations usually do it."

"I see. I believe, though, we'd prefer to have Mr. Toops shown as the winner and let him handle the division of the money."

"Certainly," Kym said. "That would be fine."

Buddy obviously liked hearing that. Kym handed him a claim form and winner's information sheet. "You can fill these out at the desk over there."

While Buddy was occupied with the forms, Norm asked, "When should we expect a check?"

"Tomorrow morning, probably about ten."

"Tomorrow?" Norm showed his disappointment.

"Yes. We transmit copies of the ticket and claim form to Olympia. Confirmation will be done first thing tomorrow."

"Guess we come back then."

Kym nodded and smiled, "Best to call first."

■□■

On the way to Haller Lake to retrieve Norm's car, Buddy jabbered away about the grand possibilities he was considering for his share of the jackpot. Norm quietly indulged him while he considered the next steps in his plan, which wouldn't please Buddy at all.

Back at the office Mary Ellen handed him his messages.

"Mr. Collins seems anxious to see you," she said.

"Uh-huh. Well, if he calls again, tell him I'll call him tomorrow. I'm not going to be available till then." Norm spent the balance of the afternoon dealing with the tedious affairs of his practice. Preoccupied by his sudden riches, though, his progress was sketchy. He shuffled paper.

Finally, realizing that he was too buzzed to continue, he stacked his neglected work to one side and left the office. He had a few portentous matters regarding the boat to take care of.

# CHAPTER 9

While Norm was out buying Buddy's aging Plymouth, Mike was wrestling with his own distractions. Work to be done sat on his desk barely touched. Les's comments at the Nite Lite disturbed him. Mike didn't know much about Norm. For eleven mil, maybe he would take off. Was that likely? Hardly. Attorneys made big money and had substantial assets that they would never walk away from. Then again, why chance it? He decided to retrieve his ticket. He thought about calling for an appointment, but it might be days before Feinberg had an opening. And it would take only a second to drop in, get the ticket, and leave.

Mary Ellen turned from her computer and smiled as he came through the door. "I just need to see Norm for a second," he said.

"I'm sorry, Mr. Collins, but Mr. Feinberg is out, and I'm not sure when he will return."

"Later this afternoon, you think? Maybe four thirty or so?"

"Possibly," she said. "Best to call, though."

The door to Feinberg's office was open, and Mike could see that Mary Ellen was telling the truth. "Well, okay, I guess I'll catch him later, then."

"I'll tell him you were in." She jotted Mike's name on message pad.

■□■

Mike finished his shift and phoned Feinberg's office at five.

"No, I'm sorry, he's still out, Mr. Collins. But I left a message on his desk that you came in. He should be getting back to you soon."

"Uh-huh. He in court or something?"

"No, just working on other matters."

"I see…well, thanks." Should he be concerned? No. It was not unusual for attorneys to be out of the office. There were lots of reasons for that. He was not running off with Mike's money. No, of course not. Still, it wouldn't hurt to be sure. He decided to go to Feinberg's home, meet him there, and they could go get the ticket. Would Feinberg be willing to do that? Maybe he'd be offended, a client coming to his home. Oh, to hell with him! At least Mike would know that he hadn't absconded. Feinberg could add the time to his fee.

The phonebook listed a Norman Feinberg on Rosemont, the Magnolia District—a nice neighborhood. Mike found a spot to park right in front of the house. There was a similarity among all the houses on Norm's block. They were all nice, one-and-half- or two-story brick homes that appeared to have been built by the same developer, probably back in the thirties. All were well kept, and because of the view and nearness to downtown, they usually sold fast. An older woman was working in a flower bed in the next yard. She looked Mike's way as he left his car.

Four cement steps led up to a small stoop at the house's front entry. A faded plastic bell button had been mounted in the brick veneer to the side of the door. Mike pressed the button and heard a chime from inside. He waited. Just before tapping the button again, he heard a latch turn and the door opened a few inches. A woman with tousled hair stood in the narrow opening. She looked about forty. Must be Norm's wife.

She squinted as if trying to remember his face. "Yes?"

"Hi. I'm here to see Norm Feinberg. I'm Mike Collins, a client of his."

She gave him a perplexed look. "Well, Mr. Collins, this isn't his office, in case you didn't know. That's downtown."

Her snappy remark amused him. "Yes, I know that, and I'm sorry to bother you. But he's been out of his office today, and it's important that I see him as soon as possible."

"Important for who? You?"

"Well, yes. Anyway, I was hoping I might catch him here. Is he home?"

"No."

"Oh." He grimaced. "Are you Mrs. Feinberg?"

"That's right." She made a sardonic smile as if she weren't entirely pleased about it.

"Well, do you expect him soon?"

"Unless he has other plans, he usually gets here about this time."

"Well, I guess I'll just wait here, in my car, then." He turned his head to point out his car at the curb.

Maxine looked mildly vexed.

"Uh-huh. Look, I can't guarantee when he'll be home. You might have a long wait." She noticed her neighbor messing with her tulip bed and glancing over their way.

"I don't mind. If he's not here by six or so, wouldn't he call?"

"Yes, most of the time, but—"

"Fine. I'll wait till he calls or shows up."

She looked him square in the eye. "You're a client, huh?"

"Yes."

"Hmm. Well, I suppose you could wait inside." She pulled the door fully open and stepped back to let him in to the entry hall. To the left, Mike noticed there was an open stairway to the upper level and beyond that the entry to the dining room. On the right, two steps led down into a sunken living room where a large window faced the street. Just beyond the window, a brick fireplace was built into the corner. Its hearth was swept clean and there was no screen; it didn't look used. A collection of figurines, mostly cats, were posed on the mantle. A Homer Winslow print in an extravagant gold frame was hung above it.

The room was modest in size, but nicely furnished. Two upholstered chairs, a floor lamp, and end table sat in the near corner to the right. Across the room, diagonally from the fireplace, they had a couch and coffee table. A narrow trestle table with an ornate lamp and a few more ceramic cats rested against the wall behind the couch. The couch and two chairs were finished with the same fabric: a beige corduroy.

The far wall, which one faced when entering, gave the room its character. An expansive floor-to-ceiling bookcase took half the wall's space. A third chair, in a bright patterned fabric, and a large TV sat alongside. Mike noticed a faint odor of lemon, maybe from furniture polish.

Mrs. Feinberg pointed to the two matching chairs. "Have a seat." She then went across the room and settled on the couch. She saw he was still standing. "Be more comfortable sitting," she said. "Oh, and I'm Maxine, by the way."

"Hi, Maxine. I'm Mike." Then he remembered he had already told her that.

Maxine was wearing a short housecoat and bedroom slippers. He couldn't tell what was underneath the housecoat, but it was snug enough to see that Maxine had a nice, full figure. He thought of Bette Midler. They could be twins. Maxine's hair, a rich amber brown, was a little mussed, but maybe she wore it that way. A scatter of magazines and a highball glass about one-third full sat on the coffee table. The television was playing a *Roseanne* rerun, the sound turned low. Neither spoke for several moments. Mike started watching the TV.

"You watch the *Roseanne* show?" she asked since he seemed interested.

"No. First time I've seen it," he said.

"Well, I guess I'm a fan. I just love that woman. She, uh, she's got attitude."

"I've heard that."

"Mmm." Maxine nodded with a slight smile. Then she reached for her drink, mostly ice. She drained off the last of it and winced as if wanting another. She set the glass back on the table. "So you're a client of Norm's, huh? What's he doing for you?"

"He's setting up a corporation."

"Business deal, huh?"

"Yes, in a way."

"Well, like I said, I can't tell when he might get here. Sometimes it's pretty late." Then she added, "And he might not be in much of a mood to see you tonight anyway." She rolled her eyes as if to indicate that Norm's moods were often testy.

"I guess I don't care what sort of mood he's in."

"Oh my," she said. "The corporation thing's not going right?"

"It's probably coming along okay. He has some property of mine, been keeping it for me. But I'd like to have it back now."

"Uh-huh." Maxine looked down at her drink and noticed the melting ice in her glass.

"Would you like a drink while you wait for Norm?"

"Sure. What are you drinking?"

"Vodka tonic."

"Sounds great."

The liquor lightened the air. Maxine explained that she met Norm when he handled her divorce. They had been married for ten years, she said. Their relationship had become benignly indifferent.

Mike finished his drink and wondered where to set the glass.

Maxine noticed. "Would you like another? I think I do."

"Well, if it's not too much trouble. You make a nice drink."

Maxine smiled and headed for the kitchen. Mike followed as far as the door and watched as she topped hers off with straight vodka. That finished the bottle. She dropped it in the trash and fetched another from under the sink. She had just sloshed a generous shot into Mike's glass when the kitchen phone rang.

"Feinbergs," she said into the phone. "Yeah…Uh-huh…So when will that be?…Oh…Well, seems like if it isn't the boat, it's something else lately…Uh-huh…No, frankly I don't really care…Okay…G'bye." She hung up the phone. "Well, that was Norm." Then she put her hand to her lips. "Oh my. I forgot to tell him you were here. Sorry."

"He say when he would be in?"

"Yeah, he said he'd be pretty late. Said he was working on his boat. Be after ten, he said."

"Oh." He wouldn't wait till then, he thought, and was about to thank Maxine for the hospitality.

"Want more ice?" she said.

"Uh, sure." He guessed he wasn't leaving for a while.

She dropped a couple of cubes into each glass. "Looks like we're having a little party." She gave him a smile.

"I guess so," he said. "Why don't I call out for some Chinese?"

She gave a coy look. "Stay for dinner, huh?"

"Just a thought."

He could feel the drinks loosening him up, more than he would have expected. He also noticed Maxine wasn't as careful about her housecoat as she moved around on the couch. It had a tendency to move up on her thighs. She had good legs, and she didn't seem to mind if he noticed. She had nice tits too; he didn't think she was wearing a bra from the way they swung and bobbed in there. When she leaned forward to pick up her drink, he got a good view of cleavage. He could imagine where they were headed. He eased up out of his chair. "Mind if I join you over there?" He motioned to the coffee table. "Place to set my glass."

"Well, I think there's room enough."

He slid onto the couch and angled himself toward her. She smiled. He took a sip of his drink, held the glass for a moment as if he were admiring it, then, using one of the magazines as a coaster, set the drink on the table.

"You're a good-looking woman, Maxine. I don't think I'd be fooling around on a boat with you here." She gave him a sideways glance through lowered lids. "And I certainly didn't expect a nice party like this," he said.

She raised her eyebrows and let her eyes close for a second, as if to say, "Maybe."

He put his right hand on her shoulder and gave it a soft massage. She didn't move away. Then he leaned forward, looking down the front of her housecoat. "You ever let those boys out to play?"

"Not lately." She rolled her eyes.

"It's been a while for me too."

■□■

He woke a little after eight, according to the bedside clock. Maxine lay there facing him, the sheet twisted around her hips. She made a soft snoring sound. Those wonderful milky pillows, each with its single dark brown eye, watching him, he thought, as if they had sight. He got up, found his clothes, and began dressing.

In the dim light, he saw his shadowy reflection in the dresser mirror. He watched as if it were another person. "Proud of yourself?" he asked. Janet was right. He was a loser. And with a vodka headache and the taste of a strange woman in his mouth, he was slinking out of another man's bedroom—his attorney's bedroom. The irony amused him.

Sweet Maxine dreamed on. Should he wake her? Would it look bad for her when Feinberg finally came home? He fluffed his imprint out of the pillow—Norm's pillow, he supposed. Then he pulled the covers up over Maxine's shoulders. It looked like she just went to bed a little early. With her vodka habit, maybe she did that.

# CHAPTER 10

The excitement of sudden wealth gave Norm a restless night. Though he hadn't slept well, he popped up before the alarm. Maxine, the lush, was snoring away like a drunk bishop. She woke finally as he was coming out of the shower. She noticed his agitation. She was in a different mood herself, but Norm was too buzzed to wonder why. He had come home after ten and expected her to be cranky or at least sullen. She was neither, though she looked a mess. "I've just had a bit of a nap," she said.

Norm fixed tea and warmed a bagel. He scanned the morning paper but found his focus scattered. He read words without processing their meaning.

Maxine wandered the kitchen in her robe and bare feet. Her slippers, forgotten, lay under the coffee table. She used the last of Norm's tea water for a cup of instant coffee. "Well, you're perky this morning," she said with a hint of curiosity.

At first he didn't answer, as if he hadn't heard. Then he looked at his watch and folded the paper. "Yes, well, lots to do," he said as if to dismiss any further conversation.

She watched him flutter about, clearing his breakfast things, then checking his watch again.

"Later," he said and headed to the garage. In a second he popped back in. "Car keys." He made an ingenuous smile and was out again. He revved the engine and shot down the driveway.

■ □ ■

Norm was in his office by 7:30. Mary Ellen would come in at nine, maybe a little earlier. He checked his messages and decided to finish some paperwork. There was a pawn broker's estate he was handling, and his filings with the court were overdue. He dithered, shuffling files and making entries in his timesheet. The clients would be billed regardless of progress. Then it occurred to him, why should he care? He wouldn't be around anyway. The thought gave him a rush.

At nine, just after Mary Ellen came in, he called the lottery office. "Hi. I'm calling regarding the Money Street Corporation. The recent lottery winner."

"And you are?"

"Mr. Keitel, the firm's attorney. I was in yesterday with Mr. Toops, the president."

"Oh, yes, Mr. Keitel. Well, we haven't received any word from Olympia yet. I don't blame you for being anxious. Why don't you call back in an hour or so?"

Shit. "Could you call them now? Maybe they'll give you the okay to cut the check."

"No, they don't like us doing that. Call back later, okay?"

"Yeah, fine, I'll do that."

Norm paced around his office. It had never seemed so small before. What to do for the next several hours? He thought about calling Buddy to give him the timing. In fact, he was a little surprised that Buddy had not already called him, as anxious as he was. Norm stepped out into the reception area. He glanced around as if nothing were familiar. Then he moved over by Mary Ellen's desk. "Hold all my calls, okay?"

"Sure."

"If that Collins fellow calls, tell him I'm out." Norm paused. "And tell him that his paperwork will be ready in two weeks and that I will call him then."

"His paperwork? I finished his will several days ago. You have his file. Was there something else we're doing for him?"

"Just tell him that, please, and that I'm not in. I just don't want to see him today." Norm sighed and wrinkled his nose as if there were an odor in the room. He tapped his fingers on her desktop, a nervous little tat-a-tat-tat—punctuation points to his thoughts. Then, feeling a need to explain, he said, "I'm in the middle of a very important matter, and I just don't want to be disturbed. No calls, no visitors." Mary Ellen nodded and watched his nervous pacing.

Finally he stalked out into the hall and headed for the elevator. Downstairs, he bought a latte at the lobby canteen. Outside the weather was warm and sunny. He thought about taking a stroll, maybe checking out a few of the nearby art galleries. Yes, that was a good idea, a way to pass the time, but first he would call Buddy and tell him the check should be ready soon. Norm didn't know that for sure, but he counted on it anyway. And he would tell Buddy not to make any plans for the evening. They would be celebrating big-time. He carried his coffee drink back upstairs and closed himself into his office.

■□■

Notwithstanding Feinberg's nice house and attractive wife, Mike still had concerns about his ticket. He took a break from work and headed to Feinberg's. He strode into the outer office reception area as Norm was making his call. Mary Ellen blanched when she saw him.

"Hi," he said. "I need to see Mr. Feinberg for a minute." He glanced over and saw the door to Norm's office was closed.

"Oh. Uh…He's not in just now, Mr. uh…Mr. Collins."

Mike winced. "Has he been in at all since yesterday morning?"

"Well, uh, yes, for just a few minutes, though."

"You gave him my message?"

"Oh, yes. I'm sure he'll be calling you. Maybe later today." Then she seemed to remember something. "Oh, he said to tell you that your paperwork should be ready in another week or two."

"Yeah, I understand that. But I have another reason to see him now. When do you expect him back?"

"He really didn't say. Later today, I suppose."

That seemed a bit odd to Mike. Secretaries generally knew their boss's schedule. "Well, if you have a piece of paper, I'll write him a note."

"Sure," she said.

As Mary Ellen was handing Mike a notepad, he noticed that one of the line buttons on her telephone was lit. Someone in the office was on the phone, and it wasn't Mary Ellen; she had been typing when he came in. "That other attorney, Feinberg's partner, he here today?"

"No, he's on vacation for several days."

Mike looked over at Norm's closed door. Mary Ellen was lying. Norm was in there. In four quick strides, he was at the door. He decided not to knock.

Mary Ellen started to stutter. "Oh no, Mr. Collins."

Feinberg was standing at the window, talking on the phone as Mike burst through his door. He turned, obviously expecting to see Mary Ellen. "What?" he snapped, then noted who had entered. He began waving his free hand. Mike couldn't tell if he meant for him to leave or sit down. Feinberg quickly concluded his call. "I can't talk anymore right now, Buddy. I'll call you a little later." He cradled the phone and gave Mike a nervous smile. "Yes, Mr. Collins, I got your message. Intended to call you today. Been terribly busy."

"Yes, that's what your secretary said. What I'm here for now, though, is the ticket. I know your safe is very secure and everything, but I decided that I'd rather hang on to it myself." Feinberg's face lost its color. Mike went on. "Anyway, here's your receipt." He dropped it on the desk.

Feinberg glanced at Mary Ellen, who stood in the doorway with a puzzled look on her face.

"Well, okay. I'll get what we have so far." Nerves caused his voice to crack rather humorously. He moved to the safe and dug out an envelope. It had Mike's name on it. "Here we go," he said and handed it to Mike.

Mike felt immediate relief. But as he took the envelope, he noticed it had more than a ticket inside. He opened it to find a two-page will. He was stunned. This couldn't be happening. "Where's the ticket?"

"What ticket is that, Mr. Collins?"

"You know damn well. The lottery ticket." Mike felt his face flush as his anger started to mount.

Feinberg tried standing a little taller, as if to assert some measure of authority. "Lottery ticket?"

"Yes, my winning ticket. What have you done with it?"

"That's your will in there, Mr. Collins. No tickets."

"I can see that. You have another envelope in there?" He started around the desk toward the safe.

"No, no, Mr. Collins, I can't have you touching the safe." He slid his chair across the floor to block Mike's path, then he stabbed his finger at Mary Ellen, trying to give her some sort of signal. She didn't move. Mike pushed the chair aside. Feinberg was getting red in the face now. "Mr. Collins, if you don't leave right now…" Then he turned to face Mary Ellen and, in a stronger voice, said, "We will have to call the police." Then he pointed her toward her desk in a frantic gesture.

Mike was at the safe, and he started dumping its contents on the floor. There wasn't much to examine. He didn't see the Lotto ticket. He stood and faced Feinberg, who began edging toward the door. Mike cut him off and backed him into a corner. "Where's my ticket, you son of a bitch?"

Feinberg stammered unintelligibly.

Then Mike grabbed his necktie and jerked him forward into an elbow butt. Blood spurted from Feinberg's nose. He touched his face, saw blood on his hand, and started swinging slapping blows at Mike's head, which landed ineffectively on Mike's forearms. Soon Feinberg was winded from the effort. Mike stepped in close and shot a short uppercut into his stomach.

The air gushed out of Feinberg's chest in a painful-sounding whoosh. He sagged against his desk and sank to the floor.

"Now, you have two seconds to tell me where that ticket is or you get a quick trip to the street." He grabbed Feinberg by the back of his shirt collar, dragged him up to the window and bumped his head against the glass. Mary Ellen could be heard screaming something into the telephone.

Feinberg struggled for air and waved his hands for Mike to stop. It was several moments before he could speak. "Okay, okay. Give me a minute," he gasped. "Okay. I…uh."

Mike continued to hold him against the glass.

"Just let me up, will you, for Christ's sake."

Mike released him.

Feinberg slumped onto his hands and knees. "Damn," he mumbled. He tried getting to his feet then collapsed again. As he hunkered there, gasping, someone had come in the reception area and Mary Ellen was screaming "In there, in there!"

Mike heard all that too. He turned toward the door just as two Seattle police officers entered heading his way.

"Arrest this man," Feinberg shouted. "He's trying to kill me."

The first officer into the room, a black man named McCullough, motioned for Mike to move. "Step away from this man, sir."

Mike didn't move.

"Sir, I told you to step clear of this man." The second officer, a Caucasian with "Willis" on his name tag, moved in closer to Mike.

Mike decided to do as McCullough had ordered. "All right, okay. All I want is my property that this bastard is trying to steal from me."

"He's crazy! Arrest him! He tried to kill me, God damn it!" Feinberg tottered to his feet and began looking for his glasses, which had been knocked off in the melee.

Mike shot a look of hate Feinberg's way. "He's a liar and a crook."

"All right, both of you settle down here." McCullough glanced at Willis. "See what the girl has to say." Willis stepped out to get a statement from Mary Ellen.

Mike knew that all she could do was corroborate Feinberg's story. She didn't know about the ticket and would be no help to him. "Look, he has my property." He pointed at Feinberg. "And he was just about to get it for me when you guys busted in." Mike started toward Feinberg again. "Now where is it, you bastard?" he shouted.

McCullough moved to restrain him. Mike attempted to wave him away and accidentally gave him a light pop in the face. Willis must have seen it from where he was talking to Mary Ellen. He bolted into the room, and the two officers wrestled Mike's arms behind his back and cuffed him. McCullough, a little hot, threw Mike into a chair. "You went too far there, mister," he said.

Feinberg put a hanky to his nose and, with a sadistic grin, said, "See, what did I tell you? This guy's crazy."

Before they left, he gave the police a brief statement. "The man is delusional and deranged," he said. "Collins's marriage has failed, he has no career, and I think he uses drugs. We've had him as a client for two weeks or so. At first he seemed okay. But now you see how he is. He makes these wild accusations about all kinds of things. He's just not rational."

Mary Ellen listened in amazement to all of it.

# CHAPTER 11

Mike and his police escort had a brief wait for the elevator. When it arrived, a man with his back to the door was talking excitedly to a woman cowering in the corner. As the doors groaned to a close, the woman whispered something and pointed at Mike. The man turned, then moved a bit to the side to get a view of Mike's face. His eyes popped in surprise. "Well, looky who's here...it's the pussy kisser."

Mike jerked his head around. There, with a leering grin, stood the Virginia Street wife slapper.

The guy noticed Mike was cuffed. "You hittin' people in this part of town now?"

McCullough gave him a cold look, but the guy continued. "Here's somethin' to think over while your jackin' off in jail, asshole. I'm suing you for assault or whatever. Take you for everything you got."

Mike closed his eyes, struggling to stay in control.

"Yes, sir. We got a lawyer, and he's gonna clean you out, Mr. Collins."

Mike thought, how wonderfully ironic it would be if Feinberg was their attorney. He tried to boil the abuser's eyes with a glare of pure hate.

McCullough had heard enough. "Okay, pal, button it up. You're interfering with police work."

"Yeah, well, you got a real asshole there. Watch he doesn't hit you in the gut."

71

They reached the lobby finally, and as the elevator doors opened, McCullough and Willis hustled Mike out to their car. As they pulled away from the curb, Willis turned to Mike. "A friend of yours?"

Mike told them about the confrontation on Virginia. "Sergeant Davis from the North Precinct can tell you about it. He saved my skin."

■ ◻ ■

Norm cleaned up as best he could in the men's lavatory. His nose was swollen and bent off to the left side, but it had stopped bleeding. His right cheek was beginning to discolor, and his shirt was splattered with blood.

He called Nathan Bloch, his doctor. "It's an emergency," he told the nurse. "I have to see Nathan right away." Then he asked Mary Ellen to call a taxi.

"Okay," she said rather disconcertedly and made the call. "The taxi will be downstairs in five minutes," she said. Norm grunted. She watched as he held a wet cloth to his face then said, "Mr. Feinberg, what was that all about? Mr. Collins ranting about a ticket and then that, uh, that statement you gave the police. That wasn't really honest, Mr. Feinberg. Could you get in trouble saying that?"

Norm sighed; it was more like a moan. "Don't worry about it, Mary Ellen. It's not your concern."

■ ◻ ■

There were two patients sitting in the waiting room when Norm burst in. The nurse receptionist gaped when she saw his condition and hustled him into a treatment room. Nathan straightened Norm's broken nose and gave him a sample packet of extra-strength Tylenol. When asked about the injuries, Norm told him he had mixed it up with a drug-crazed robber. "This is in your office?" Nathan asked rather skeptically.

"Uh, yeah," Norm replied.

"So, what's to steal in an attorney's office? Your imaginative time log? He likes to read fiction?"

Norm sighed and lightly studied his nose with his fingers. "Nathan, you have a wonderful sense of humor, and it's expressed vividly in your fee schedule."

Nathan smiled. "Good that we understand each other. It's maintained our friendship all these years."

"You call this a friendship?" Norm said satirically.

"As close to it as either one of us will ever get."

"You are probably right. I'd smile, but my face hurts."

"You want hurt? Wait for my bill. Office visit, outpatient surgery, anesthetic, dressings, post-op observation, and examination. Oh, yes, and professional advice."

"Professional advice?"

"Yes. Stop representing drug-crazed felons."

■□■

Mike was wise enough to apologize to McCullough as they rode to the West Precinct. "I'm sorry about all of this," he said. "I should have been more cooperative. I lost it. You'd think you could trust your attorney. Well, mine has taken property that I entrusted to him and denies it. It's ironic, isn't it? I lose eleven million dollars and go to jail while he keeps my money."

McCullough chuckled. "And don't forget your friend there in the elevator. Sounded like he will be adding to your happiness."

Willis started to laugh at that, and McCullough's chuckle expanded to join in.

Mike considered the irony. "Yeah, this has really been my day. What could I do to top it off? Bribe you with a dime bag?"

Willis blinked. "Huh?" Then he realized Mike was kidding and they laughed together.

McCullough gave Mike a break. He wrote up the charges as a class-four assault. He didn't mention resisting arrest. Mike was booked into King County jail and placed in a cell with two other men—both innocent victims, they said, just like him.

■□■

Norm walked the short distance to the Macy's department store for a new shirt. He changed in the dressing room and tossed his blood-stained shirt in the wastebasket. On Third Avenue he flagged a taxi and returned to his office, wondering how soon he'd be seeing Collins again. If Collins was released today, he'd probably be back. Oh God.

Norm had a friend in the prosecutor's office. He called him the instant he reached his phone. Norm explained his request. "This guy, Collins, was arrested this morning. Assaulted me here in my office. I'm wondering how long you're going to hold him."

"You concerned he'll come at you again?"

"Yeah."

"Okay, I'll see what I can find out. Be a few minutes."

"Thanks, Dwight."

Ten minutes later, Dwight called back. "Looks like he'll see a judge this afternoon in Municipal. They tagged him for fourth-degree assault."

"Fourth degree? He broke my nose, for Christ's sake." Norm shook his head at the irony. "Okay, thanks, Dwight."

"Sure."

Norm thought he might get sick. Collins would be out that afternoon. He called the lottery office.

"Good news, Mr. Keitel. We have received the okay from Olympia and your check is ready. After the deduction for income tax, the amount is eight million six hundred twenty-five thousand dollars."

Norm forgot about his nose and called Buddy.

"Your voice sounds a little different, Norm. You getting a cold?"

Norm could kick the little shit for noticing. So he didn't answer. "I'll see you in twenty minutes. Be outside. I don't want to have to park, and we don't have any time to waste here. Oh yeah, do you have a bank account?"

"Well, sure. Checking."

"Bring your checkbook."

He checked his briefcase for the lottery file, saw it was there, and asked Mary Ellen for Michael Collins's cell phone number. She pulled the file, wrote the number on a Post-It, and with a puzzled look, brought it to him.

"I'll be out for the rest of day," he said as he lightly palpated his nose. On his way out, he stopped in the men's room down the hall for a pee. At the urinal he noticed his urine was slightly discolored as if from blood. Collins must have kidney punched him. He reached around to the small of his back, feeling for pain and wondering if he should ask Nathan about it. Then he realized he wouldn't be seeing Nathan ever again—or his outrageous bill.

■□■

Buddy was sitting on his front steps as Norm drove up. He hustled across the lawn that his neighbor had cut that morning and hopped into the car. He clapped his hands at the thought of the money. "Let's go!" Then he noticed Norm's new look. "Geez, Norm, what happened to your face?"

Norm's nose had started to hurt again. The Tylenol was losing its effect. And his mood, in spite of the forthcoming bonanza, had curdled. "Little trouble with a client. And I don't want to talk about it."

"Ooh. Looks like he may have got the best of it."

"He landed in jail, that's what he got. But I said I don't want to talk about it, okay?"

■□■

The state's regional lottery office was located in a modest retail complex on Corson, just a couple of blocks off the freeway. Norm pulled into their lot at a little after two.

Inside, they immediately received a warm greeting by the three lady staff members. "We wondered what kept you," one of them said. Norm winced.

Buddy had his picture taken holding a giant-sized replica of a lottery check. They snapped a couple of shots with Buddy and the staff, and were given some gifts and the big winning check. At 2:40, they left and headed for the bank.

On the way, Norm explained the remainder of his plan. "When we deposit the check, we will also fill out two wire transfer forms. You sign them as the president. One will put one hundred thousand dollars in your bank account." He glanced over at Buddy. "You brought your checkbook?"

"Yeah, got it right here. But why one hundred? I thought my cut was a million."

"It is. But you don't get it all at once."

"Oh?"

"Here's why. The press are going to want a story. They'll come to you for an interview. Now you're going to tell them that you are just one of several winners that are sharing the jackpot and that the others, for various reasons, want to remain anonymous."

"So?"

"So if you stick with that, after a few weeks things settle—the lottery thing isn't a story anymore—then you get the remaining nine hundred. You blab and let the truth out, my wife hears about it, then the single hundred is all you get. Your sticking with the story is how you earn your money. Understand?"

Buddy sat there, rubbing his chin, considering what Norm had just said. "I thought all along that a million was a lot for my part in this."

"Well, it is. But you've got to hold up your end now to get it."

"Right." Buddy nodded. "You said there will be two of these forms?"

"Yes. The remaining amount will go to another account for the time being."

Buddy obviously didn't understand the reason for that. "Huh."

■ □ ■

Full of himself, in spite of his beat-up look, Norm waved lavishly to Jeff Nelson as he marched up to the nearest teller. He handed her the check that Buddy had just endorsed and a deposit slip. The check stunned her. "My goodness," she said. "I've never had a deposit this big." Then she noticed the Lottery Commission logo. "Wow! This is that jackpot, isn't it?"

"That's right," Norm said. Buddy, almost wetting his pants and doing a sort of jig, gave Norm a coconspirator's chuck on the shoulder. Norm winced, then smiled as if he were hip to that macho crap. The teller had the deposit approved and handed Norm the receipt. Jeff Nelson had overheard the excitement and came over to offer his congratulations. They all shook hands. "Before we leave, Jeff, we would like two of your wire transfer forms to fill out and sign. Then, after the lottery check clears, you can transfer money accordingly. Okay?"

"Certainly."

Jeff had them take a seat in his office and gave Norm the forms.

Norm completed the form for Buddy's $100,000 and slid it across Jeff's desk. "Okay," he said to Jeff. "I have to get the identifier code for this one." He pointed to the second form, which showed Money Street Corporation as the beneficiary recipient, but lacked a receiving bank name or ID code. "But we'll sign both now. I'll call you when I get the numbers." Jeff nodded and Buddy signed both forms.

As they were leaving, Buddy asked Norm about the second form.

"I have to set up a new account. Can't use the one I have now. Maxine would sure as hell notice eight million dollars."

"Oh."

They piled into the Acura. Norm put the car in gear and pulled out into traffic. Then he smiled and turned to Buddy. "Now tonight you and I are going to celebrate big-time. We're going to Ray's for the top of their menu and all the booze we can drink."

"Hey." Buddy scrubbed his hands together. "Sounds great."

"Right." Norm looked down the street for a moment, half expecting to see Collins running at him with guns or a baseball bat. He heaved a deep sigh. He'd never experienced such conflicting emotions—gut-wrenching stress and giddy elation. "I've got a couple things at the office I have to take care of first. So I'll drop you at your place. Let's meet about 6:30. You can come over in your new car."

As they eased to a stop at Buddy's, Norm looked around for the Plymouth. "Where's your car?"

"Got it out in back."

"Oh. It's runnin' okay, isn't it?" he asked with a little concern.

"Yeah, fine."

"Good. I'll see you at 6:30, then."

"Right." Buddy knitted his brow. "Sure you want to make it Ray's? I was thinking Metropolitan Grill. Great steaks."

"Yeah, I know. But I have to meet a guy later at the marina. Ray's is handy."

"Okay. Ray's it is, then." Buddy climbed out of the Acura, stood, and held the door ajar for a second, looking in, studying Norm's eyes. He closed the door finally and headed to his house.

Norm pulled around and headed back to the bank. Jeff was back working on his computer as Norm moved to his desk and smiled. "Well, I found the information for the other bank. If that form is handy, I will complete it."

"Got it right here."

Norm filled in the missing information for Barrington Bank. "How soon can you wire the funds?"

Jeff scanned the form, "You're moving the entire balance?"

"Yes. We decided it would be simpler to do it that way."

"Well, it will take at least a day for the lottery check to clear."

"It shouldn't. It's on your bank."

"Well, then, tomorrow would be the soonest."

"You couldn't confirm the funds and do it now?"

"I can confirm the funds, Mr. Van Brocklin, but today's wires have already been sent. This order must wait until tomorrow."

Norm shrugged. He felt he should give Nelson an incentive for prompt service. "Well, okay. Now in a month, most of this money is coming back to Washington, and we will be making some large deposits in a local bank. I'd really appreciate your expediting this transfer, and then we can talk about your rates and so forth in a few days."

Nelson smiled. "I'll do my best."

# CHAPTER 12

Mike was given a hearing before a municipal judge that afternoon. The court was clearing business for the weekend, and the judge didn't waste any time. He ordered Mike released pending bail as posted for his offense, which in his case was five thousand dollars. The judge told him he would be notified by mail when further proceedings were scheduled.

Mike tried to convince himself that he would either recover the ticket or, if it had been cashed, then sue Feinberg for conversion. He also hoped to keep the news of his fortune from Janet.

He called her office. She answered with a sweet smile, thinking it was a client. He went right to the point and blurted that he was in jail and needed bail. She was stunned, but not hesitant to believe it. "Pull it out of savings and get a cashier's check," he said.

"That's damn near all we have in there. I'll get a bond instead."

"That'll cost five hundred dollars, Janet. Why would you want to do that when we don't have to?"

"The savings is half mine," she said. "Why should I risk it? You might do something dumb."

"It would be at risk anyway. If I did something dumb, the bond firm would go after the savings first thing."

"Oh. I didn't know that. Okay, I'll get it out of savings, then. But tell me, what the hell are you doing in jail anyway?"

He gave her a sketchy explanation.

"You were drunk, weren't you?"

"No."

"No? Well, what prompted you to lose your head and get in a fight, then? Though, now that I think about it, it'd be better if you were drunk. You'd have some kind of excuse, not just stupidity. And who the hell is Feinberg? He handling the divorce for you?"

"No. It's another matter…that he…uh—"

Janet burst in. "Another matter? You don't have any other matters, other than getting your next drink."

"I'm beginning to feel I'd like one right now."

"Yeah, I'll bet you do."

"Janet, look, I'm sorry I have to ask for your help like this, but could you please just get the cash and get me out of here?"

■ □ ■

Later that afternoon, she purchased a cashier's check. The bank teller smiled. "I hope this is for something nice," she said.

Janet stood rather dull witted for a second then just shook her head and left.

A public affairs assistant at Adult Detentions gave her directions to the reception area where she could present bailment. She expected it could all be done in a matter of minutes. It was exasperating when she saw the amount of paperwork involved. Why should she be doing this? It was humiliating just being in that place. A guy in a cheap suit sat across the room, and each time she looked, he was leering her way. Two seats away, a distressed, overweight woman sat disconsolately, reeking of alcohol—one of Mike's fellow travelers.

They met in the release area. She greeted him with a look of disgust. "Don't ever ask me to do this again."

"I wouldn't expect to."

Janet rolled her eyes. "Marriage to you has been a slow slide to the bottom, Mike. Now you're picking up speed. Can it get any worse?"

He didn't answer.

"So this attorney is doing some work on 'other matters' and you decide to beat him up, huh? Quarreling over his fee?"

"No, it was a business matter. A disagreement."

She pursed her lips and thought for a moment. "I guess I'm just curious, but I can't imagine you involved in any business matters."

■□■

Janet drove to the lot where he kept his car. Along the way, neither spoke. Mike was grateful for that. Finally, as she pulled to a stop at the curb, she turned and with cold eyes watched him climb out. He thanked her for her help.

"You know, Mike, you haven't done all that well career-wise these last couple of years. This criminal business might get you bounced out. You ever think of that?"

Mike dropped his gaze and studied his hands as they rested on the door frame. "I'm not really worried about that now. But I don't think they would anyway."

"Well, you should be worrying about it. They probably know you're a boozer. They'll figure you've started drinking on the job now."

He started to reply but didn't feel like discussing it. The lottery ticket occupied his mind. He nodded and closed the door.

■□■

At the lottery office, Mike introduced himself to Kym Jones and explained his dilemma.

"Well," she said. "This has happened before, where the legitimacy of ownership has been challenged. Fortunately, not often, though."

"If it's any proof, I can tell you where the ticket was purchased. I bought it at the Admiral Way 7-Eleven. Feinberg wouldn't know that."

Kym pulled the winner's file and inserted the ticket into their bar code reader. "Yes, you're right. That's where the ticket was sold."

"Has he picked up the check yet?"

"Who?"

"Feinberg, the attorney."

"I don't know anything about a Feinberg. The winning draft was issued to a Buddy Toops, who accepted the check on behalf of a corporation. An attorney named Kites, or something like that, was here also, said he represented them."

"Kites?"

"Yes."

"Was he about five six, average build, thinning reddish brown hair, wore glasses?"

"Yes. That sounds pretty close."

"That was Feinberg. When did he get the draft?"

"Today."

"Can you stop payment?"

"I'm not sure. I'd have to talk to my supervisor. You see, we can't be an intervener in cases like this. These disputes are settled in the courts. I believe that's where you will have to go with this."

Her answer didn't come as a surprise. "Well, can you tell me the name of the corporation and whatever you have on Toops?"

"Sure. That's public information." She glanced at the winner's declarations. "It was the Money Street Corporation, and Buddy Toops is the president. Here's his address."

"One more request: after the draft clears, could you tell me which bank they used?"

"Yes, I believe I could do that."

Mike thanked her, returned to his car, and called Feinberg's office. Mary Ellen was finishing her work for the day. At first she didn't recognize his voice. "Mr. Feinberg is not in just now," she said. "Who may I say is calling?"

Mike ignored her questions. "He expected back today?"

She hedged. "I'm not sure. Can I take a message?"

"How about tomorrow? He say he'd be in then?"

Then she recognized the voice. "Is this Mr. Collins?"

"Yes, it is, Mary Ellen. And I'd like to see Mr. Feinberg."

"Well, I'm sure he won't want to see you, Mr. Collins, after the terrible way you were this morning. I just can't believe what you did."

"He had it coming, Mary Ellen. That bastard has stolen valuable property. I could kill him."

She hung up.

After a shower and shave, Buddy found a fresh shirt that looked good enough for their little celebration. He popped a cold Coors and took it out to his back porch. He took a swallow and looked, almost in wonder, at the Plymouth. He still couldn't figure it out. Why did Norm buy him a car? He didn't believe the story about the needy cousin. Then he saw Lorene come out to dump some trash. He shouted over to her. "Hey, want to go for a ride?"

"Where to?"

"Anywhere you like. I got me a car now."

"Really. That Plymouth there?"

"Yeah."

Lorene dumped a sack of garbage in the trash can and crossed the yard over to Buddy sitting there on his porch. She gave him a conspiratorial smile, "Spending your money already, huh?"

"Well, that's the funny part. I didn't buy it. My attorney did. Gave it to me."

Lorene blinked. "Your attorney? That Feinberg fellow gave it to you?"

"Yeah. Strange, isn't it?"

"I'll say. What prompted him to do that?"

Buddy shook his head, "Tell you the truth, I'm not really sure."

"Anything to do with that money scheme of his?"

"Possibly." He lifted his bottle. "Want a beer?"

Lorene declined.

Buddy finished his in one last swallow and then related the details of the lottery deal that he hadn't shared before. Then he mentioned that he had some doubts about Norm. "There's something about him I just can't get my mind around. He brought me in as the mule for his corporation, which he says will keep the money from his wife. But how will that work? He gonna hide it forever? Or is he planning to take off? He does, he might not want to leave my cut behind. A million dollars is a lot of money for doing practically nothing. It's almost too much to believe." Lorene shook her head at the mystery of it. Buddy stood, set his empty can aside. "Want to take a ride to the bank?"

■□■

Norm didn't go to his office. He never intended to; Collins might be there. Mary Ellen seemed a little flustered when she answered the phone. "Oh, I'm glad it's you, Mr. Feinberg," she said. "Mr. Collins called. He says he wants to see you again. Can you imagine that? After what he did." Norm could imagine her pursing her lips and shaking her head at the astonishment of it. "I was afraid this was him calling again."

"Well, I want to see him too. Straighten out his misunderstandings."

Mary Ellen was flabbergasted. "You'll meet him…in person?"

"Sure."

"Oh, Mr. Feinberg, I don't think that's wise. He's a dangerous man. He said he could kill you."

Norm chuckled as if amused. "I'm not worried, Mary Ellen. Collins is just frustrated, that's all, making silly threats."

Next, Norm dialed Collins's cell phone number. Mike answered on the second ring.

"Mr. Collins, this is Norman Feinberg."

Mike was stunned. "Well, this is a surprise. Enjoying my money?"

"That's what I want to talk to you about. I'd like to propose a deal."

"Oh, yeah?"

"Yes. It was rash to use your ticket, but that's water over the bridge or dam or whatever. Anyway, I've decided that a lawsuit over this would be unpleasant for both of us and there's no telling how it might turn out. You might prevail, but then again, maybe not. I can tell you this from my many years dealing with capricious juries."

"I don't share your opinion. I'm certain I could establish ownership."

"Yes. Well, believe whatever you like. But what I propose would really be best for both of us."

"And that is?"

"We meet tonight. I will give you the winning proceeds less two hundred thousand dollars."

"That's your incentive for integrity?"

"Call it my fee. It could cost you that much to go to trial. And it would be months, maybe years, before you got a court date. This way you avoid all that and don't really come out behind."

There was a long pause as Collins thought it over—probably trying to find a hole in the logic.

"The interest on eight million would be about thirty-five thousand a month," Norm added. "That adds up fast."

"Okay," Collins finally said. "Where do you want to meet?"

"I'm out of town right now. On my boat actually. I'll be back about ten. Let's meet at the Shilshole parking lot."

"Ten o'clock."

"Yes. Park near G gate."

Collins said he would be there.

Norm then called Maxine. He explained that he would be meeting with Michael Collins, a client. Since he would be working on the boat, he was going to meet him there at the marina.

"Collins?" she echoed faintly. "Okay."

"Accordingly," he added. "I will be late coming home." He knew she didn't care.

"Fine," she said.

# CHAPTER 13

**M**ike pulled into the Shilshole lot at 9:45. He found G gate and took a space in the front row. Shilshole was the largest marina on Puget Sound. It was a boaters' favorite because it was on saltwater and only twenty minutes from downtown. Owned and operated by the Port of Seattle, the marina had a major restaurant, two boatyards, a fuel dock, pump outs, acres of parking, and slips for fifteen hundred boats.

Mike admired the view. A billion-dollar array of yachts, sail and power, lay silent before him, gleaming under the dock lights. Minutes later, he noticed a marina security attendant moving through the lot checking cars. He came up, saw Mike inside, and tapped on the driver's window. Mike buzzed it halfway down. "Yes?"

"Sir, you're in a space reserved for permit holders."

"I know. I'm meeting someone in a few minutes."

"Okay. Just so you know you can't leave your car here overnight."

"No, I won't, thanks."

The guard waved and moved on.

Periodically, Mike turned on the dome light to check his watch. At 10:30, he tuned the radio to a jazz station. At eleven he decided to leave. Feinberg never intended to meet him. It was a hoax to keep him from the office or his home.

As he was starting the engine, he saw a man coming his way. At first he thought it was Feinberg. As he drew closer, though, Mike could see that the guy was taller than Norm, huskier too. He came up and stood by the driver's side window. "Excuse me, are you Mr. Collins?" he asked.

Mike lowered the window. "Yes."

"Mr. Feinberg sent me. He couldn't make it."

"Yeah…so?"

The man grabbed the handle and jerked the door open. Before Mike could react, the guy reached in, took Mike's shirt in his left hand, and pulled him toward the door opening. "He said to give you this." He slammed a stiff right-hand shot into Mike's left cheek. The blow scrambled Mike's vision, and he felt a dizzying sickness as he was pulled out of the car. Before he went down, he took another punch to the head. "And this," the man said as he stepped in and slammed a sharp shot to the ribs. Mike collapsed on the pavement.

In a semiconscious state, he thought he was back on Virginia Street with the bully and his bimbo wife. As he wondered about Officer Davis, his head cleared enough to register pain and cognizance. "Oh yeah," he said to himself. "I'm at Shilshole."

He pulled himself into his car and sat for several minutes. The throb in his left cheek felt it would burst through his skin. His thoughts were jumbled. He'd like to lie down somewhere, but realized he couldn't. He had to get moving…get home…plan something .What was next? "Well, a shot of Early Times would be nice right now." He said to himself. "I should keep a bottle in the car for times like this." He made a warped smile at the irony.

■□■

At 6:30, his alarm pulled him out of a restless sleep. He got up to pee and checked himself in the mirror. He looked terrible and felt worse. There were bruises on both cheeks. He took two Aleves and called his supervisor's voice mail number. "I'll be in at noon," he said, and went back to bed. Later he could hear Janet as she dressed and readied for work.

At ten Mike got up and took a bath as hot as he could get it. Soaking in the warm water seemed to help. He dressed and called Feinberg's office. Mary Ellen said Mr. Feinberg wasn't in; then she recognized Mike's voice and hung up. Next Mike tried Feinberg's home number. Maxine answered on the second ring. She must have been near the phone. There was no point in hostility toward her or venting his frustration. He spoke in a friendly voice. "It's Mike Collins, Maxine. Is he there?"

"No. In fact, I haven't seen him since yesterday morning. You tried his office?"

"Just did. His secretary says he's out. But she could be lying." Mike groaned; breathing was a pain. "And he hasn't called you, huh?"

"No. Just now I thought this call might be him." Then, in a skeptical voice, she added, "I thought you were going to meet him last night."

Mike grimaced. "Yes, at Shilshole. He didn't show up, but one of his goons did."

Maxine didn't understand and just said, "Oh. Well, he said he was going to do some work on his boat. That's probably where he was. Spent the night there too, I guess."

Mike doubted it.

"This about something he has been keeping for you?"

"Yes, a valuable item I left with him for safekeeping, and now I want it back."

"A valuable item?"

"My winning lottery ticket."

He made it to the office by noon, as he said he would. As he was hanging his jacket, his supervisor came over. He started to say something about attendance when he saw Mike's face. "Jesus, what happened to you?"

"Got mugged."

"In a bar?"

Mike sighed. His drinking was always blamed for everything. "No. I was actually in my car."

"Huh?"

"Yeah. Out at Shilshole. Don't go there at night. Dangerous place." His supervisor shook his head and walked away.

■□■

After his shift at Qwest, Mike headed for Toops's place. There was a parking spot right in front. He climbed the three steps to the porch and rang the bell. When he received no answer, he rang again. Then he peered in the front window. There were no signs of life that he could see. He walked around the house and tried the back door. It wasn't locked.

As he was about to enter, a young woman in the next yard startled him by calling out. "You looking for someone?"

"Uh, yes. I'm looking for Mr. Toops."

"You try his front doorbell?"

"Yes."

"Well, since there was no answer, what did that tell you?"

This was a saucy young lady. Good-looking too. "I thought he might be out back here and not hear his bell."

"Oh. Well, he's not home just now."

"You know where I might find him? He at work?"

She chuckled. "No, he's not at work. I'm sure of that."

Mike could see that the woman didn't know where Toops was or didn't care to say if she did. Toops had left, taken off, maybe for good. He might even be with Feinberg. The two of them could be living big on the Lotto money. The thought made him a little dizzy, almost nauseated. He was fucked. He wondered if there might be any clues in the house as to where Toops had gone. The sweetie would call the police first thing if he broke in, though. He had to get her cooperation. "Are you a friend of Mr. Toops?" he asked.

"Well, we're neighbors. And I guess you could say friends." She paused for a moment. "You don't know Buddy, do you?"

"No. I don't. But I'm concerned for his welfare. I'm afraid that he has been taken in on an attorney's illicit scheme, and his life is in danger." He noticed the little giveaway signals in her face. She had some concerns too.

She studied Mike's face. "Looks like you've been in an accident."

Mike didn't want to bother explaining. "Yes."

"Uh-huh. So why should you be concerned about Buddy?" she asked.

"Because this attorney, Feinberg, has victimized me as well. I know he will do the same to Buddy." Then, to add urgency, he said, "We must warn him at once." Mike noticed her doubt.

Finally, she said, "Feinberg did that to you?"

"No, a hired goon did."

"Oh. And now you are here to warn Buddy?"

"Yes. Do you suppose there may be some clue inside as to where he has gone?"

"Possibly. I don't suppose Buddy would mind. I should feed the cat anyway."

Mike introduced himself as the woman came up on the porch. "I'm Michael Collins. Just call me Mike." He extended his hand.

"I'm Lorene, Lorene White," she said and shook his hand.

In the kitchen, they found travel brochures sitting on the table next to an ashtray full of pistachio shells. Mike moaned. A hotel in Cuenca, Ecuador, was circled in ink. Lorene nodded. "He left me a note, said he was going to Ecuador. Guess he did. It seemed strange, though. He didn't say anything about it yesterday. And he really loved Gigi Girl, his cat. I couldn't believe he would leave and not ask me to take care of her." At the mention of her name, Gigi Girl appeared from the bedroom hall. She came right to Lorene and rubbed against her leg. "You hungry, girl?" Lorene asked the cat.

Mike stared blankly at the brochure. Had his money gone to Ecuador? He looked around the room while Lorene shook some kibbles into the cat's dish.

"Looks like he left in a rush, doesn't it? Dishes in the sink. Trash in the waste can."

"Well, Buddy never was too neat. But it does seem odd, just leaving the house like this."

Without looking for her approval, Mike began checking the other rooms. The back bedroom didn't appear to be used except for storage. A dusty desk, card table, and unmatched chairs sat pushed up against the wall. Heavy drapes and a shade on each window darkened the front bedroom. Apparently Buddy didn't like to wake early. Mike found the light switch. The bed was unmade, and a loose pile of clothes had been tossed on a chair. The bedroom closet held some more clothes, not much, though, and maybe not worth taking. Two suitcases were stacked up on the overhead shelf. Mike noticed an electric shaver, toothbrush, and some personal toiletries in the bathroom. He called to Lorene, "His shaver and stuff are still here."

She came into the bedroom, looked in the open closet, then went into the bathroom. "You'd think he'd take them with him. And his suitcases are still in the closet."

"I don't think Buddy has gone to Ecuador, Lorene. I don't think he really planned to go anywhere."

"But why would he leave that note?"

"Maybe he didn't leave it."

"You think his attorney left it?"

"He could have."

"Buddy said he and his attorney were sharing the Lotto jackpot. You know anything about that?"

"Yes. My ticket was the winner." Lorene blinked. "And Feinberg was keeping it in his safe while he did some paperwork for me. He took the ticket and cashed it."

"You gave the winning ticket to Feinberg?"

Mike sighed. "Yeah. Stupid, huh?"

"Seems that it was." They went back into the kitchen. Lorene picked up the brochure for Ecuador. "You think this could be a plant too?"

"I don't know. Did he ever talk about going to South America?"

"No. In fact, he said if he had the money, he'd sell the house and go to Vegas or maybe Hawaii. I can't see him going to Ecuador. I doubt he even knows where it is. You think he's with the attorney?"

"If he is, he must have known the ticket was stolen. I can't see that he'd have any reason to leave otherwise. Which would also mean that Buddy got a hefty share of the money."

"Buddy said he was getting one million."

"Well, that's enough to leave home for. When did he tell you this?"

"He mentioned getting some big money several days ago, and then yesterday he said it would be a million."

"He might be with Feinberg, then, but I doubt it will be for long. Feinberg won't have Buddy tagging along. From the looks of things here, I'd say they aren't the type to be traveling pals. Buddy'll get dumped or even worse."

"Worse? You mean like killed?"

"Possibly. Especially if Feinberg decides to retrieve Buddy's share."

"Huh." Lorene slid her gaze to Gigi Girl then said, "He wasn't really a friend. I kinda liked him, though. He had a funny sense of humor. Sometimes we'd have a beer together after I came home from class. I hate to think he's in serious danger."

"Yeah, well, let's hope Buddy is just off on a little spree and will be back soon. You'd think he'd take his shaver, though. He ever explain why he was involved in the first place?"

"His attorney told him he was setting up a corporation which would somehow keep his wife from learning about the money." Mike winced. Lorene went on. "That seemed odd to me, but anyway, he needed participants other than himself, so he used Buddy. For his part, Buddy said he was getting one million dollars. Unbelievable, isn't it?"

"Yes…and Buddy believed that? Believed what Feinberg said?"

"He had some doubts. He thought Feinberg might take off with all the cash, including his share."

"If I were Buddy, I'd think that too. But it looks like Buddy made out after all…got his share. Otherwise he'd be here."

"I suppose."

"Well, thanks, Lorene. I appreciate your telling me all this."

She nodded. "So what do you plan to do?"

"Try and find Feinberg. Buddy may know where he is…or Feinberg's wife. If she's involved, she'd know. Right now those two are the only people that would have a clue." He shrugged. "So if you see Buddy, I'd appreciate it if you gave me a call." He wrote his cell number on a Qwest card and handed it to her.

"Okay," she said.

■□■

Larry had been attending a convention at the Salishan resort in Oregon. He found the meetings humdrum and spent most of his day on the golf course with three buddies from Century Twenty-One. His wife, Felicia, and two sons came down on Sunday after the convention closed. Together they spent the next four days sightseeing the Oregon coast.

Larry and the boys were gregarious, a welcome change from the often cantankerous temperament at home. Felicia seemed a bit aroused by it. Larry mistakenly fancied a carnal aspect to her mood until she coldly advised him that sex would diminish a family event. "This is a time to enjoy the boys, Larry. Even if we're not all in the same room, my thoughts are with them. Sneaking in a quickie would be so prurient."

"Oh," he said. He was thinking of more than a quickie.

So Larry was ready for action when he returned to the office, action in the sack with Janet. He was a little extra sweet about it and took her to Palisades for lunch. They shared a planked salmon entrée and a bottle of wine. Janet might have mistaken his lust for affection and entertained thoughts of a future as Mrs. Weston. To heighten his interest, at the motel she suggested a shower together. She'd give him head; then after a couple of drinks, they could do an encore in the bed. Larry was ecstatic.

# CHAPTER 14

Norm had spent a few nights on the boat in its slip before, but never on the eve of a workday. He was too fussy to go to the office in yesterday's clothes. Maxine finished a light lunch and, out of curiosity as much as concern, called the office.

"It's Maxine, Mary Ellen. Is Norm there?"

"No, Mrs. Feinberg. He hasn't been in yet today, or called either, and I'm getting worried." Mary Ellen finished some notes in a client file as she talked.

"Worried, why?" Maxine asked.

"Well, Wednesday evening he said he was going to meet with one of our clients on his boat."

"Mike Collins?"

"Yes. How did you know that?"

"He told me the same thing. But why would that worry you?"

"I was afraid they'd get in a fight again."

Maxine's jaw dropped. "A fight?"

"Yes. Didn't Mr. Feinberg tell you about it?"

"No, he didn't say anything about a fight."

"Oh, it was terrible, Mrs. Feinberg. The police had to come to break it up, and they took Mr. Collins away. I couldn't believe it was happening. Mr. Feinberg had to see the doctor about his nose."

It was hard for Maxine to believe as well. Norm, Mr. Metamucil, in a fight? He'd run. Then again, Collins didn't seem the type to start something like that either. But if he did, why was Norm meeting with him again, and on the boat of all places? Mike had called her earlier, though, just that morning. He said that Norm didn't show up for their evening meeting. Was that the truth? She supposed it could be, but it seemed odd. "Well, when he comes in, ask him to call me, okay?"

■□■

It was Friday morning, and Maxine still had not heard from Norm. If they had been quarrelling, she might expect him to go off and sulk for a couple of days. He had done that before. But the air between them, if not sunny, at least had been composed. In fact, Norm had been in an energized mood, as if in anticipation of some good fortune.

Maxine had slept late and was just getting into her housecoat when the call came in. "This is Lieutenant McDowell with the U.S. Coast Guard, ma'am. Is Mr. Feinberg there?"

"No," she said. The thought flashed in her mind: Norm had an accident with the boat.

"Is this Mrs. Feinberg?"

"Yes."

"Mrs. Feinberg, we have reason to believe that your yacht, the *Jezebel*, burned and sank Wednesday night. Your husband may have been aboard. Have you heard from him since then?"

Maxine felt a sudden weakness in her legs. She pulled a chair over to the phone.

"No…No. I haven't."

"When last you talked, did he say anything about going out on the boat?"

Maxine sat stunned and silent, her mind spinning.

"Ma'am?"

"Uh…yes?"

"Did your husband say anything about going out on the boat?"

"Well, yes, he said he would be working on it."

"Uh-huh. Well, as I say, he may have been aboard. And, if so, he could have survived the accident. His dinghy was found in the *Jezebel*'s slip at Shilshole. It's possible he's in a dazed state somewhere, a clinic or hospital."

"You say the boat burned and sank?"

"Yes, ma'am. Actually an explosion preceded the fire, according to our reports. Our helicopter was dispatched and a Seattle fireboat as well, but the *Jezebel* sank as it arrived on the scene."

"If it sank, how could you be sure it was the *Jezebel*?"

"Debris with the boat name on it."

"Oh. Well, if my husband had survived, wouldn't he have been there, in the water or something?"

"Yes, you would think so. The presence of his dinghy in the marina, though, gives some hope that he might have managed to get away."

"Oh...what should I do?"

"Well, you should file a missing persons report with the police. However, we are sending them an accident report ourselves. So it is certain they will be contacting you."

"And you are sure it was the *Jezebel*?"

"Pretty certain, ma'am. Now if you do hear from your husband, please ask him to contact us as soon as possible."

"Yes...I will," she said softly.

Maxine didn't think that would happen—Lieutenant McDowell hadn't sounded optimistic either. Norm was gone, gone down with the boat. She was stunned. Their marriage had withered, but Norm didn't seem to be bothered by it, and she admitted that she wasn't either. But now it was suddenly over, and in a tragic way. Perhaps there wasn't much love between them, but there wasn't hate either. In their accommodating way, they had gotten along.

She began to feel sentimental and wondered if he suffered much; maybe the explosion had killed him outright. She hoped so. "Oh, Norman Daniel, you sad little bastard," she said to herself. "Life didn't quite work out for you." She mixed up a stiff drink, a triple, and stared out the kitchen window, not recognizing anything, while the alcohol seeped, slow and warm, into her blood.

# CHAPTER 15

The telephone roused Maxine from a hangover sleep. She got up to pee and ignored the phone. Thirty minutes later, it rang again. She answered that time.

"Mrs. Feinberg?"

"Yes."

"I'm Detective Baldwin with the Seattle Police."

"Yeah?"

"The Coast Guard has referred the loss of your boat to my department."

"Yes, they said they would."

"Right. Now have you seen or heard from your husband since the accident?"

"No. I don't expect to. I believe he's dead. The Coast Guard man said they didn't see any survivors. So I guess Norm died in the explosion."

"That appears likely." Baldwin paused then said, "As you may know, it is our job to investigate these matters, especially where a missing person or death is involved."

"Uh-huh."

"So if it isn't a bad time for you, I would like to come by this morning. I'll bring a copy of the Coast Guard report."

"Well, okay, but I don't know how I can be of any help."

"Possibly not, we'll find out. Would ten thirty be all right?"

"Make it eleven."

That gave Maxine time to dress, arrange her hair, and neaten up the house. She noticed her eyes were puffy and shaded. She tried extra mascara, which didn't help. She thought she looked like a burned-out dance hall queen.

■□■

Baldwin arrived at eleven ten. Maxine offered coffee, which he accepted. They settled themselves at the dining room table. "I appreciate your seeing me on such short notice, Mrs. Feinberg. And I realize this is not an easy time for you."

She nodded.

"Let me apologize in advance, then, if some of my questions seem insensitive, but police work is sometimes like that."

Maxine wondered where Baldwin was headed. It seemed like a simple matter to her. The boat burned, sank, and Norm died. "Sure," she said.

"The Coast Guard report raises a few questions. First, do you know what Mr. Feinberg was planning? It seems that was a late hour to set out on a cruise."

Maxine winced. What the hell difference did his plans make? She sighed. "No, he was doing some work on the boat, getting it ready to sell. He was on the boat Tuesday evening, came home rather late. Then he called me Wednesday and said he would be there again."

"Did he say what sort of work he was doing? Engine maintenance perhaps?"

"No, he didn't say. I doubt it would be anything on the engines, though. He wasn't much of a mechanic."

"The engines, were they gasoline or diesel?"

"Diesel, I think…but I'm not sure."

"How about the propane system?"

"Propane system?"

"Yes, did the boat have a propane galley stove?"

100

"Oh, yeah, gas of some kind. Propane, I guess."

"Had you been having any trouble with it?"

"Not that I know of." Maxine slid her gaze across the room then back to Baldwin. "Look, I don't know much about the boat. It was mostly Norm's thing. He'd go out with a few of his friends now and then. Not often. I didn't care much for boating, so we didn't do many cruises together."

"Mr. Feinberg a fisherman?"

Maxine sighed and made a wan smile. "Norm? No. He said it was boring."

"Oh."

"You're wondering now why he had a boat, right?"

"Well, no. A lot of boaters just like to cruise, visit different marinas, that sort of thing."

"Yeah, well, it seemed Norm used it to entertain as much as anything. He and one or two of his Jewish lawyer friends would go out. Sometimes with girls. Women from the office. Little overnighters."

Baldwin's eyes widened. Maxine shrugged.

"Although, I don't think there's been any of that the last two years or so."

"Do you suppose he had anybody with him Tuesday night?"

"I don't know. He had said he was going to meet a client that night. On the boat or in the marina someplace, I guess. Anyway the client called here the next day, and he said the same thing. He said they had a meeting scheduled, but Norm didn't show up. And that seemed really strange to me."

"That Mr. Feinberg didn't show up?"

"No. That he planned to meet with this client. They, apparently, had had a fight earlier in Norm's office."

"A quarrel?"

"No, a fight…hitting. The office girl said Norm got a broken nose. The police had to come to stop it."

That piece of news widened Baldwin's eyes even further. He made some hurried notes. "You say the police came?"

"That's what Mary Ellen said."

"Mr. Feinberg's office girl?"

"Yes."

"Do you know if they made an arrest?"

"She said they did."

"Did Mr. Feinberg mention the client's name to you?"

"Yes. He said it was Michael Collins. When he told me that, I didn't know about the row in his office. He didn't mention that. I was quite surprised when Mary Ellen told me about it."

Baldwin noted the name. "Yes, that does seem odd. If Collins was actually arrested, he obviously was released that same day. But you wouldn't expect Mr. Feinberg to set up a meeting with him, at least not right away like that, would you?" He slowly shook his head as the visual corollary to his remark. "And you say this Mr. Collins called here?"

"Yes, the next day. He asked if Norm was here. Then he said that they were to meet Wednesday night at Shilshole, like I mentioned, but Norm didn't show."

"Uh-huh."

"Yeah. Collins said they were to meet around ten or so. Coast Guard says that's about when the boat blew up."

"Do you think it's unusual for Collins to call here, rather than Mr. Feinberg's office?"

"I think he did try the office first."

"I see." Baldwin paused for a moment, fussing a bit with his note-book. "While this seems pretty clearly a case of accidental death, I'm sure you understand that we must consider all angles."

"Uh-huh."

"Yes. Now, here's a copy of the Coast Guard report." Baldwin placed it next to Maxine's cup.

She looked at the cover sheet. "Do I need this for anything?"

"Probably not. But it does give the time and location of the sinking in case you ever need that. You might file it away for a while."

"Oh…okay."

"Now in that report," Baldwin pointed to it. "The Coast Guard suggests that the sinking may have been intentional, that the attitude of the boat indicated the aft sea cocks were open."

Maxine blinked.

Baldwin continued. "Would Mr. Feinberg have any reason to cause this accident himself? Has he been depressed or acting in any strange way recently?"

"You think he might have committed suicide?" Maxine stared openmouthed.

"Well, I'm trying to rule that out."

"That's a crazy idea. No matter how bad things got, Norm would never do that. We've never had money trouble. But if we did, his fantasies would keep him going. Norm has always felt that one way or another he would, someday, somehow, get rich. Besides, he doesn't have the guts to do anything like that."

Baldwin looked down at the remains of his coffee, cold now from sitting so long. "The Coast Guard coordinates put the *Jezebel's* location within the police dive limit, one hundred feet. So we will be sending a dive team down in the next day or so. We may learn then the cause of the explosion and fire."

Maxine sensed the implication in Baldwin's ominous tone. But she couldn't believe Norm would deliberately sink his boat.

"The divers may also recover your husband's body."

That thought stunned her. So far, there had been a remoteness to Norm's death. She was adjusting to the idea of his absence, but now they might be delivering a grisly corpse.

That afternoon the *Post-Intelligencer* picked up the story. Their Saturday edition carried a brief piece identifying Norman Feinberg, a local attorney, as the tragic boat owner. Mike saw the article and his heart stopped.

# CHAPTER 16

Tuesday morning, just before nine, Mary Ellen called Maxine. There was no answer. She tried again at ten thirty. Maxine picked up after the third ring. "It's Mary Ellen, Mrs. Feinberg. What should we be doing with Mr. Feinberg's things, his practice and all?"

"Oh God. I'm sorry, Mary Ellen. I can't seem to get organized here. I'll come to the office, and we'll figure out what must be done. I'll really need your help on this. Expect me in about an hour or so."

When Maxine arrived, Mary Ellen had opened the mail and stacked it according to action to be taken. There were three checks from clients, a settlement offer, a lease to review, and a short stack of junk mail. She also had Norm's docket calendar and had highlighted two items that were imminent. "We should refer these to Mr. Levine," she said. "So he can handle them. In fact, I believe he and Mr. Feinberg have some sort of an agreement."

"I believe you are right, Mary Ellen. Norm had said something about that. Must have it in a file here someplace."

"I think he keeps that sort of thing in his personal file cabinet. The one in his office. I've never seen it out here." She pointed to the six filing cabinets. "These are client files." She paused for a moment then added, "He also has a few things in the safe, but I don't have the combination."

Maxine checked the safe. It wasn't locked, but it contained nothing of value that she could see. The file cabinet, though, was locked. Maxine started going through Norm's desk, looking for the key.

Mary Ellen stood by, watching. "Maybe the key to the office cabinets would work," she said. They tried it. It worked.

Maxine started with the top drawer. Most of the files held papers related to business matters long since closed, bar association newsletters, old tax returns, and several files relating to his divorce. The next drawer held the pertinent stuff, including the office lease, expense records, and the buy-sell agreement. Under its terms, the survivor agreed to buy the decedent's share of the office furniture, fixtures, and reference books. In addition, a nominal sum would be paid for the client list. Accounts receivable would be paid to the seller as payments were received. The buyer also agreed to accept full responsibility for the office lease. Since Bernard Levine was out for the day, Maxine left a note on his desk stating she wished to proceed with the transfer of Norm's practice.

In a separate folder, she found corporate papers for Jezebel, Inc. "Jezebel, Inc.?" Maxine remarked. "That's the name of our boat...or what used to be our boat." She set the file aside as a thought struck her. "It just now occurred to me, I think Norm had the boat insured. Do you know where he keeps insurance policies, Mary Ellen?"

"I've never seen them out here. They'd be in the cabinet there or maybe in his desk."

"Well, I hope he didn't have it on the boat."

Maxine moved to Norm's desk. Things were more orderly there. In the large side drawer, she found the file for a stock brokerage account. Statements indicated the account had grown to $640,000 mostly by client deposits. Then, eighteen months ago, it began showing losses. Each statement listed numerous trades. It had been an active account, and following his broker's advice, losing trades had whittled it down to $83,000. Maxine blinked. "Jesus, look at this, Mary Ellen. The broker made as much as $5,000 one month for bad trades. How could Norm put up with that?"

Mary Ellen remembered Mr. Feinberg's exasperation. "Yes, he complained from time to time and would call the broker, but the next trade would get it all back, the broker said. Apparently Mr. Feinberg believed him until a few days ago. Something about a margin call, he said."

The drawer also held the mortgage papers for the house and Norm's will. He appointed Levine as executor and instructed that all proceeds were to go to Maxine, nothing to his first wife. Both marriages were childless. Mary Ellen made a photocopy of it, which they left on Bernard's desk with Maxine's note. In a file tabbed *Insurance*, Norm had their homeowner policy, the policy for the boat, and two life insurance contracts. The original beneficiary had been Norm's first wife. An endorsement made after the divorce directed the proceeds to his estate. Each policy had a death benefit of one hundred thousand dollars. One also had a double indemnity clause operative in case of accidental death. Maxine put the policies in a large envelope to take home.

If she sold the house, she'd have about three hundred fifty to four hundred thousand after paying off the mortgage. And there still should be about $80,000 in the stock account, she thought, unless the broker had pissed it all away by then. With the life insurance proceeds, another three hundred thousand, she thought the interest income would be enough to live on.

Bernard would be paying for the practice in monthly installments, but it wouldn't be much. She would have to review the boat insurance to see what to expect there. Norm had paid $70,000 for the boat if that meant anything. She pawed through the desk drawers, looking for evidence of other assets. Surely Norm had more than this. An IRA or something. What did he expect to retire on? She thought she had hit a winner when she came across a file marked *Key Bank Acct.* The file had the initial deposit slip dated September 1992, but nothing else. "Do we have an account at Key Bank?"

Mary Ellen shook her head. "Not for the office. Both the trust account and the operating account are with Wells Fargo. I think Mr. Feinberg had some kind of personal account there, though. But he handled that himself. I didn't have anything to do with it."

"Huh." Maxine put the slip in with the insurance policies. "I'll give the bank a call." She continued rummaging through the desk then remarked, "You know, looking through all this stuff, it seems Norm could have been a stranger. You'd think I would know more about his business, wouldn't you?"

"Well, Mr. Feinberg was always rather private about things, especially anything to do with money."

■□■

The dive request was faxed to the commander of the Seattle Harbor Patrol. The Search and Rescue unit loaded a remote-operated vehicle, ROV, and a side scanning sonar unit onto the boat they kept at the Elliott Bay marina. Fifty minutes later, working from the Coast Guard's coordinates and allowing for drift and current, the sonar picked up a ping.

They had timed their search to the tide's ebb, when there would be little current to contend with. The helmsman faced their boat into a slight southwesterly breeze. At a dead slow throttle, he held that position as they lowered the anchor. Once the anchor was set, the crew launched the ROV and activated its propulsion system. Gradually it descended to a depth of ninety-eight feet. Minutes later the ROV's camera spotted the resting remains of Feinberg's yacht. *Jezebel* sat upright as if parked there. Two divers suited up and stepped off into the cool water. They followed the anchor line down and, on the bottom, attached a strobe to it. Visibility was quite limited at that depth, but lights from the ROV pointed them to the sunken wreck.

One diver swam into the view of the ROV's front-mounted camera and gave a thumbs-up sign to the attendant in the boat above. Their inspection was brief. They first circled the hull and examined the interior through the blown-out windows. Sooty ash from the upholstery fabric, headliner, and paneling had settled uneasily over the cabin floor.

They swam to the aft cockpit for entry into the salon. As the first diver came inside, a sudden inky cloud exploded in his face. He jerked back from the shock of it, almost losing his mouthpiece. He looked back at his partner, who pointed toward the bow. They had disturbed a large Pacific octopus that had jetted to the boat's forward V.

They eased into the salon. The slight action from their fins swirled the silty ash, which then hung suspended in the cabin's dark water as if it would never again settle. There were no bodies in the salon. A propane tank sat on its side near the dinette. That would be the likely source of the explosion and fire.

The second diver eased himself up to the salon's forward bulkhead. Fire had blackened and burned away most of the teak paneling and melted the plastic grips on the throttles and shifters. The helm station seat was just a metal frame.

Next he glided down into the galley. Smoke-stained glassware sat in the sink. The portside head was clear with surprisingly little fire damage. He moved forward and shined his light into the V, which euphemistically was called the forward stateroom. The octopus was wedged tight against the access hatch to the anchor chain locker. Its arms curled and flexed slowly, as if readying for action. Aside from the cephalopod, the forward sleeping space was empty.

The other diver had checked the aft stateroom, so just the engine compartment remained for their inspection. The nylon carpet fibers had melted and turned into blackened plastic patches on the cabin floor. But the engine room hatch was intact, and they managed to lift it. The fire had not reached the engine area, and the twin Hino engines sat there, looking ready to go. They saw that the raw water intake hoses had been loosened and the sea cocks were open.

The evidence was clear. It was intended that the boat sink regardless of damage from the explosion or fire. And if the owner went down with the boat, his body had apparently drifted off.

The strobe guided them back to the anchor line, which they followed in their ascent. Though the time on the bottom had been brief, just fifteen minutes, they stopped at thirty feet for a few moments to decompress. Back aboard their boat, they relayed their findings to the sergeant in charge. His report was subsequently forwarded to the arson unit.

# CHAPTER 17

Maxine was home in time for a late lunch and a double G and T. She reheated yesterday's soup to go with the gin. When she finished, she rinsed her dish, sweetened her drink, and got the phonebook. She had two calls to make. The first was to the life insurance agent whose name was on a sticker attached to Norm's insurance policies. The agent was out, the receptionist said, but he would return the call. "Tell him it's Mrs. Feinberg and I would like to file a claim." Maxine heard a slight gasp.

Her next call was to Key Bank. After going through three computer prompts, she reached a person. Maxine explained she would like to know the balance in her husband's account. She gave the account number.

The customer rep, a pleasant-sounding woman, had the account on her screen in three seconds. "That account has been closed, ma'am," she said.

"When was that?"

The woman was reluctant to answer, but offered, "About a week ago."

"Can you tell me how much was in the account then, when it was closed?"

"No, I'm sorry, ma'am. Since your name is not on the account, I can't give out information like that."

"Well, I'm his wife...his widow, for Christ's sake."

"Yes, well, the bank would need to see a power of attorney or a letter from the court instructing to us to honor your requests."

"Uh-huh. That seems crazy to me. The account is closed and your customer is dead. I can't see who would care at this point." Maxine didn't wait for a response. "Good-bye."

"Well, since this is going so well," she said to herself, "I'll give the stock broker a call." The receptionist put her call through to his extension. Thinking it was a client with an order, he answered with just the right professional yet friendly tone to his voice. He put just a hint of impatience in it, as if he were in a rush making money for his clients. Maxine introduced herself, and the friendly part faded.

"I see from the trend in my husband's account that you would have had it down to zero in another six or seven months, maybe sooner."

She could hear the sneer in his voice. "Well, Mrs. Feinberg, your husband did make a few unfortunate trades." He was giving the credit to Norm as if he had no role in the matter.

"Uh-huh. Well, it appears you've been the only beneficiary here, whether the trades were good or bad."

He didn't respond to her cut. For a moment the line was silent.

"Well, you may be aware that my husband was killed on his boat a few days ago, but in any case, I'm calling to request you close his account."

"Your husband's account is now in an inactive status."

"I can imagine, since he's not available to agree to your marvelous advice. But did you understand the request I made just now?"

"We will take no further action on this account until we have received instructions from the court. Until then, good day, Mrs. Feinberg."

Maxine finished her gin and tonic and was thinking about fixing another when the phone rang. She snatched it off its cradle and answered.

"Maxine, this is Bernard Levine."

"Bernard, I'm glad you called."

"Yes. I'm back in the office, and I found your note."

"Uh-huh."

"First let me say how sorry I am about Norman. I just can't believe it."

"Well, it was a shock to me too."

"Yes, I'm sure it was." He paused for a moment. Maxine didn't sound broken with grief, and she was sure he noticed. But then, he knew their marriage wasn't the best. "You doing okay?"

"Maybe the reality hasn't hit quite yet. I don't know. But, yeah, I'm all right."

"Good. Now regarding the will and purchase agreement, I have to tell you we can't proceed with any of that quite yet. Norman's death has not been established. What we have at this point is a missing person."

"But we know he was on the *Jezebel* when it blew up and sank. It's obvious, isn't it, that he's dead?"

"Yes, you would think so. It's obvious to us, but not as far as the law is concerned. Death is not automatically assumed in cases such as this. Statute provides that a court must first consider the circumstances surrounding his disappearance and any other facts that lead to the conclusion of death."

Maxine sighed. "Oh my."

"Now in this case, I believe the court will be reasonable and will rule accordingly."

"Is it possible that they wouldn't?"

"Well, yes, it's possible. But I don't think it's likely. In any event, we are not in a position to dispose of Norman's estate at this time. We must first petition the court."

"How about the life insurance?"

"Same thing. Unless you get a ruling from the court, there is a seven-year wait before payout." Bernard waited as Maxine absorbed all that. "Now if you do not have another attorney you'd like handling this, I will be glad to do it for you."

That sounded fine to Maxine. Bernard's fee might even be a little lighter, given his relationship with Norm. Did attorneys have a tradition of professional courtesy like doctors? "That would be fine, Bernard," she said.

"I'll start tomorrow. Oh, yes, Mary Ellen has referred a couple of matters to me which I will take care of. It might be best if I review the rest of his current stuff too, just as I would under the buy-out agreement."

"I would appreciate that, Bernard."

"Meanwhile if there is anything else, let me know. I want to help as much as I can."

Mike took his morning coffee break at 9:30. With his cup and the morning paper, he settled in a quiet corner of the break room. Six other employees, two tables away, were discussing last night's Mariners game. They were obviously elated with the results, loudly relating key plays. One of them called over to him. "Mike, you're a Mariners fan. Do you think they should trade Turner?"

Mike didn't answer, didn't hear, just stared into his coffee.

"Mike."

"Huh?"

"You okay?"

After an awkward pause, he said, "Yeah."

"I asked if you thought they should trade Turner."

"Oh…I don't know."

The group resumed their banter then fell silent as Mike's supervisor, a uniformed policeman, and a man in a suit entered the room. They stopped at Mike's table. "These men would like to talk to you," his boss said.

Mike looked at the suit and started to ask why when the reason came to him.

The guy flashed his shield. "I'm Detective Baldwin," he said. "And this is Officer Rogers. We realize this could be inconvenient for you, but we hope you can help us clear up a few details regarding the boat that burned and sank last Wednesday."

"Well, sure. But I don't know how."

"You might be right. But if you don't mind, then, would you come with us? These interviews are best when held in our office."

Mike glanced up at his supervisor to see if he had any objection. Apparently he didn't.

■□■

At the West Precinct headquarters, Mike was led through the lobby to an interrogation room. The room was small, about ten by fifteen. It was furnished with a scratched-up table and four straight-back chairs. The uniformed cop left them at the door. Baldwin asked Mike to take a seat. "The chair over there," he said.

After a moment, another plainclothes officer joined them. He brought a compact digital recorder, which he set in the center of the table. Baldwin introduced the other officer as Sergeant Scalzo. He went on to explain that he was investigating the disappearance of the attorney Norman Feinberg. "Your presence here is voluntary; you are not under arrest. We would like whatever information you can furnish which might help our investigation. We are hoping for your cooperation here. But if you choose, you can have your attorney join us."

Mike felt that he was just as interested in Feinberg's disappearance as they were, but for different reasons, of course. He realized, though, that he was probably there as a suspect. His blowup in Feinberg's office had tagged him. But surely, since he was innocent, they couldn't come up with any case against him. He didn't have an attorney to call anyway. His cooperation and honest statements should clear whatever suspicions the police might have. "Sure. I hope I can help."

Detective Baldwin pointed to the recorder. "Now, with your permission, this conversation will be recorded. Okay?"

"Sure."

"Good." Speaking toward the microphone, Baldwin recited the date, time, and names of those in attendance for the recorder. "Now first I would like to review the information that I have gathered so far. I understand that you are or were a client of Mr. Feinberg."

"Yes, that's right." Mike moved up closer to the table and rested his arms.

"And he was preparing, or had prepared, a will for you?"

"No. He was forming a corporation."

"A corporation, not a will?" Baldwin raised his eyebrows.

"Yes."

Sergeant Scalzo had been studying his cuticles, now he looked up, watching Mike's eyes.

Baldwin continued, "But he did, in fact, prepare a will. Had your name on it."

"That's what he said that morning, when we had the altercation. But I had never asked him to do a will. That was a ruse. He couldn't admit anything about the corporation because he had already planned to keep my ticket."

"Your ticket?"

"Yes. I won the big Lotto jackpot." Baldwin blinked. Scalzo made a silent "Oh." Mike went on. "I wanted to keep my winning confidential. He was referred to me as an attorney that could arrange that."

"Keep your winnings private?"

"Yes. He said he would set up a corporation. My name wouldn't appear as the winner." Mike glanced at Scalzo, who was jotting some notes on a small pad. Scalzo finished and resumed his focus on Mike. They locked eyes. For a moment no one spoke.

Baldwin wrinkled his brow and resumed the interrogation. "Okay, and…he had your ticket?"

"Yes. He convinced me that it would be more secure in his safe. I fell for it, gave him the ticket. He put it in an envelope, gave me a receipt." While he answered Mike kept his eye on Scalzo. This guy was cool, Mike thought. Wasn't giving away a thing.

"Did the receipt identify the ticket?" Baldwin asked.

Mike grimaced and studied the scratches on the table for a moment. *Shit, did he have to ask that?*

"No, I'm embarrassed to say. It didn't. I was so damned excited about winning, I was careless, I guess." Mike started tapping his finger tips together. The room was getting stuffy as if the air had lost its oxygen. He could feel himself tightening up. Were they believing all this?

Baldwin picked up on it. Moved in a little closer.

"So then what happened on Wednesday?"

"I began to have concerns about the ticket. I didn't think he would take it, but I felt it would be best to have it myself. I went to his office to get it."

"Uh-huh."

Mike rolled his gaze around the room as if he were pricing a paint job. He looked at the digital recorder. It was getting all the discourse. Could it be used when he was tried for assault? He wondered how much more information to offer. He studied Scalzo and Baldwin. They were waiting for him to continue.

"Yes. Go on," Baldwin said.

"Will this recording be used at my assault trial?"

"No. It would not be admissible," Scalzo said.

Mike decided to believe him. He probably would plead guilty, so it wouldn't matter anyway. "I hadn't called for an appointment, so his girl was a little surprised to see me. She told me Feinberg wasn't in. But then I noticed a line button on the phone was lit. I thought it was probably Feinberg. She was lying. So I bounced into his office, caught him on the phone. When I asked him for the ticket, he said he didn't have it. Acted like he didn't know what I was talking about."

"And then you decided to beat him up?"

Mike rolled his head and sighed. "Look, I realize I lost it. But I had just learned that my attorney was stealing eight million dollars from me. That gets you excited." He looked at Baldwin then Scalzo to see if they agreed. They showed no emotion or sympathy. "I knew he was lying," Mike continued. "I thought if I threatened him, he would get the ticket. The threat became a punch in the nose."

"His girl said there was more to it than that, more than just a punch to the nose."

"Yeah, we wrestled around for a bit. He threw a bunch of harmless punches. I told him I was going to toss him out the window. I wouldn't have, of course, but he might have believed it. He said he would get the ticket. Then the police arrived."

"Did they or the office girl, Mary Ellen, hear him say he would get the ticket?"

"I don't know. She might have."

"Okay. Now are you aware of what happened to his boat?"

"I read that it burned and sank."

"Yes. That's right. Happened Wednesday night, same day you had your fight."

"That's what the paper said."

"Did you meet with Mr. Feinberg that night?"

"No, I was supposed to, though. He called me about five in the evening. I had been to the lottery office to see if my ticket had been cashed. Found out a Mr. Toops had presented it on behalf of a corporation." Mike clenched his fists. "Can you imagine that? I was paying him to set one up for me…instead he arranged one for himself and cashed the damn ticket. Toops was somebody Feinberg brought in to keep his name out of it. I was on my way to Toops's place when I got his call. I was quite surprised."

"Why did he call? What did he say?"

"He said he realized he had made a mistake thinking he could keep my ticket. He suggested there could be a lengthy trial over ownership, but if I agreed to a two hundred thousand–dollar fee for him, he would turn over the Lotto check. We were going to meet at Shilshole."

Baldwin kept his focus on Mike's eyes. Scalzo let his gaze drift.

"At first it sounded phony, late at night at a marina, maybe a hit to get me out of the way. Then I thought no, Feinberg's not that rough. This whole deal was a scam to get a big fee. He knew he couldn't get away with keeping the money, the eight mil, so he set me up for two hundred thou, more than I would have paid him otherwise.

"He said he was out on the water and would be back in the marina about ten. Anyway, I got to the marina about a quarter to and waited until after eleven. I was about to leave when a guy walks up. I thought it was Feinberg at first. He comes up to the car and says that Norm sent him. Next thing I know he pops the door and gives me a straight hard right to the face." Mike lightly patted his swollen cheek.

"That's how you got that bruise?"

"Yes. The guy was pretty fast. Could be an ex-boxer. Anyway, he pulled me out of the car and finished me with a couple solid punches. I blacked out." Mike moved his eyes from Baldwin to Scalzo then back to Baldwin. They didn't seem touched by his story.

"And you think Feinberg sent him?"

"That's what the guy said."

"Uh-huh." Baldwin hardened his gaze, locked onto to Mike's eyes. "Any witnesses?"

"No. I don't think so. I didn't see anybody."

"How about the watchman?"

"If he was anywhere nearby, he sure didn't let me know."

"So you're sitting there in your car and some tough guy comes up, smacks you out, then just leaves. Doesn't take your wallet or anything?"

"He wasn't a mugger, for God's sake. Didn't you hear what I just said? He came to even things up for Feinberg's nose."

"A revenge thing?"

"Yeah. A goon that Feinberg hired." He touched his cheek again. "Pretty good one too."

"Well, it seems more likely to me that you got that cheek someplace else."

"Huh?"

"We have the impression that you joined Feinberg and went out on the boat with him. Maybe there was some rough stuff out there."

That hit Mike like an electric shock. "How could you think that? I never saw his boat or him that night." He was getting nervous now.

"You don't seem to have much of an alibi," Baldwin said.

Mike studied his hands as if he had never seen them before. He had become a fictional character to observe as an amusement. What began as a million-to-one stroke of luck had turned into a nightmare. It was unbelievable. He imagined himself going to prison or worse. Nothing would seem unusual after all that had happened.

He shook his head. Baldwin was waiting for a response. In a soft voice that tasted of despair, he said, "Look, I can prove that the winning ticket was mine. Talk to the lottery office and Les, the bartender at the Nite Lite. And if you check it out, I'm sure you'll find that Feinberg was in the corporation that cashed it. That should establish that he stole it and that he's a liar." He looked to see if either Baldwin or Scalzo agreed. He couldn't tell. "Killing Feinberg would be contrary to my own interest. My only chance of recovery is in the courts. Charge Feinberg with conversion. And he has to be alive for that."

"You say you would sue Feinberg, but somebody named Toops was actually the winner, isn't that what you said? Isn't he the one you'd go after?"

Mike saw the implication. "Toops would be included in the suit, sure, but it would principally involve Feinberg. He's the only one that had access to my ticket. Now with him gone, I'm screwed." He locked on to Baldwin's eyes. The detective's almost hidden smile agreed: *You're screwed, all right, but for a capital crime, not a lost lottery ticket.* Mike could see it in his face.

He pulled in a deep breath and exhaled through his lips like a fatigued trombone player. He continued. "I went over to Toops's place and found that he's gone, left for Ecuador. Seems to me he would be the suspect here. He didn't want to share with Feinberg."

Baldwin leaned forward, closer to Mike's face. "You think Toops has gone to Ecuador. How would you know that?"

"He left a note with his next-door neighbor. She showed it to me."

Mike was released and ordered not to leave the state. Baldwin explained that their investigation would continue and even suggested that he should see a lawyer. Mike tried to smile at the irony. "Yes, I'm having wonderful luck with lawyers. My wife's lawyer is probably going to screw me over, and Feinberg, my attorney, took my money and set me up for a murder."

He dragged his way out of the precinct offices and went to the nearest bar.

# CHAPTER 18

Sergeant Scalzo suggested they check out what little there was to verify in Collins's story. "He didn't give you much that would clear him as a suspect, but talk to someone at the lottery office and the bartender. They may be able to confirm Collins's story about the ticket, that he was the owner. At this point, I tend to believe he was. I can't see him killing an attorney over a simple will.

"Then find the money. If this Toops guy has it, he's a suspect too. Feinberg told his office girl and his wife that he was going to meet with Collins, and Collins said so as well. But at this point, we don't know who set it up. If Collins did, though I can't imagine Feinberg going for it, we've got Collins in a lie and a stronger case. Get the Telco records for both Collins and Feinberg. That should tell us who set up the meeting. If Feinberg did, that would corroborate Collins."

"If Feinberg made the call, does it matter from where?"

"You mean from his boat or his office?"

"Yes."

"I don't see that it matters."

Baldwin nodded and picked up the recorder. They moved out of the room, and just as they were about to part in the hallway, Scalzo turned and said, "You want this guy, right?"

"He looks good for it. He threatened to kill Feinberg. Said so to the secretary. We know he loses his temper. Just let it go too far this time."

Scalzo nodded. "You may be right. But, you know, Collins sounded dumb and honest to me."

■□■

When the telephone company was told that Detective Baldwin's request for call records involved a murder investigation, they gave it their prompt attention. Copies were faxed to Baldwin Thursday morning. He noticed Mike made a call to Feinberg's office at 4:30 p.m. on the day of the sinking. That checked with what Feinberg's secretary had said. He punched up Feinberg's office number. Mary Ellen answered in her soft, almost shy way.

"This Mary Ellen?" he asked.

"Yes."

"Mary Ellen, this is Detective Baldwin. We talked the other day."

"Yes."

"A couple more details I think you can help me with. Now when we talked last Friday, you said that Collins called Wednesday sometime."

"Yes." She paused for a moment. "My note says 4:30."

"And he didn't talk to Feinberg then?"

"No. Mr. Feinberg was out of the office."

"What was it again that Collins said?"

"He asked to speak to Mr. Feinberg. I didn't know who it was calling at first. I just said that he was out. Then he asked when he would be back in. I recognized Mr. Collins's voice then, though, and didn't think it would be a good idea to tell him anything."

"He say he would call back later?"

"I don't recall. But it was then that he made that awful threat."

"That he'd kill Mr. Feinberg?"

"Yes."

"And when Mr. Feinberg returned, you told him that Collins had called?"

"Well, when he called in, I did."

"And you mentioned the threat?"

"Yes. But Mr. Feinberg said he wasn't worried."

"Hmm. So apparently Mr. Feinberg agreed to a meeting in spite of the confrontation earlier in the day?"

"And what a mistake that was."

"Yes. Now did Mr. Feinberg say that he was going to call Collins?"

"Hmm. I don't remember that, but he had Mr. Collins's number. He said he wanted to meet with him to straighten out their misunderstandings or something like that."

"Did Mr. Feinberg have a cell phone?"

"Yes."

"Would Collins have the number?"

"I doubt it. Mr. Feinberg didn't give that out to anybody."

"I see. Well, thanks again, Mary Ellen. You've been very helpful."

"You're welcome." She paused. "Can I ask you a question?"

"Sure."

"Will you be arresting Mr. Collins, then?"

"I can't say for sure at this point, Mary Ellen."

"Oh…I was wondering if I should send him an invoice for the will."

Baldwin had Toops's address from the lottery claim form. He found the house and parked his unmarked sedan in the closest open spot, three doors away. He tried the bell and could hear it ringing inside. There was no answer. The neighbor to the north was out fertilizing his lawn; he looked up for a moment, studying Baldwin as he rang the bell again. There was still no answer. Baldwin waited a few seconds, listening for signs of life. There were none. Then he went over and introduced himself to the neighbor, who said his name was Karstetter. They shook hands. Baldwin asked him if he knew Mr. Toops.

"Well, of course. He's my neighbor," Karstetter said.

"Had he said anything about leaving, going away for a while, perhaps to Ecuador?"

"Ecuador?" The neighbor chuckled. "A big trip for Buddy was out to the Auburn race track. I can't imagine him going to Ecuador. But we didn't talk all that much anyway. So I wouldn't be the one to know his plans."

"Uh-huh. He have anyone living there with him? Wife, girlfriend, relative, anything like that?"

"No, he's lived alone since his mother died. Used to be her house."

"Hmmm. Toops have any relatives in this area that you know of?"

"A sister. I think she lives in Renton."

"You know her name?"

"First name's Gladys. Believe her last name is Speckle or something like that."

Baldwin made a note of it. "No other relatives?"

"Not that I know of." Karstetter watched Baldwin pocket his pen then asked, "What's this about anyway? He in some kind of trouble?"

"No. We just want to talk with him."

"Well, he seemed to be on friendly terms with the young woman that lives on the other side there. She might know where he is."

"You know her name?"

"Lorene. She's been living there at her aunt and uncle's house while they're away. She might be home now."

"Thank you, Mr. Karstetter." They shook hands again, and Baldwin headed for Lorene's. The front door was open, and from inside he heard the sound of a vacuum cleaner. The bell chime was a little soft and the vacuum droned on. He shouted through the doorway, "Hello!"

Lorene clicked off the vacuum and peeked out from the hallway, "Yes?"

Baldwin introduced himself and mentioned his interest in locating her neighbor Toops.

Lorene came through the front room, studying Baldwin as he stood in the doorway. "You say you're a detective?" Lorene was wearing shorts, little more than panties, and a Tee shirt.

Baldwin measured every inch as she approached. He almost stammered, "That's right." Baldwin showed her his shield.

Lorene glanced at it then nodded. "Well, Buddy left me a note. Said he was going to Ecuador."

"You have the note?"

"I'm not sure. I didn't think it needed to be kept. But I'll look." She turned and went to the back of the house. In a minute, she returned. "Guess I didn't throw it away after all." She handed him the note.

Baldwin read it. It was brief. *I'm going to Ecuador and wish you were with me.* "Mind if I keep it?" he asked.

"I have no need for it. Can I ask why you're looking for him?"

"He might be able to help with an investigation we're conducting."

"Oh...the Feinberg boat accident?" She folded her arms over her chest.

Baldwin wondered if she'd noticed his wandering eyes. "Uh...Yes. Why did you think that?" Now he kept his focus on her face.

"Well, Buddy was in some arrangement with Mr. Feinberg. They won the big Lotto prize, he said."

Baldwin pulled a small notepad from his jacket pocket and began taking notes. "They won jointly?"

"No. The winning ticket was Feinberg's." Baldwin noted it.

A cat that had been lying on the back of the living room couch hopped down and came over to Lorene, rubbed against her leg. Then it moved to Baldwin and rubbed against his trousers.

"Friendly cat, He said and reached down to scratch its ears.

"That's Gigi Girl. Toops's cat. He left it."

"Oh, uh-huh." He watched the cat for a moment. Then lifted his gaze back to Lorene, "Well did Buddy say why he was involved?"

"Feinberg told him that he was setting up a corporation to keep the money from his wife, and he needed Buddy to be shown as the winner"

Baldwin nodded to indicate understanding and added her answer to his notes. "Did Buddy know that Feinberg might not actually own the ticket?"

"I don't know. That other fellow asked that too. Said it was his, that Feinberg stole it."

"Collins?"

"Yes."

"Collins said he talked to you and he either saw Buddy's note or you told him about it. Is that right?"

"Yes, I showed it to him."

"When was that?"

Lorene pursed her lips while she recollected. "Last Thursday."

"And the last time you saw Toops?"

"Wednesday afternoon." She looked across the yard, where Karstetter seemed to have an interest, and then back to Baldwin. "Look, is this going to take any more time? I have an appointment in thirty minutes."

Baldwin jotted down the date and squinted a bit as if in doubt about something. "No, I don't think so. Just a couple more questions. Why do you think Toops might have gone to Ecuador?"

"I don't know." She shrugged.

"He and Feinberg close friends?"

"I don't think so. In fact, Buddy was leery about their lottery deal." Lorene began shifting her weight from foot to foot.

Baldwin wondered if she had to go to the bathroom. He'd love to help her in there. He sighed and then went to his final question. "He didn't trust Feinberg?"

"Thought Feinberg might skip and not give him his share. And Collins thought that too. Said Buddy could be in danger. Do you suppose he is?"

"I don't think so. Not from Feinberg anyway." Baldwin pocketed his pen and pad and thanked Lorene for her time and the helpful information. He almost stumbled on the first step as he backed away to leave.

# CHAPTER 19

Thursday afternoon the police beat reporter learned that the Seattle PD was investigating the accident as an arson and potential homicide. He also learned of the altercation in Feinberg's office and that Collins had been questioned as a person of interest. The story appeared in the Friday edition. Mike saw it on his morning break. He was depressed, but not surprised.

He dreaded facing Janet. The flimsy story he gave when she bailed him out of jail wouldn't do it now. She would demand a full account...or at least most of it. The lottery matter was out in the open. The newspapers would soon get the gist of his police interview. The contention over the winning ticket would make a big splash.

He had hardened to her rants about his drinking; he rationalized that life with her almost justified it. The zingers about his job were tougher to ignore, but he managed. Till that moment, he had felt no guilt about his plan. The winning ticket was his, not hers. Would he have expected half if the ticket had been hers? No. And she would have done her best to deny him if he had suggested a split. He knew that. But he saw the matter in a different light now. By subterfuge he intended to deprive her of her legal, if not merited, rights and screwed himself in the process. Was that the final punition, the grand retribution for the lottery contrivance and all his past transgressions?

At the end of his shift, he was ready for a bracer. He could have stopped by the Nite Lite for his usual evening libations, but felt too moody to deal with Les. Getting closer to home, though, he began to feel the need. There was a lounge on California Avenue; he could try that. But parking would probably be a problem. To hell with it. He continued on home.

He pulled in the driveway and, expecting the worst, he slunk into the kitchen. The house was quiet: no TV, nothing cooking, not even a takeout package on the counter. Janet wasn't home. Good, he had a brief reprieve. He fixed a drink, three ounces of bourbon over ice. He checked the refrigerator for dinner prospects and saw he would have to defrost something. He put a pot pie in the oven, took a swallow of his drink, and went into the den.

He turned on the TV and flipped channels to ESPN. Then he heard her car in the driveway and the door slam as she came in. He raised the audio a little and focused on the set. Two talking heads seemed terribly anxious over some player's batting slump. Then their inane observations were eclipsed by Janet's resolute footsteps coming down the hall. He could feel the condemnation resounding off each footfall.

"What the hell is this I read in the paper?" she blared from the den doorway. "'Michael Collins, a person of interest in the Feinberg boat matter.' What's going on, Mike?"

He slowly turned to face her. "Well, not much really. I'm a murder suspect is all."

"Oh great. As long as it's nothing serious." She shook her head at the frustration of dealing with an insufferable husband. "You're just a bundle of laughs."

He took a big pull on his drink.

"I've become the gossip object at the office. 'Gee, Janet, I see your husband is in some kind of trouble,'" she whined in a sarcastic voice. "I don't give a damn what your drunken stumbling is doing to your sorry career, but it's certainly not helping mine. Weren't you satisfied beating up that attorney? You have to kill him?"

Mike ignored her question.

"Talk to me, God damn it! What the hell are you into?"

He was almost ready to say, but her rancor edged him off. He sighed and, with a patronizing smile, said, "I'm sorry about your career. But if you are the office goat, it might be because you've got Larry's dong in your mouth once or twice a week."

She slammed the door on her way out.

His smartass remark didn't leave him feeling amused or diverted. He knew there would be more to deal with in the morning.

■□■

While Mike numbed himself in the den, Janet found the Early Times and poured a strong shot into a coffee cup without ice. That was uncharacteristic of her. She rarely resorted to alcohol, but her life was taking a sour turn. She hadn't made a sale in several weeks, and Mike, like a stupid terrorist, was destroying himself and splattering shit on anyone nearby.

Once she got rolling, her real estate career had gone quite well. She had begun in a hot market. Sales were easy. Show a house and fill out the papers. Buyers were eager and offered the full asking price. And Larry had sent some listing prospects her way. Her commissions were inconsistent, but averaged four thousand a month—not bad for a beginner.

Because it came relatively easily, though, she had not developed a strong work ethic. She didn't know how or was unwilling to dig for listings. And she was light on the ability to induce buyers and sellers to negotiated settlements. Early on, she could bring Larry in to help close a sale. For a while he was happy to do it. He didn't take a slice of her commission either. The celebrations at the motel seemed to suffice. Whether any of that peeved his other agents didn't matter.

Even in a hot market, a salesperson can have a slump. With skill and determination, they work through it. But Janet struggled, and to divert responsibility, she blamed Mike. He was a pain and a distraction. Then the market cooled a bit. Buyers were becoming less anxious, but sellers were hard to budge on price. Janet needed motivation and training. Larry wasn't patient enough to do much of either. He gave her a set of Xerox sales training tapes. "Listen to these at home," he said. "Take notes. Repeat a tape to be sure of its lesson. They should help you."

She took the tapes and listened to the first lesson. Qualify your prospects, it said. Determine their needs and identify the key feature essential to close a sale. Did she do any of that? No. She drove them around and showed houses. She felt discouraged. Her job was becoming a job.

Married to Larry, though, that would be much nicer. He was very likable, good-looking, had a pleasant sophistication, was a little older, and made good money. She didn't love him, but he shouldn't be hard to live with, and maybe love would come later.

She doubted there was much affection left in his marriage to Felicia. She had been in the office a few times, and Janet had seen how she had let herself go, putting on the pounds, too many desserts. Janet wondered how Larry would respond to a suggestion of marriage. Would he divorce Felicia? His two boys were in high school. One would graduate next year, probably go on to college. Larry might be reluctant, perhaps unwilling to upset them. Yes, that seemed likely. She could hear him say, "I can't hurt the boys, but you and I can still have our love life." Larry would need a little push, a push from Felicia.

# CHAPTER 20

The next morning, before Janet could start in on him, Mike gave her the full story. He was tempted to gloss over the intent behind the corporation, say it was to reduce taxes or something, but he didn't. The truth seemed easier than another hazy, misleading evasion. Janet was stunned. She had questions about the money and how he planned to get it. Mike's predicament with the law didn't seem to concern her.

"So what do you plan to do?"

"Try and find Toops. And ironically, I need police help to do that." He grimaced. "Or a sharp attorney."

"What do you mean?"

"The police can follow the money. I can't. An attorney might be able to get a court order to serve on the bank. I don't know."

With a cold look and clipped words, she told him, "Look, as far as your problem with the law goes, you are on your own. Don't expect any help or sympathy from me."

"I didn't expect it," he said quietly.

"Good. And that means that whatever you need for additional bail or attorney fees, none of it comes from my half of anything."

He nodded.

"Next, I want you to move out. You'll have to anyway when the house sells, but I want you out now."

He started to object, but she cut him off. "I'm informing my attorney about all this and will ask that the divorce be settled immediately. The papers have been filed for a couple of months now, so it seems to me he should be able to do it. I want the final decree before any more shit hits your fan." As if a drawstring had tightened them, she pursed her lips and gave him a hard stare.

He was too disheartened to complain or object. Janet was in the driver's seat. He had fucked up; he probably deserved it.

■□■

On Monday morning, Baldwin ran a records check on Toops. He learned that Bradley Alvin Toops had been arrested in 2002 for possession, resisting arrest, and a DUI. In 2003, he had been charged with passing bad checks. He noticed that Gladys Spreckle, with a Renton address, had posted bail for Buddy in 2003. Baldwin found her number in the greater Seattle directory. His call, after four rings, went to an answering machine. He left his name and number. Her return call was almost immediate.

"This is Gladys Spreckle," the woman said. "You just called me."

"Yes, Mrs. Spreckle, I'm calling in connection with your brother, Bradley Toops."

"My brother! Not my husband?" She seemed a little puzzled.

"No, ma'am, your brother."

"What about him? He in trouble again?"

"I don't believe he is. We would like to talk to him is all."

"Well, he doesn't live here. Why call me?"

"He seems to have left town, and I thought you might know his whereabouts or when he is expected to return."

Gladys sounded impatient. "I have no idea. We don't see Buddy much or talk to him either."

"I see. Well, I understand he might have gone to Ecuador and would have made arrangements with you regarding the house and all."

"Ecuador!" The level of her voice stung Baldwin's ear.

"Yes. That's what he told his neighbor."

"I can't believe that. He doesn't have enough money to go any-where. And why in hell would he go to Ecuador?" After a moment's pause: "You know when he left?"

"Last Wednesday, according to the neighbor."

Gladys didn't sound too worried about her brother. "And he just walked off and left the house?"

"Apparently."

"Well, we own that house jointly. Inherited it from Mom. Guess I better see about it."

Baldwin was impatient as well. The call wasn't netting him any-thing, except a further glimpse of Buddy's character. "Yes, I think you should. Now in the meantime, Mrs. Spreckle, keep my number there and call me if you hear from your brother. Okay?"

"Sure."

■□■

Gladys didn't waste any time. She found her set of house keys and headed for Seattle. Midmorning traffic was light, and she made the trip in thirty minutes. She let herself in the front and left the door fully open to give the house some air. It smelled of tobacco and dirty laundry. Mail dropped through the door slot lay scattered on the floor. She picked it up and moved into the kitchen. She noticed the travel brochure for Ecuador sitting there on the table. Dirty dishes lay in the sink. A paper sack, half full of empty beer cans, sat next to the back door. She found three TV dinners in the freezer and some molding cheese in the fridge. Buddy wasn't much of a cook.

She made a quick tour through the rest of the house. The bed was unmade, and it appeared that most of Buddy's clothes were still in the closet. His suitcases were there too. He must be traveling light.

Back in the kitchen, she started sorting through the mail, most of it junk. The offers from credit card companies amazed her. "Don't they know who they send these things to?" She set aside an overdue utility bill then, out of curiosity, opened an envelope from the Holiday Inn in Portland. The letter stated that a 1995 Plymouth, registered in Toops's name, had been left in their lot. As he was no longer a guest at the inn, he must make arrangements for the vehicle or they would be obliged to have it towed and impounded at his expense. Their deadline was Wednesday noon, two days away. He was asked to contact the manager to confirm his intent to move the vehicle or to make other acceptable arrangements. The letter closed thanking him for choosing their hotel.

Gladys stared at the letter. She didn't know Buddy owned a car. He hadn't had one since he lost his license two years ago. And why would he leave it in Portland? It just didn't make sense, especially if he were going to Ecuador, though she still couldn't believe that, travel brochures or no. There seemed to be a lot that she didn't know about her brother.

Buddy's phone was still in service, and she considered calling Holiday Inn as suggested in their letter. But then she wondered, what could she say? She doubted she could do much with the car. She wasn't the owner. A locksmith wouldn't make a key for her, and if she called to have it stored someplace, she'd be stuck for the bill. To hell with it. It was Buddy's problem.

She couldn't remember Baldwin's number, but after three attempts, she reached his voice mail. She told him about her brother's car in Portland.

# CHAPTER 21

It was as nice as June days can be in Seattle. The skies were solid blue and sunny. A soft breeze off Elliot Bay carried a light smell of the sea. Scalzo stopped by Baldwin's desk. "Got time for lunch? I was thinking Ivar's. Check out the waterfront."

Baldwin smiled. "Sure. I'll fill you in on Feinberg."

Alaskan Way, the thoroughfare along the downtown waterfront, had a mix of commercial wharves with shops, restaurants, and tour boats. Ye Olde Curiosity Shop, a waterfront business since 1939 with a coastwise reputation, was one of the star attractions. The sidewalk was busy, mostly locals who had come down to enjoy the sights and have a seafood lunch. "A sunny day brings forth the adder…and the tourists," Scalzo said. "I read that somewhere."

Baldwin nodded. "I believe Caesar said something like that."

"My favorite comedian. Loved his routines with Imogene."

Baldwin chuckled.

They picked up their lunch at Ivar's outside counter and took a table under the canopy. They could look at the fireboat in the next dock or at three attractive girls in hot pants at a nearby table. "Nice view."

"The fireboat?" Baldwin said in mock innocence.

"That too. You can't see from where you're sitting, but this one gal just put her feet up on an empty seat."

135

"Yeah?"

"I'm getting a view of her panties. Flesh tone. You think she's doing that deliberately?"

"Resting her legs?"

"No. Shining me like that."

Baldwin swung around to take a quick look. The girl smiled. "Tony, you know how old they are?"

"They're built like twenty."

"Fifteen would be closer. They might go to school with your daughter."

"Wouldn't that be nice. 'Hi, we flashed your dad down at Ivar's today.'" Tony shook his head. "Those little nymphs. Look at that; they know we're talking about them."

"Tony, I hate to break the spell, but there's two young studs sitting behind you. I think they're the attraction."

"Oh. Thought maybe I still had it. Too bad." He took a bite of fish.

Baldwin nodded toward the fireboat. "Probably the one that went to the *Jezebel*."

"Too bad they couldn't stop it from sinking."

"We'd have more of a case if they did."

"We'd have a body, you're saying."

"I believe so."

"So…is there anything new?"

"One tenuous break. A witness."

"Oh yeah? Witness to what?"

"A local accountant and a few of his friends were on his boat at the end of M dock Wednesday night. They watched a guy in a dinghy come into the marina from out on the bay. He goes by their boat and turns in to the L fairway. The accountant, fellow named Johansen, called to the guy, asked if he had come from the burning boat out there. The guy wouldn't answer."

"They get a good look?"

"Just fair. He said the dock lights didn't help much, but get this, the guy was wearing a baseball cap. Mariners. Had to be Collins. He wears a hat like that."

"Well, at least he did when he came in for questioning. But maybe Toops or Feinberg do as well. Lot of those hats around. So what do you want to do?"

"Good question. Without a body, I've got an arson and a missing person. My homicide suspect has no clear motive that makes sense. He apparently expressed a threatening intention to Feinberg's secretary, but I'm a little soft on that. And would a baseball cap and the pen I found in the dinghy put him on the boat? Jury might not think so. Even with a body, I've got an iffy case."

"I agree. So where are you with Toops?"

"I doubt he's in Portland. He wired the money to Antigua and from there someplace else. The bank down there won't say. He could have gone to Ecuador like he said in that note."

Scalzo pursed his lips and slowly nodded. "Here's the way I see it: from the dive report, we know the boat was deliberately sunk. Three people could have done it: Collins, Toops, or Feinberg. One of them came back to the marina in the dinghy. The baseball cap and the pen point to Collins. If that's so, then we know that Feinberg went down with the boat. Feinberg would have been with him, alive or dead. Maybe he intended to strike some kind of bargain, make a deal. It got out of hand and Collins killed him. Toops probably left town before any of this happened, but we don't know for sure. He was supposed to meet up someplace and share with Feinberg. But it's all his now."

Tony continued. "The defense will propose that Feinberg went out alone and sank his boat to fake his death and set Collins up. Or that Toops was with him and he is the culprit. Didn't want to share with Feinberg. Feinberg may be out in the bay somewhere feeding the fish, or he may even be with Toops." He stopped to drain his coffee. "Your case hangs on a Mariners cap, a ballpoint pen, and a soft witness. Not enough." He watched the girls get up from their table and carry their trash to the waste can. "Bye, girls," he said. The flesh-toned undies gave him a smile. Tony watched them walk away.

"I'd like to take one more shot at Collins," Baldwin said.

"Arrest?"

"No. Not yet. A voluntary appearance for further questions. See if he can establish that he was at G dock. Then brace him…and give him an offer."

"Manslaughter."

"Yes. Think the captain would go for it? I believe it's the only way with what we've got to close this one."

"I'll find out. You might ask Feinberg's widow if he had a baseball cap. I doubt it, though. Oh, and Toops's neighbor, the young woman next door, she might know if Toops wore one. It wouldn't mean much in court, but it would ease our minds.

# CHAPTER 22

Sheldon Mains, Janet's attorney, explained that she had three more weeks to wait before the final decree. He spoke rather curtly; he had told her that before.

Janet was irked. She leaned forward in her chair as if to add emphasis, "Well, what the hell can I do, then?"

"About what?"

"Mike getting us both in debt."

"Does he have an attorney?"

"I don't know. He hasn't said. I don't think so."

"I don't mean for the divorce, the Feinberg matter."

"I knew what you meant." Her answer was crusty.

"Well, he'll need one. Find out who he'll use. Ask him. Then let me know. I'll write the guy a letter." As if his letter would carry weight, he looked to see if the offer softened her.

"Okay."

"When is the hearing on the assault charge?"

"Next month. The fifteenth."

"Make sure he shows up. You'll lose your cash bond if he doesn't. He still hitting the bottle?"

"Oh, sure. Not as much the last week or so."

"Uh-huh. The paper said he's a person of interest regarding Feinberg's disappearance. How serious is that?"

"The police think Feinberg was murdered, went down with his boat. I guess Mike is their prime suspect."

"Jesus." Mains shook his head. "You think he really had the winning ticket?"

"He says he did. There'd be no reason for his confrontation with Feinberg otherwise."

"Why'd he give it to Feinberg?"

"He said Feinberg was setting up a corporation or something. He was trying to keep it from me, the bastard."

Mains spreads his fingers then tapped his hands together, just the fingertips touching. He looked over them and studied Janet as she crossed her legs. Her short skirt exposed a tempting four inches of thigh; she wondered if he noticed.

"Any chance he'll recover the cash?"

"He thinks Toops wired it outside the country."

"Toops?"

"He cashed the Lotto check. Apparently he and Feinberg had a partnership of sorts."

"Is Toops a suspect?" His eyes drifted lower and lingered.

"Mike thinks he should be. But the police don't say." Janet noticed Mains interest and thought of twisting her position off to the side to deflect his view. Decided not to, moved a bit, and gave him a better peek instead.

Mains seemed to read her thoughts. Damn. After a pause: "You think Mike killed Feinberg?"

"No. He's dumb, but not that dumb."

"If Toops is also a suspect, the police will trace the money and find him. If Mike could prove it, the money would go to him. Half would be yours, you know."

"Yes."

"And then if he were prosecuted for Feinberg, it's possible that all would be yours." Mains leered at her.

"You suggesting I add something to the police case against him? Something incriminating?"

"Oh, no. No, nothing like that. But I think that we should keep an eye on old Mike."

■□■

Baldwin called Qwest to confirm that Mike was at work. He was. As before, Mike's supervisor met him in the lobby. Baldwin explained that he needed Collins for further questioning. The supervisor asked if it could be done in one of Qwest's private offices. Baldwin said no, they would be going to the West Precinct.

They used the same interrogation room as before. Scalzo had driven up from arson and joined them. Baldwin set up the recorder. "Okay," he said. "As I explained to you at your office, you are not under arrest and are here voluntarily. Right?" He didn't mention that he had also told Mike that they would arrest him if he didn't want to come voluntarily.

"Yes."

"And do I have your permission to record our conversation here?"

Mike thought about it. "No."

Baldwin seemed surprised. He glanced at Scalzo. "No?" he said sharply.

"That's right. I'm willing to chat with you here. I don't know how it will help your investigation, but before we do any more recording, I would like an attorney with me."

Scalzo spoke up. "Well, that is certainly your prerogative, Mr. Collins. So we will just talk off the record here. Now you said that Feinberg proposed a meeting at the marina."

"Yes."

"That's a big place. He say exactly where you were to meet?"

"By the G dock gate. He said he was coming in on his boat."

"G dock."

"Yes."

"What sort of boats are on that dock? You notice? Anything like Feinberg's?"

"I don't know what sort of boat he had. Never saw it."

"Uh-huh. Anybody see you there?"

"Yes, the security guy…and, of course, the mugger."

"The security guy?"

"Yeah. He came and told me I was parked in a permit-only spot."

"Okay, we'll want to talk to him."

Mike shrugged.

"Okay, here's what we've got." Scalzo held his right hand up in a fist and one by one straightened his fingers as he made his points against Collins. "One, you assaulted Feinberg in his office. Two, you admit you were to meet him that night and we are sure you did."

Mike started to object. Scalzo waved him off. "Let me finish. Three, we have a statement from his secretary that in the course of a phone conversation with her you threatened to kill Feinberg."

Mike rolled his eyes. He couldn't believe it.

Scalzo continued. "And four, we have a witness that saw you that night...returning to the marina in the dinghy."

Mike erupted. "That's crazy. First, I didn't say I was going to kill him. I said I was almost mad enough to. It was a figure of speech. And your witness is a liar or just plain mistaken. I was not in that dinghy. Nor ever on Feinberg's boat."

Scalzo lowered his eyelids and shook his head as if Mike's resistance were pointless. "Look, Collins, all the evidence points to you. Any jury will see that. You had motive, opportunity, and the evidence links you to the crime. You and Feinberg were out on that boat that night. The boat blew up. You came back. Feinberg didn't. It's a pretty simple case."

Mike was flustered and afraid he would lose control. He sputtered, "For God's sakes! Yes, it's a simple case all right. Only you seem too blind to see it. I had no motive to kill Feinberg. Do you think I'd get my money that way? The guy that had motive is the one that ended up with the money. Eight mil was his motive. But are you talking to him? No. He's out of the country, so you're trying to hang this on me just to close your damn case. And how do you know Feinberg's dead? He could be south with Toops."

"How do we know he's dead?" Scalzo said, speaking louder. "You came back alone in the dinghy. We know that. You going to suggest to a jury that you were out there on his boat alone? He wasn't with you. Or that he went for a swim and you were so mad you sank his boat? Get real, Collins. Feinberg's body will show up sooner or later. They always do. And that will ice it." He paused to let all that sink in. He studied Mike's eyes. "But you are right about one thing. We do want to close this case. And I believe that at this point, we would be easier for you to deal with."

Mike slowly shook his head. How ironic—Janet was right. He was on a skid to the bottom. He was going to hell but wouldn't be dead.

Scalzo nodded to Baldwin then pointed to the briefcase. "You have a pen with you, Mr. Collins?"

"Huh? Sure."

"Could I see it please?"

Mike sat quietly for a moment, wondering about Scalzo's request. Then he took a pen from his shirt pocket and placed it on the table.

Scalzo glanced at the pen then turned to Mike. "I see it has the Qwest logo. The company give you these?"

"Yes."

"And you have a piece of adhesive tape around the barrel, there. The pen broken?"

"No, a short piece of tape like that gives my thumb and fingers a better grip."

"That's interesting. I don't think I've ever seen that before." Scalzo's voice had mellowed and was quite pleasant.

Mike shrugged.

Baldwin placed the case on the table. While Mike watched, wondering, Scalzo opened the case and withdrew a plastic evidence bag. "We found this in Feinberg's dinghy." He slid the bag across the table to Mike. Inside the bag, Mike saw a Qwest pen. It had adhesive tape around the barrel. Mike's heart froze.

Scalzo retrieved the bag and returned it to the briefcase. "Now, Mr. Collins, you may establish that the Lotto ticket was yours. I think it was. But you have nothing that clears you of murder. The jury won't have any trouble seeing that."

Mike tried to respond, but couldn't speak.

Scalzo slid his gaze to Baldwin then back to Mike. Silence amplified the tension.

Finally he continued. "Well, here's what I believe you should do. Discuss this with your attorney."

Mike nodded. "Yes, I'll discuss this with my attorney, of course. But..." His voice trailed away.

"Yes, well, listen to what he tells you. Going the hard way will just make it worse for you."

Mike rolled a bewildered gaze around the room as if looking for something. Everything, including the two policemen, had become alien to him.

Baldwin asked Mike if he wanted a ride back to work. He almost accepted; then, still stunned, he answered morosely, "No...I don't think so." He fetched his cap and headed for a bar.

■□■

The next morning he awoke to find he had slept on the living room floor. He couldn't remember how he had gotten home. He checked his watch. It was six in the morning. Janet would be asleep. Good. He shambled into the bathroom and tried to resurrect an appearance of sobriety. He shaved, showered, and dressed for work. He thought he would stop at Starbucks for a latte and croissant. Outside, though, he saw that his car wasn't in the driveway. "Was it stolen? No. Where the hell did I leave it?" he asked himself. Then he decided he must have left it in the lot downtown. He headed for the bus stop on Thirty-fifth.

Bus service was pretty good. He had time to stop by Elsie's for coffee and a danish and still arrive at the office twenty minutes early. He found a morning paper in the break room and began looking to see if his name was in the news again. It wasn't, thankfully. He went to his desk to begin the day, wondering what the point was.

An hour into his shift, his supervisor came over, a dark look on his face. "Goodman would like to see you in his office," he said. Then he turned and started to walk off, as if concerned about exposure to a disease.

Mike called after him, "Right now?"

"Yes. He's down there expecting you."

Mike got up and headed for the stairs.

Hal Goodman, the district office superintendent, had an office one floor below on the west side of the building. The office was not large or fancy. It had a nondescript vinyl floor and easy-to-clean semi-gloss beige walls. Goodman had a gray metal desk, one guest chair, and two steel file cabinets. It was spartan, but his window gave him a nice view.

Mike stopped at the doorway and looked in. "You wanted to see me?"

"Yes, Mike, come on in." He pointed to the chair and shuffled some papers off to the side of his desk. Then he centered a file folder on his desk pad. Mike sat while Goodman opened the folder and glanced for a moment at the top sheet. It was Mike's personnel file. He looked up, studying Mike's face as though not sure how to begin. "I understand that you are involved in a police matter that could be quite serious."

"Yes, that's right. It's crazy, but I am a person of interest in the disappearance of a local attorney," he said. "Person of interest" that sounded better than "suspect."

"I see. And you have been arrested?"

"No. Not in the disappearance case. But I was charged regarding a confrontation in the attorney's office. He had property that was mine and was attempting to steal it. Which he managed to do, as it turns out."

"You are referring to the Lotto ticket?"

"Yes."

Goodman went back to perusing Mike's file then closed the folder. "Mike, here's our problem: We can't have the police coming in here continually and hauling you off the job. It leaves us shorthanded in your department, and it agitates the other personnel."

"Agitates?"

"Perhaps that's not the right word. But they start to buzz around with gossip and speculation. It detracts them from their work."

"Oh."

"Yes. Now I've been reviewing your file, and I can't say I'm very impressed, at least by the last twelve months. You started well. Got good appraisals. Eventually advanced a grade to district staff. But then things changed. Your supervisor is disappointed with your attitude. You were tardy for a spell there. He thinks you might have a drinking . problem. It could affect your work, though he doesn't think so yet. You should be at supervisor level by now. Instead you're just putting in time. And you are not showing the initiative or leadership that we like." He paused and measured Mike's response.

Mike tightened his lips. He could feel what was coming. "I guess I can't argue with most of that, Hal. Things started going bad at home. We tried having my mother live with us. That didn't work out. She and my wife didn't get along. Mom moved to a nursing home. Only there for a few months till she died. My marriage probably wouldn't have lasted anyway, but it really went sour then. I started stopping off for a few after work…more than I should maybe. But never on the job. I never showed up under the influence." Mike didn't mention that he came in twice with a hangover, though.

Goodman opened his mouth to speak. Mike lifted a hand to dissuade him. "I know, none of this is an excuse, and personal problems are not to be company problems, but that's what's been screwing me up."

The room fell silent for a moment. Mike wondered if what he had said even mattered. Probably not, he decided, but he pressed on. "Now we are in the process of getting a divorce, so the marital side of it will soon be over. No more misery there. And the police matter…they're wasting their time with me. They don't have a case and can't build one. I will have my attorney advise that they can't come here anymore while I am on the job."

Goodman waited to see if he had anything else to say. "Well, Mike, that all sounds fine, and perhaps things will work out for you. But we can't go on the way things are right now. It's been decided that, as of now, you are on administrative leave."

Mike blanched. "No."

"Yes. Your salary will continue until September first. Then you will receive pay for accrued vacation and sick leave."

"That'll give me about ten weeks total."

"That's right."

"Jesus."

"You may think this is harsh, but it really gives you a better chance to clear up your different problems. Now if you have resolved the police matter by then, we will discuss your return to work. And, Mike…"

"Yes?"

"I suggest you see someone about the booze. Your doctor, a clinic, or whatever. This really isn't the place for you otherwise."

Mike clenched his fists as if to lock in his emotion. He lowered his head, defeated. That was the final blow.

Goodman stood to let him know that the meeting was over. He offered his hand. Mike gazed blankly, distracted and depressed, then took it and they shook. He turned quietly and headed upstairs to clean out his locker.

# CHAPTER 23

Mike scraped his few personal things into a small trash bag. His chief had explained to Mike's coworkers that he would be on leave for a few weeks, so there were no sorrowful good-byes. Mike was grateful for that. The men knew, of course, that Mike had gotten himself into serious trouble. There were mixed emotions about it, some sympathetic, some not. But he was sure all were struck by the irony: a multimillionaire one day, a potential convict the next. The general opinion, he figured, was "Too much drink will do that."

He thought about stopping at the Nite Lite. Then it occurred to him that they may not be open that early. And Les wouldn't be there anyway. He didn't come in until three. Curiously, he realized that there was a futility in drinking. He was too depressed to get drunk. He headed for home, the home he would be leaving soon.

Janet had left for work, a small blessing. He didn't relish facing her just then. He fixed a cup of instant coffee and perused the "for rent" ads. He had roughed out a budget for himself as a single. It allowed enough for a nice apartment close in or a newer, larger unit in one of the suburbs. After losing his job, though, his budget was irrelevant. Unless he found another job, his income would cease in ten weeks. Unemployment compensation didn't occur to him. His pride might have vetoed that anyway. Yes, he had better see what was out there. Who would hire him? What would he say? *Hi there.*

*I'm a murder suspect and an alcoholic and I'd like a job.* Sure. That would work.

He began amending the allowance for rent. Then booze, should he eliminate it? No, that would be unrealistic. He cut the amount in half. He wouldn't be drinking at the Nite Lite for a while. Legal expense had been left as an open item. The divorce shouldn't take much. It hadn't so far. He didn't expect Janet to get greedy or unreasonable. She just wanted out as soon as possible. He'd need an attorney for the assault charge, of course, but he thought that shouldn't go over one, maybe two thousand max.

The elephant in the room, though, was his position as a murder suspect. Would he be arrested, jailed again, and ultimately put to trial? What could that cost? It would take everything he had, most likely: savings and his half of the proceeds from the sale of the house. How much rent could he pay then? He smiled, amused by his black sense of humor, as a facetious thought came to him—now that Feinberg was gone, maybe he could move in with Maxine.

He circled three ads for apartments on Capitol Hill. It was close to work, he thought, then realized that didn't matter anymore.

Mike signed an application for a one-bedroom unit in an older building near the Group Health hospital. He gave the manager a check for the damage deposit and the first month's rent. He would know the next day if he was acceptable. On the way home, he stopped at a moving company and bought some used packing boxes.

Thankfully, his mother's things were still in the garage. He had not gotten around to giving them to charity, as Janet had requested then later demanded. Well, she wouldn't have to look at them much longer. He selected the things he'd need for the apartment. The rest he set aside for Goodwill Industries.

He wondered how he and Janet might split what they had accumulated during their marriage. Most of it was pretty nice. She would probably want it all. Except for the bed he'd been using and a couple of things in the den, he'd let her have it. He didn't feel like fighting about it.

On the first of July, he rented a pickup, and with a neighbor's help, he moved into his apartment. Janet had hung around for a while, not helping, but watching to see that he didn't take anything she wanted. He didn't.

The next several days he kept busy settling in. He repainted the woodwork and kitchen cabinets, hung a few pictures, and washed the windows. He gave the post office and his credit card company his new address. In the evenings he walked to one of the cafés on Fifteenth for dinner.

Except for a glass of wine with his meal, he eased up on the booze. He hadn't felt the urge, the need. Could the habit just leave like that? It surprised him a little. He had thought that living alone, he would get even worse, souse up every night. Perhaps he wasn't an alcoholic after all. He didn't need alcohol to make his life worse now. It couldn't get worse.

■□■

A friend referred him to John Adkins, a young attorney who, with three partners, had offices in the Norton Building. Mike hired him to handle the assault matter and explained that they may be discussing a murder charge later. John was sharp and so well prepared that the overworked prosecutor acquiesced almost willingly to a deferred sentence. The bail bond was released. Janet was relieved if not cordial about it.

■□■

Mike found the telephone number for Lorene's uncle. The aunt answered and, after Mike's introduction, he heard her hold the phone away from her mouth and call her niece.

Lorene picked up a few seconds later. "Yes?"

"Hi, Lorene. It's Mike Collins."

"Oh," she said after a moment's hesitation.

He noticed. "Am I interrupting something?"

"I'm packing to go home. To Panama."

"I'll be quick, then. I wondered if you've seen or heard from Buddy."

"No. Not a thing. I saw his sister the other day. She's getting ready to sell the house...or maybe rent it."

"She heard anything? Know where he is?"

"I don't think so."

"Huh." If the sister was selling the house, she must have gotten Buddy's permission.

"His sister says he apparently went to Portland. But she doesn't know if he went anywhere beyond that."

"Portland? How'd she know that?"

"He left his car there."

# CHAPTER 24

Unlike most women, Maxine had had only cursory interest in the mail. She would peruse the ads and set the bills aside for Norm to handle. At first, as if she expected him to return, she continued to do that. Finally, though, as she began reorganizing her life, she accepted the task and sorted through items to be paid, several of them overdue. A window envelope from Nathan Bloch's office was among them. She had forgotten about Norm's nose. The statement listed the charges for the prior month. The fee for treating the nose was there along with an earlier charge of seventy-five dollars for a "Health Letter." The statement indicated that it had been paid two days prior to the charge. That seemed odd. Norm never paid anything up front like that. She thumbed through the check register. There were no checks listed for that amount and none for more than four months made to Bloch's office. It must be an error, an item for some other patient. Out of curiosity more than concern, she called Helen, Dr. Bloch's bookkeeper.

"Hi, Helen, it's Maxine Feinberg."

"Oh, Mrs. Feinberg, we were so distressed about your husband's terrible accident."

"Yes, it has distressed me too. Anyway, I'm trying to get my life together now and move on."

"That's the spirit." Helen paused for a moment. "How may I help you?"

"Well, I am getting ready to pay your bill for June, and I noticed one item that might be for another patient."

"Oh my."

"The amount has been paid, so you're not charging me now, but I thought I should call you about it."

"Certainly. Let me pull up your husband's file...Well, for June I show a charge for the letter of health and then the one for treating Mr. Feinberg's nose."

"The letter of health was for Norm?"

"Yes."

"Uh...well, in the records that I have here, I can't see we ever paid for it."

"I believe your husband paid with cash."

"Hmm. My. He didn't usually do that." Norm had a habit of paying all bills with a check. He always wanted a record. "What is a 'Health Letter' anyway?"

Helen was getting a little uneasy. "Dr. Bloch could answer that for you."

"I hate to bother him about such a minor matter. But perhaps he could call me when he has a moment. Guess I'm just curious."

Shortly after noon, he called. "It's Nathan Bloch, Maxine. First let me say how sorry I am about Norman. I can't believe it."

"Yes, a shock to me as well."

"I know it must be terrible for you now, but if there is any way that I can be of help, you'll let me know, won't you?"

She wondered how sincere he was. Whenever she'd stopped by the office, his eyes had always lingered a little lower than her face. "You're very kind, Nathan," she said.

"It's nothing. Oh, and, Maxine, please disregard that bill from my office. It was for Norman's nose. I didn't realize they had sent it."

"Oh my, I was just now writing a check," she said.

"Tear it up. Don't send it, please. I don't want you to."

"Well, as you say, then. Thank you, Nathan."

"You're very welcome, my dear. Now, Helen said you had a question about one of the items on the June statement."

"Yes, I wondered about the 'Health Letter.' Is that something that Norm subscribed to through your office?"

"Uh…no. It was a letter that gave a general description of his health."

"Uh-huh. Just for his own edification?" Maxine asked.

"I believe it was addressed to some official in Panama."

"Panama?"

"Yes, that's what I recall."

"Some official in Panama wanted to know about Norm's health?"

For several seconds, Nathan didn't speak. "Well, Norman told me you were going to Panama for a while. 'For an indefinite period,' he said. And a letter of health, among other things, was needed for a visa. It seemed strange to me. I asked him, why Panama? He didn't really answer. I assumed the two of you would be going and am quite surprised you didn't know about it." He paused as if wondering what to say next. "I'm so sorry, Maxine."

As if she hadn't been breathing, she exhaled in a long, slow press. "When was this, Nathan? When did Norm request that letter?"

"I could look it up to be certain, but I believe it was about a week before the boating accident."

■□■

Maxine moved to the kitchen counter and topped off her drink. She set it on the table there in the breakfast nook and eased onto a chair. She moved in slow motion. The pieces were falling into place. The sudden closing of his secret bank account—the bastard. His fiddling with the boat. He wasn't repairing anything. He was getting it ready to sink. And that claim by Collins that Norm had kept his Lotto ticket? That could be true. "So where does that leave me?" she asked aloud. Norm cashed the ticket and sank the boat to fake his death. He set Collins up for the blame. Norm wasn't going to float up on some beach…ever. Then she wondered, could she ever sell the house or his car? Probably not. And Norm's practice would sit in limbo. Her widow's estate just dropped big-time. In fact, it disappeared. "I'm not a widow."

Maxine sipped her drink and pondered the possibilities. If she didn't say anything, what would happen? Would Bernard get the court to declare Norm dead? How long would that take? Would Collins get hung for murder? No, she couldn't allow that. Besides, what if Norm was found to be alive? He might need to use his Social Security number to open accounts down there, buy real estate, renew his visa...or get married, the son of a bitch. There were too many liabilities. Maxine decided to play it straight. She looked for Collins's number in the phonebook. There were nine Collinses that used just the initial *M* and seven listings for Michael, sixteen possibilities altogether. On a hunch, she called the office. Mary Ellen picked up on the second ring.

"Hi, Mary Ellen, it's Maxine."

"Oh, how are you, Mrs. Feinberg?"

"I'm fine. Everything okay down there?"

"Yes. It's working quite well with Mr. Levine."

"Good. Reason I called, though, do you have Mike Collins's telephone number?"

Mary Ellen was aghast. "Michael Collins? Oh, Mrs. Feinberg, are you sure you want to talk to him? I'd be afraid to do that."

"Yes. I appreciate your concern, Mary Ellen, but it has become important now to speak to him."

"Well, if you think you must." Maxine heard typing on the other end. "He has two numbers, home and a cell phone," Mary Ellen said after a moment.

"Give me both." Mary Ellen did.

Maxine imagined that Mike would be at work, but could have his cell phone with him and on standby. She keyed in the number. He answered on the fourth ring.

Maxine felt no reason to be formal. "Mike, this is Maxine."

"Maxine...uh...hi. Believe me, Maxine, I'm sorry about Norm. And I want you to know I had nothing to do with it."

"I'm inclined to believe you."

"Oh." Mike obviously didn't expect that.

"Yes. For reasons I'll go into later, I believe Norm is alive."

"Norm, alive?" He sounded flabbergasted.

"That's right. I don't have proof, but I'm pretty sure."

"Well, that's damn good news."

"Thought you'd think so. Anyway I think we should meet to discuss this and make some plans. Plans that would work for both of us."

Maxine wondered if they should meet at the house. Would Mike think there was to be hanky-panky along with their discussion? She wasn't in the mood for that right then. He might not be either. They could meet in a restaurant or a bar, but she didn't want to risk their conversation being overheard, by anybody. So she said, "Let's meet here. This afternoon, okay?"

"I'll be there about two."

"Make it two thirty. I'm having lunch with Norm's partner."

She finished with the mail and then dressed for her trip to the office. She had forgotten her drink, and it sat warming on the counter.

# CHAPTER 25

At the office, Mary Ellen had prepared her salary check for Maxine's signature.

Bernard was in his office and came out when he heard her voice. "Whenever you're ready," he said. "At lunch, I'll give you an update on our progress with the court."

It turned out there wasn't much to report, and Bernard made their luncheon more of a social engagement than one of business. Like a bee near flowers, he was getting interested. Maxine noticed. He held her chair, ordered wine, and from time to time during the meal, he touched her hand. She enjoyed it. Bernard was nice looking; he had kept himself trim, not like some men who go to pot after the wife dies. The fact that he had a nice income didn't hurt either. She wondered if she should tell him about Panama. No, she decided—at least not until after she had met with Collins.

■□■

Maxine had just gotten back from her lunch with Bernard when Mike arrived at the door. His eyes popped in surprise as she let him in. Maxine was in a pricey silver-gray skirt with a matching jacket over a dove-gray cashmere sweater. The whole effect dramatized her dark titian hair, which was nicely styled. "My, don't you look nice," he said.

"Oh, thanks," she said almost impassively. Maxine, since her youth, had felt herself rather plain and feigned an indifference regarding her appearance. She was nice looking, but not beautiful. Her features were not delicately pretty. She pretended not to care, but actually she was very particular when she put herself together. "Guess you've never seen me dressed." The remark amused her.

She was still a little mellow from the wine at lunch. She liked that pleasant warmth, which softened the edges of her current circumstances. To keep the float, she suggested a gin and tonic. Mike's eyes sparkled a little, and a quiet smile tugged his lips. She caught the look. "No, I'm not promoting a romp…just a drink. Okay?"

"Of course." He moseyed about in the living room, looking at her bric-a-brac, while she mixed the drinks.

She came in from the kitchen and set his glass on a coaster that had been left on the coffee table. "Day off today?" she asked as she settled on the couch.

"Yes, today, tomorrow, and until who knows when."

"Retired and just waiting for your money," she said facetiously.

"Be nice if that were so. No, I've been fired. Well, not fired exactly. I'm on administrative leave. Almost the same thing." Mike settled himself and took a sip of his drink. "You said you thought Norm was alive?"

"Yes." Maxine studied her glass for a moment, wondering where to begin. "I got this statement from Norm's doctor that summarized charges for the nose you gave him."

Mike winced.

"Yeah, two hundred thirty dollars. Anyway, there was another charge and credit on there that didn't seem right, so I called Nathan's office—that's his doctor, Nathan Bloch." Maxine took a pull on her G and T. "Anyway, it turns out Norm needed a health statement or letter to get a visa."

Mike opened his mouth to speak, paused, and took a drink instead.

"And there had been some other things too. They didn't seem to mean much at the time."

"What kind of things?"

"He was acting different for a week or so, as if he had just won a big case or something. Then, while I was going through his stuff at the office, I found out he had an account at Key Bank. He'd never told me about that. He closed the account and took the cash a few days before the boat went down."

"Hmm."

"Yeah. After I found out about the letter, I looked for his passport. He kept it in the desk there in the den. Wasn't there."

"Could it be at the office?"

"I looked there too. Been through his stuff twice now. It's not there either. He wouldn't keep it there anyway. He wanted it handy when he packed."

"So you think he's alive someplace…some other country?"

"Well, at least it looks like he planned it that way."

"He could still have gone down with the boat, never got to use his visa."

"I thought of that. But if that's the case, who went out there with him? Somebody brought the dinghy back."

"Toops."

"Yeah, Toops or you."

"Wasn't me, Maxine."

"For some reason, I believe you. But Toops wasn't with him either."

"No?"

"No. Norm went out alone. He took the boat out, set it afire, and sank it. Then he came back in the dinghy. He had told his secretary and me that he was going to meet you at the marina. That was to aim suspicion your way. He never intended to meet with you at all."

"You don't think he and Toops could have argued over the split? Toops kills him and then does the boat to cover the crime."

"No. Think about it. Why would he and Toops go out in the boat? That doesn't make sense. And if Toops did him in someplace else, he could never get to the boat anyway. He'd need keys to the gate and the boat. Plus, I doubt he knows how to run a boat. He'd dump the body in a trash bin or something. No, Norm went out alone. He wouldn't take Toops along. Norm had to be the only one in the dinghy, just in case somebody saw him when he came back to the marina. It had to look like it was you. Two guys in the dinghy wouldn't fit his scheme."

"If that's the case, he played it right," Mike said. "He was seen by some people. The police have a statement where this fellow says he and some friends were on his boat when the dinghy came in the marina. They couldn't see the guy's face, but the police, of course, think it was me. I guess that would have been Norm. He might even have met Toops and gone to Portland with him."

"Portland?"

"Yeah. Toops left his car down there."

"Norm's car was left at Shilshole. I wondered how he got out of there without it. Toops was waiting for him in the marina lot. That's how he did it. Then he took a plane from Portland."

"Might've. The police could check."

"Could we?"

"No." Mike shook his head. "Only the police can do that."

"Would they?"

"Well, you'd think so. It would resolve the murder case. I think they would want to do that. And they'd like to talk to Toops as well." He tilted his glass to finish his drink.

"Want another?" Maxine asked.

"No, thanks. That was fine, though." He set his glass on the coaster. "You haven't said where you think he's gone."

"That's right. But since I'm sharing all this, you probably have figured that I'm going to."

Mike shrugged.

"Okay, here's the deal." Maxine took another sip. "What would it be worth to you to find Norm?"

Mike smiled. "Well, that would save me from facing a murder rap and might mean I get my Lotto money. It would be worth a lot."

"I thought it would. Now here's the way it works for me. First, if I'm quiet, there's a good chance the court will declare Norm dead. Then I can collect his life insurance, sell his car, the house, and his law practice. I'd have a comfortable life. I'd probably get a job anyhow, but wouldn't have to. And Norm could just rot down there with your money."

"And I might face a trial for murder. Would that bother you?"

"Sure. I don't think they have a good case, though, and I would speak up if it looked like they did. You'd have a hefty attorney bill, though."

Mike nodded.

"So now for the second possibility. I share this info with the police. They should be interested enough to check it out...or maybe have locals down there do it. Anyway, Norm is found. Maybe extradited. I don't care. They're off your case and you can sue for your money. Meantime, though, I'm out in the cold. There's no insurance, and I can't sell anything. And I sure as hell don't want Norm back. You get the picture?"

"I think I do. We agree to some kind of split, and you talk to the police."

"That's right. I wouldn't expect too big a cut, say four hundred thousand."

"Four hundred, huh?"

She nodded.

"Well, Maxine, here's the way I see it." He paused and looked at the melting ice in his glass as if there were a message there.

She lowered her eyes, expecting disappointment.

"Norm screwed me and dumped you. He did us both. I think you deserve more than four."

She blinked.

"How about eight?"

"What? Eight hundred thousand?"

"Yes."

"Oh my." She grinned. "For a second I thought you were turning me down. Oh Jesus, oh my, I'm getting juicy. Um...how about a jump?"

# CHAPTER 26

Maxine's call came in just as Detective Baldwin was preparing to leave for the day. After a somewhat baffling start, she said she thought her husband was alive and in Panama. Baldwin was stunned. "What makes you think that, Mrs. Feinberg?"

"Several things point that way."

"I see. I guess we had better discuss them, then. Are you home now?"

"Yes."

"Well, I was just getting ready to leave my office. I could come by on my way home."

"That would be fine."

■□■

Detective Baldwin was on Maxine's stoop at 5:25. She greeted him at the door. "Hi, thanks for coming," she said. "I fixed us some coffee. It's in the dining room."

Maxine told him about the health statement, the missing passport, and the closed bank account. Then she mentioned Norm's perky attitude in the few days before the accident. Baldwin rolled his eyes at that. She noticed. She finished by suggesting he check the airline's passenger lists out of Seattle and Portland. She thought that Norm may have gone to Portland with Toops and on to Panama from there.

"All right, we'll check the airlines for all outgoing flights. Now can you think of any reason that your husband would choose Panama?"

"No. It rather surprises me."

"Does he have any relatives or friends there?"

"Relatives? I don't think so, none that I've ever heard of. Friends, maybe, I don't know. I doubt it, though."

"No one you can think of contacting?"

"No."

"How have things been between the two of you?"

Maxine sighed. She had been waiting for that. "We don't fight. We have a settled, indifferent relationship. Norm has his practice. I have my friends. We don't get in each other's way."

"I see." He paused. "What can you tell me about your financial situation? You have a nice home here. Would you say you were well off?"

Maxine frowned. "Comfortable, I guess. Not what I'd call rich."

"Mr. Feinberg had his practice. How about other assets: real estate, stocks, business interests?"

"What does that have to do with anything?"

"Just that it seems strange to me that he would walk off and leave everything."

"Well, he had the Lotto money. And I can't find that he left much."

"I believe Toops had the Lotto money."

"Toops? Why do you say that?"

"I checked with the bank that took the Lotto check. Toops had the money wired to Antigua."

"Antigua? Not Panama."

"It could end up there, I suppose. It didn't stay in Antigua very long."

"Well, where did the Antigua bank send it?"

"They won't say, at least not to me."

How clever of Norm. He dead-ended the money trail.

She noticed skepticism on Baldwin's face. "You think I'm crazy, right?"

"Not at all, Mrs. Feinberg. You could be right about Panama and your husband's plans." He studied his coffee, then, "It appears that Collins did buy the Lotto ticket. He and your husband may have had some kind of scheme cooked up; I don't know. But it obviously went sour. Mr. Toops got involved and eventually ended up with the money. Collins got aced out." He paused, watching her reactions. "And…your husband as well. The evidence indicates he died on the boat." He stood.

Maxine started to say something, but stopped.

"Well, thank you for giving us this information, Mrs. Feinberg. I will check with the airlines. If Mr. Feinberg left that way, they would know. It's pretty difficult these days to fly under an alias. He could use the train or a bus, though."

"Can you check with them?"

"Yes, but it's been a month now since the disappearance. Showing ticket clerks a picture seldom works, but if you have a recent one…"

Maxine thought for a moment then went to a drawer in the buffet. "This snapshot is probably the best I have."

Baldwin studied the picture for a moment. "You don't have anything larger?"

"Not that's recent."

"Okay. Now I will also request Panamanian Immigration to notify us if he has entered their country. They say they have a pretty good system of monitoring incoming tourist and visa travelers. Perhaps they do."

"But you don't think he's there, do you?"

Baldwin looked away for a second. "The evidence doesn't point that way, Mrs. Feinberg."

"Hmm."

Baldwin nodded.

"Look, I don't mean to sound critical, but it seems Norm is just slipping away and we're letting him do it because we think he's dead."

Baldwin sighed. "It may seem that way because we move cautiously and must be thorough. But if your husband is alive, no matter where, we will find him, Mrs. Feinberg. Please be assured of that. We don't just quit on these things."

"Well, if you say so. So what happens next?"

"We'll see what we learn from the airlines and Panama."

Maxine carried the empty cups back to the kitchen. Her gaze went to the window above the sink and out to the side of the house next door. They had a bedroom on that side. The owner, an older widower, would occasionally stand naked by the window. The level of the sill was just a few inches above his knees. She was sure he was waiting for her to come to the sink and see him there. Sad, she thought.

She next thought about a drink. The gin bottle was right there under the sink. "No," she said to herself. "Let's not get started on that right now." She fixed another cup of coffee instead. She could see that Detective Baldwin didn't believe her husband was headed for Panama or was even alive. Could he be right? Was Collins a killer? Jesus, what a cool guy, and she'd been in the sack with him twice. She chuckled at the thought. He seemed so straight, so believable.

Bernard felt that the court would give her a favorable decision. Norm would be declared officially dead. But it could be a while before they came to that decision. They might await the outcome of Collins's trial, if it was ever held. A verdict against Mike would probably help her case. Meanwhile, she faced an indefinite future and should keep her own welfare in mind. In spite of the evidence, though, she didn't think Collins was a murderer.

If she had a few more clues, more details confirming Norm's plans, perhaps Baldwin would pursue them more aggressively. Or maybe Mike would.

She called Mary Ellen.

"It's Maxine, Mary Ellen." She always identified herself to Norm's assistant, even though she didn't need to; Mary Ellen readily recognized the voice. "Do we have a computer service person we call for technical stuff?"

"You mean for repairs or software problems?"

"No, not repairs. A software expert, I guess."

"Well, there's the guy that installed our PCs and the local network stuff."

"Yeah, he might do. What's his number?"

# CHAPTER 27

Bert Russell, no relation to Bertrand Russell, agreed to meet Maxine the next morning. He had been to Feinberg's office before and remembered Mary Ellen. She introduced him to Maxine. Maxine smiled, more from a private thought than courtesy, as they met, and she took in Bert's appearance. He had an endomorphic physique and wore thick-lensed glasses. His clothes were a bit large and nothing matched; shirt, trousers, and socks all seemed to belong to different sets. Bert was just what she expected a computer geek to look like.

When Maxine explained what she wanted, he rolled his eyes upward and sighed. "That's so easy, you could do it yourself," he said, which was nowhere near the truth. Maxine wasn't sure how to turn a PC on, and Mary Ellen's skills were limited to Microsoft Office and legal software.

It took him thirty minutes to hit on Norm's access code, "masada." Once in, he went right to Outlook Express and brought up the received and sent messages that were still in the folder. Then he retrieved the items that Norm had deleted and mistakenly thought were permanently erased.

There weren't that many items to sort through. There were messages to and from an Antigua bank, a Zurich bond broker, and a Panama realtor. Bert then went into the hard drive to review Internet traffic. There he found the searches that led Norm to his banker and broker. He had also scanned sites for three realtors and various airline schedules. Maxine made copies of the Outlook messages and felt she had enough for the next step in her plan.

She called Mike. His voice mail picked up. "It's Maxine," she said. "I'm down at the office and will be here for another half hour or so. Then I'm going home. Call me back. It's important."

Mary Ellen prepared a check for Bert's fee, and as Maxine was signing, he asked, "Do you mind telling me what this is all about?"

"I'm trying to find my husband."

"Feinberg, the attorney?"

"Yes."

"Seems I saw his name in the paper a few weeks ago."

"You could have."

"A plane crash?"

"No, boat."

"That's right. His boat burned and sank out in the sound someplace."

"Yes."

Bert blinked. "Well…didn't he, uh, go down with the boat?" He gave Maxine a cautious look. "But you don't think so."

"I'm not sure."

"I see." He smiled at the novelty of it. "Well, good luck."

Maxine reviewed a few things that Mary Ellen had set aside then asked, "Bernard coming in today?"

"I believe he's in court."

"Oh."

"On one of Mr. Feinberg's cases."

"Thank God for Bernard."

Mary Ellen nodded and gave her a wry smile.

■□■

Maxine was loading her coffee maker as Mike's call came in.

"I got your message."

"Good. I just got in. I've been at the office, like I said. We went through Norm's PC."

"Yeah?"

"He left a trail."

"That's good news."

"I think so. He's in Panama City. He bought a condo through a realtor down there. I've got the guy's name and address."

"You give it to the police?"

She decided to shade things a bit. "I've talked to Baldwin. He says it's a dead lead. He's certain Norm is not there."

"He could pass it on to the local police. They could check. Wouldn't he do that?"

"No," Maxine lied. "He's got you for a murder. Just needs to tie up one or two loose ends."

"Great."

"Yeah, I think it will be up to you."

"You mean go down there…to Panama?"

"Yes. That's the only way I can see you getting clear and getting your money."

"Our money."

"Yeah, our money."

"Uh-huh. Without police help, I'm wondering how easy it will be finding Norm. Must be a couple million people down there."

"The realtor will have his address."

"Might have, you mean. Norm could have bought from someone else."

"From their messages, it looks pretty certain he planned to use this guy. He had already selected a unit."

"Should we call this realtor to confirm that?"

"We could call him, of course, but I doubt he'd give us anything over the phone. Those people are leery. We call him and he'd probably tell Norm. Then we'd be in the dark again." Maxine began to wonder if Mike's reticence was genuine. Was he not interested in going to Panama because he knew Norm wasn't there? Was that it? Was he a killer after all? "Can you travel?"

"I guess so. Baldwin wouldn't like it. Claim I was fleeing to avoid arrest. He said not to leave the state, but he didn't take my passport."

"Then you'd better get moving before he does."

Mike didn't respond at first. The line was ominously silent. "Okay, what's the realtor's name and address?"

# CHAPTER 28

If he found Norm, Mike said he would telephone the address to Maxine, who would then pass it on to Baldwin. They expected that Baldwin would arrange extradition proceedings and Norm would be charged with arson and fraud. But then he wondered, if Norm were brought back to Seattle, what were the chances he would bring the eight million with him or tell anybody where he stashed it? It seemed more likely to Mike that Norm would either act dumb or not talk. Mike would win an uncollectible award. And for a first offense, Norm's prison time, if he got any, would likely be just a year or two. Then he could return to his cache of riches. Perhaps they'd leave Baldwin out of it for a while.

Mike went online and purchased his tickets, a confirmed seat going down and an open date for his return. He didn't know how long he would be in Panama. Finding Norm might not be as easy as Maxine had implied. He thought about Lorene. Perhaps she could be of some help. She might have contacts with access to information not available to him. If Norm had bought a condo, as Maxine said, he probably had a telephone, electric utility, maybe even cable TV. He called Lorene's aunt.

"Hello, Mrs. Hermosa, this is Michael Collins, an acquaintance of your niece. You might remember, I called and talked with Lorene just before she left for Panama."

"Michael Collins?"

"Yes."

"Lorene mentioned your name, but I don't remember why."

"It would have been in connection with your neighbor, Toops. We were both suspicious about his sudden leaving and were concerned for his welfare."

"Yes, I remember now. I think she said that Buddy might have money of yours. He stole it or something."

"He didn't. His lawyer did and he included Buddy in the scam to keep his own name out of it. Anyway, Buddy didn't go to Ecuador. And I believe he is in real danger."

"Oh, really?" She gasped. "You think he's in danger now? He's been gone for several weeks."

"Yes. Anyway, I'm leaving for Panama in a few days to find the attorney and have him arrested." Mike was really getting fancy. "Hopefully before he does serious harm to Buddy. I would like to contact Lorene and let her know all this. She was very helpful before, when we first became concerned about Buddy's disappearance." He paused for a second. "And it would be nice to see her again. Do you have her phone number or address?"

"Well, of course. Let me see where I have it." She left the phone for a moment to fetch her address book. Mike could hear a radio playing in the background. "I will give you her work number," she said as she returned to the phone. "If she wants to see you, she can give you her address."

"That would be fine."

She gave him the number for an orphanage.

Mike placed the call. An answering machine picked it up and announced in Spanish that the office was closed for the day. He had forgotten the difference in time. Panama City was in the eastern standard time zone. He didn't leave a message. He tried again the next morning. A woman answered in Spanish.

"Lorene White, *por favor*," he said.

He didn't understand her answer. "*Habla inglés?*" he asked.

"*Sí*...yes," she said.

"I'm calling for Lorene White. I understand she works there."

"Yes, that's right. But she is in a meeting just now."

"Please tell her that Michael Collins called. I'm coming down to Panama City and will call again after I arrive."

# CHAPTER 29

At 6:45 p.m., local time, Continental flight 888 touched down at Tocumen International Airport. The flight had been comfortable, as air travel goes. Warm, humid air rushed into the passenger cabin as attendants pushed open the fuselage door. Mike retrieved his single piece of luggage from the overhead and joined the slow-moving line exiting the plane.

There was much more to Panama City than what he had expected. High-rise condos and office towers stretched along the bay front. Nearby shops and malls were open and busy. The streets and boulevards close to his hotel swarmed with pedestrians and auto traffic. The cooler evening air made it a good time to be out.

After a shower and a change of clothes, he went down to the hotel café for a cocktail and light dinner. He borrowed a telephone directory, and while he nursed his drink, he scanned through the real estate section of the yellow pages. He found Norm's agent, Vista Realty, prominently listed, though he didn't understand much of their ad.

■□■

The next morning, Mike called the orphanage. Lorene held the phone in her hand indecisively for a few long seconds before she put it up to her ear and said hello.

"It's Mike Collins, Lorene. I got in last night. I'm hoping we can get together. I'll fill you in on Feinberg and Toops and hopefully get some advice. I'm not sure how to proceed here."

Lorene was reluctant. She had gotten his message and wondered why he was calling her. Feinberg and Toops were not important issues to her. While Buddy was an interesting neighbor in Seattle, she really had little concern about his situation. And what advice could she offer Collins? He had seemed like a decent guy, but was he still a suspect? He said he wasn't, but that might not be true. Then it occurred to her that Collins wouldn't come down here looking for Feinberg if he had, in fact, killed him. "Well, yeah…I guess that would be okay. What did you have in mind?"

"I was thinking dinner, tonight."

"Dinner…tonight?"

"Yes."

"Hmm." Was this to be a date or a meeting? "Yeah, I guess tonight would be okay."

"Should we meet at your home, then…or what?"

"Be easier for me to come to your hotel."

"Okay. I'm at the Riande Granada on Morales."

"All right, Mr. Collins, er, Mike. I'll be there at seven."

■□■

Lorene picked a restaurant within walking distance of Mike's hotel. It was not fancy or romantic, but the food was very good. It was obviously not a date for her; Mike, though, acted as if it were for him. He hardly knew her, yet there was a powerful attraction, a magnetism in her presence.

During dinner, he explained how Maxine had discovered Norm's secret move to Panama. Then he went on to relate the elaborate ruse

Feinberg set up to fake his death. "He set up a corporation as the Lotto winner and involved Buddy, as you know. It appears that Buddy knew the ticket was not Norm's."

"He never said that to me."

"He may not have known it at first or preferred not to share that with you. But he would have no reason to leave Seattle otherwise. Plus, he helped Norm with the boat scenario."

"How did he do that?"

"He stood by in the marina lot, and when Norm returned from sinking the boat, Buddy drove them both to Portland in his car. That way they left Norm's car abandoned in the lot to further indicate that he went down with the boat."

"I guess that's why Feinberg bought Buddy that car."

"Feinberg bought it?"

"Yeah. That's what Buddy said. At the time, though, he didn't know why."

"Guess he found out."

"Well, have the police been told all this? It seems to me they would be the ones looking for Feinberg. Why are you here?"

"Maxine did tell them. They checked airline records and have requested help from Panamanian authorities. So far nothing has turned up, at least that I'm aware of. She says the police doubt her theory and do not seem too interested in pursuing it. She and I are the only ones convinced that he's down here. But you have to understand, the only charge against Feinberg would be arson for burning the boat and fraud. And Seattle PD wouldn't send someone down here until they get word from Panamanian immigration. Maybe not even then. I don't know."

"How about theft? Stealing your ticket?"

"Yeah, there'd be that. Technically it's conversion, not theft."

"Conversion?"

"Yeah. He converted my property to his own use. Which brings up the real motive for me being here. If the police were to extradite and convict Feinberg, he would probably face a minimum sentence, maybe just a year or two. Who knows? Expecting something like that, he'd leave the money here, hidden someplace. Don't know if

Seattle police could force him to return it even if they find it. He'd probably deny he had it. Then when he's out, come down and continue a rich lifestyle."

"Well, if the police couldn't get it out of him, why do you think you could?"

"I actually think my best chance comes with the police out of it. I could threaten to expose him. Give Seattle his address. They would probably attempt extradition. It would be a hassle for him. I could also sue him down here, though I'm not sure how that would work. But if a judgment goes against him in a Panamanian court, I understand they can penetrate bank secrecy. He wouldn't want that. But whether that's the case or not, I plan to give him an offer. He keeps half, say four million, and I get the rest. Four mil down here is a lot of money. His lifestyle shouldn't change. Out of my share, I'd give his wife $800,000. He might appreciate that."

"He says no deal, then what?"

"Carry out my threat. Send his address to Seattle and hire a local attorney to sue him."

"He wouldn't have it all in cash, would he?"

"He probably doesn't. My guess is stocks, bonds, or some income-producing asset. Going through his bank records, though, I believe they could find it."

Lorene studied the interior of her wine glass as if seeing runes. "You haven't said much about Buddy or even if he is really in peril. You don't know, do you? You held that out to just get my interest and agree to meet."

"Yes."

# CHAPTER 30

Still adjusting to the time change, Mike rose late and missed the complimentary breakfast. He grabbed a danish and coffee; that seemed enough anyway. The memory of his evening with Lorene occupied his mind. Without intending to, she had enchanted him. Was it her physical beauty? No, there was much more to it than that. He was smitten with a woman that he would probably never see again once he left Panama.

He bought a pound of chocolates and had it gift wrapped at the hotel lobby shop. He selected a card, and on the outside of the envelope he wrote, *To Norman Feinberg, c/o Vista Realty.* Then, in bold print, he added, *Open on your birthday, Dad.* He then taped the envelope to the wrapped package, with the printed message showing plainly.

He asked the bell captain for an English-speaking cab driver and was told that almost all cabbies spoke reasonably good English. The bell captain was right. Mike's driver, a charming young man named Isais, understood his directions and was a pleasant conversationalist as well.

Vista had a street-front office with a prominent sign in the window. Isais pulled in to the passenger load zone and parked. Mike repeated his instructions and handed him the parcel. Mike watched as his driver entered the realty office and was greeted by the receptionist. Whatever Isais said seemed to confuse the woman, and she left her desk. After a few moments, she returned and handed him a slip of paper. He was smiling when he returned to the cab. "*Bueno*. She gives me the address," he said. "Number twenty-two, Valle Escondido."

"Great." Mike smiled as well.

"But one thing, *señor*."

"Yes?"

"It is in Boquete."

"Boquete?" Mike asked.

"Yes," the driver said. "It is in the hills, north of here."

"Very far?"

"Three hundred kilos, maybe more. Is best to fly to David." He pronounced it "Daveed." "Then you hire a car."

"You can keep the chocolates," Mike said. "Give them to your wife. Oh, if I can get a seat, I will be flying to David tomorrow morning. I'll call and let you know."

■□■

Aeroplas had space, and Mike booked a seat on their 9:00 a.m. flight. He called his driver. "I'll be at your hotel by eight," Isais said.

"Eight? I don't want to miss my flight."

"Okay, seven forty-five. But not to worry. The municipal airport is just fifteen minutes away."

■□■

The flight was half booked, and Mike found a window seat in the rear of the plane. At nine sharp, just as the schedule said, they lifted off. Miles and miles of verdant forest slid away under his vision as the flight skirted the southern edge of the Central Cordillera. Aside from an occasional ranchero, there were no signs of humanity to be seen until they began the descent to David. They landed at ten fifteen.

Outside the modest terminal building, Mike found three waiting taxis. He quickly learned that none of the drivers spoke English, and he was a little uncertain about his one semester of high school Spanish. A local man, perhaps an airport employee, offered to help. Mike explained he wanted a car for a day trip to Boquete and back. His request was translated to the curious drivers. The first guy in line said, "*Sesenta*."

Mike understood the number and shook his head. "Fifty…uh *cincuentena*…and I'll buy lunch."

The driver nodded and they shook hands. Mike pointed to himself, "*Mi llamo* Mike."

The driver smiled, tapped to his chest, "Jorge, Jorge Gomez." He then pointed to the front passenger seat and Mike climbed in.

Boquete lay thirty-eight miles to the north, nestled in the rampart range of the mountains. Outside David, the highway passed through a stretch of modest rural homes. Small houses set back from the road were fronted by grassy yards and large elm-like shade trees. Some places had little sheds for chickens or garden tools. Not so different from the States. A woman standing by her mailbox looked up and waved as they passed.

Further out the land opened up. Large spaces once cleared for grazing, but with no visible livestock now, spread out on both sides of the road. Prominent signs indicated the land was available for development. Development to what? Finally the highway moved into a sparse riparian forest of espavé and cocobolo trees. It dipped and crossed a small shady stream. They were at the scratchy edge of Boquete. In town, the highway became the main street for two blocks, before it narrowed and wandered into the town's older residential area. An eccentric row of small, single-story clapboard and adobe buildings shouldered along each side—Boquete's original business district. A few newer and larger retail operations and a school were situated one street over. Several building sites were in various stages of development, attesting to Boquete's expectations. The town was responding to the slow influx of retiring Anglos from Europe and North America. Graveled lanes edged along the valley slopes, where expats perched and viewed the village. After getting directions from a local, they continued the short distance to the upper edge of town. The valley narrowed here as it climbed to its provenance in the mountains. Valle Escondido's was a gated community and its entry was controlled at a guard station, where a fee was charged for admittance. "It keeps the curious out," the guard said. They paid the fee, and he gave them directions to Feinberg's unit. A fast-moving stream raced down through the development and furnished year-round water for irrigation. New duplex and single-family homes, in a modern adobe style, randomly bordered a nine-hole golf course.

Jorge pulled to the curb as they spied unit twenty-two.

There were no vehicles in Feinberg's carport. Mike went to the door and rang the bell anyway. There was no answer. He rang again. Then an older woman, Feinberg's duplex neighbor probably, called over from her yard. "There's no one living there now," she said in perfect English. "Who are you looking for?"

"Norman Feinberg."

"He moved. The place is for sale again."

"Moved? Do you know where?"

"I think he went to PC."

"PC?"

"Panama City. But I'm not sure. He only lived here a few weeks. We really didn't get to know him."

Mike gritted his teeth. Shit. "Do you know who he listed with? Which realtor?"

"Probably one of the locals."

"Mmm. Well, thank you for your help."

Back in town, they found the offices of Boquete Highlands Realty. Two men, probably agents, were chatting as Mike entered. The younger of the two smiled, came over, and introduced himself. "I am Luis Tomasa," he said. "How can I help you?"

Mike explained that he was moving to Boquete and wished to purchase a home. Luis brightened right up. Mike went on to say that he understood they had a listing on a property in the Valle Escondido subdivision.

"Certainly," Luis said. "I will get the key. And your name?"

"Homer, Homer Simpson. I have a car and driver right outside," Mike said. "We can go in it."

"Might be easier if we use mine," Luis said.

They pulled up to unit twenty-two and parked in the same spot that Mike and Jorge had left just minutes ago. Luis opened the entry door from the carport and led them up a flight of stairs to the home's main level. The kitchen, dining area, and living room formed one large great room, with a slider that led out to an expansive deck. Luis moved over by the cooktop. "First-class appliances…real nice."

Mike agreed. "How long has it been for sale?"

"Since the fifteenth. It's rather strange. The seller lived here just a few weeks."

"He didn't like Boquete?"

"Maybe. I don't know."

"What did he say when he gave you the listing?"

"He didn't talk to us. He's using a broker in Panama City. We have a joint listing with him since we are close to the property."

"The same agent that sold this to him?"

"No, a different one, I believe."

"Oh."

They made a quick tour of the unit; it was quite nice, as Luis had said. Mike faked an interest and asked about utilities, taxes, and the seller's price.

"It's a real bargain. Two twenty-five U.S."

"Hmm. Well, I was thinking something a little less."

"Give me your offer. I'll present it."

"To the broker in Panama City?"

"Yes."

"I'm going back there this evening. I'd like to negotiate with him directly. That wouldn't reduce your commission, would it?"

"No. But perhaps you should look at some other properties before you leave. I do have some at a lower price." It was a tease, Mike thought. Luis suspected that he didn't really intend to buy anything.

# CHAPTER 31

It seemed strange that Norm would leave Boquete after so short a stay, especially after Mike read through some of the brochures extolling the area's virtues. The climate at that altitude was ideal. Spring-like temperatures persisted for most of the year. It was rarely as hot or humid as Panama City. A fair-sized colony of expats had retired there, and the retail trade had accommodated their tastes and preferences. Boquete did not have the sophistication or cultural opportunities of Panama City, but how much would that mean to Norm anyway? And if that was important to him, why did he go there in the first place? Was all that merely to confuse his trail? That didn't seem sensible to Mike.

The last flight back to Panama City, or PC as Norm's ex-neighbor called it, left David at 5:25. His taxi dropped him off at four. He paid the driver, went inside, and bought an apple drink. A double bourbon would have suited him, but there was no bar or lounge at the airport. Finally, at 5:15 they began boarding the plane. Mike took a seat next to an attractive woman whom he had noticed earlier in the waiting area. She smiled as he settled himself. He nodded in return.

"What brings you to David?" she asked.

"A fool's errand, I guess," he said flatly.

"Oh." Assuming he preferred privacy, she turned to the window. The engines began their preignition whine, then belched and revved, proud of their power.

Mike sat, dumbly staring at the seat back in front of him, beginning to wonder if he'd ever connect with Feinberg. Then it occurred to him that his response to the woman just then had been rather curt. "I'm sorry if I seemed a bit flip there. Frustration, I guess. I'm trying to find a guy that stole eight million dollars and not making much progress."

"Oh my," she said. "So…you're with the police?"

"No, not the police. I'm the victim."

She blinked. "Well, if you're not the police, what do you expect to do if you find this guy?" She studied Mike's face. "If you don't mind my asking."

"Try and strike a bargain with him."

"Not notify the police?"

"Not if I'm lucky. Sounds crazy, doesn't it?"

"Well…yes."

"Would you like to hear the whole story?"

"Sure."

"It's longer than an Irish funeral."

"I guess we've got the time."

"Well, okay. Oh, I'm Mike, by the way." He extended his hand.

"And I'm Zoraida. Friends call me Zee."

They shook, and Mike launched into a somewhat abbreviated version of his odyssey. Zee was a good listener and soon was offering encouraging suggestions. As they touched down at Panama Municipal, Mike touched her hand. "Thank you for being such a good seat mate. I don't feel so discouraged now."

■□■

The next morning, he bought another box of chocolates. It was wrapped and addressed to *Dad, in care of Balboa Realty.* Then, with Isais again as his driver, they headed for their second "delivery." Balboa was located in an older, but well-kept office building off Brasil Boulevard. They pulled in to the passenger load zone, and Isais took the package.

When he returned, he was empty-handed.

Mike blinked. "What happened?"

"They wouldn't give me the address. I said, 'But this is from his son.' Then this woman took the package and said they would see that he got it."

Isais was getting into the game they were playing, and he seemed just as disappointed as Mike.

■□■

After a G and T at the hotel bar, Mike went up to his room and called the information operator for TelCA Panama. Surely Norm had a telephone. He did, but his number was unlisted. He wasn't surprised. "Well, could I have his address? I'll send him a telegraph message." He said it was an emergency regarding Feinberg's brother. The operator instructed him to wait on the line. She would call Feinberg and see if he would take the call. Mike hung up.

"I guess I'm a phony condo buyer again," he said to himself.

■□■

He found a waiting taxi and headed back to Balboa Realty. Mike found their office on the second floor. A glass door with discreet lettering led into a large, oblong-shaped room. Immediately inside the door, Balboa had a receptionist's desk, a settee, and two modern chairs for visitors. The room was wide enough beyond the reception area to accommodate eight sales desks, four along each of the two longer walls. Toward the back, Mike could see a bank of file cabinets and, to the rear of that, two private offices. Four tall windows gave the room an open and airy feeling.

Mike spotted three people, a woman and two men, conversing by one of the sales desks. The rest of the staff must be out for the day. The woman came forward and greeted him. After he explained that he was interested in one of their properties, she introduced him to a pleasant young man named Jules something-or-other. Mike didn't get the last name, but he smiled and mumbled that his name was Homer Simpson. They shook hands.

"I've just come from Boquete, where I met your correspondent agent, fellow named Luis."

Jules nodded. "Yes, at Boquete Highlands."

"Right. He showed me the Feinberg property, which I understand you represent."

"Yes, that is correct," Jules said. "That is a new listing for us. Very nice, I understand. Did you make an offer?"

"No, not to Luis. I told him I would prefer dealing directly with you."

"I see. So you have an offer for me to present, then?"

"Yes."

Jules took an earnest money form from the side drawer of his desk. "This is the form we use. You may read it, then enter your offer here." He pointed toward the bottom of the form. "And sign here." He pointed again.

Mike quickly scanned the form, entered his bid, and signed as Homer Simpson.

Jules glanced at his offer. "One hundred fifty thousand dollars?"

"Yes."

"Hmm. Excuse me one moment." Jules turned to his computer and brought up the Feinberg listing. The monitor was angled in such a way that the screen was out of Mike's view.

"Well," he said. "That is quite a bit under the asking price. I can present your offer, but I am certain it will be declined. This seller is not pressed for funds. He has no compunction to take an offer such as you are proposing here. Now, Mr. Simpson, if you saw much of Boquete, I'm sure you noticed how that community is developing. Many, many foreign citizens, such as yourself, are eager to buy there. There is a strong demand for first-class properties. Mr. Feinberg's home will sell at his price."

"Uh-huh. I understand that he lived there for just a few weeks. I thought that he might be a speculator, buying and selling properties for a profit."

"Oh, no. Not that it matters, but I think it is fair to tell you that he paid more than his asking price when he purchased the property just a short time ago. I have not met Mr. Feinberg, myself, but I understand that he is a retired American, quite comfortable financially, and is not a real estate speculator."

Yes, Feinberg was comfortable financially all right. Mike was sure of that. Then, in an abrupt move, he leaned toward Jules to get a sight angle on the monitor screen and asked in a hushed voice, "What do you think it will take to move this seller?"

Jules might have noticed Mike's attempt to peek at his monitor, but it didn't matter. It had gone to screen saver. "He might accept two fifteen."

"Huh. Has he bought another home here? He may want some quick cash."

"No, I don't believe so. At least not through us. I think he is renting. But as I said, he is not short of money."

"Well, I suppose you are right about my offer being too low. I am willing to raise it, but I'd like to talk to the seller first. Find out why he's selling."

"I suggest you give me a more reasonable offer contingent on an acceptable inspection. A qualified third-party opinion would be more reliable than the seller's, don't you think?" Jules reached for another form, then added, "But I'm sure you noticed that the condo is new. Barely lived in. I doubt that there would be any problems with it."

"Yes, I suppose you are right." Damn, he was beginning to sound like a fool. He just was not getting around this guy, and he was beginning to catch on. "Could you give me a few minutes to talk to my banker?"

"Certainly."

"And would you have any coffee? Or water? A glass of water would be just fine."

"We have both."

"Well, coffee, then. And while you are getting it, could I use the phone on the desk over there?" Mike pointed to an empty desk over by the office windows. "It's local, to my bank."

"You can use mine."

"Umm. Well…"

Jules noticed Mike's hesitancy. "But if you prefer, yes, use that phone. You have the bank's number?"

Mike made a nervous little laugh. "Yes, have it right here."

While Jules was getting coffee, Mike moved across the room and dialed his hotel. When the receptionist operator answered, Mike introduced himself and said he wanted to talk to Mr. Disney, hoping there was no one there with that name. While she checked their guest list, Mike rattled on as if talking to a banker. Finally, quite confused, she told Mike that she thought he had the wrong number and disconnected.

Mike continued his monologue, all the while checking the window for alarm wires. Fortunately, there were none, and the windows at that level were not barred on the outside like those on the ground floor. He made a furtive glance about the room and moved up against the glass. No one seemed to be paying particular attention as he quietly unlatched one of the window locks. He noticed that that side of the building faced a narrow parking lot that was twelve feet below where he stood. Getting up to the window from ground level would be a problem. Maybe his faithful cabbie friend could help him. Perhaps he had a ladder.

When Jules returned, Mike said, "Well, my banker has asked me to come to the bank to review my total plans for investment down here."

Jules looked on as if he had expected something like that.

"So thank you for your time and help, Jules. I'll consider a better offer and let you know."

Jules smiled, gave him a business card, and said he looked forward to their next meeting.

# CHAPTER 32

Before leaving, Mike took a brief tour of the building. From Balboa's office, he followed the hallway to the rear of the building. There, a second set of stairs descended to ground level. A large window, at the second-floor landing, swung inward when opened to provide access to the outside fire escape. He opened the window and saw that the bottom flight of the fire stairs was cantilevered to keep it out of reach from the ground. He also noticed that, as an architectural embellishment, a belt of white granite blocks girded the building at the second- and fourth-floor levels. Each block extended two inches out beyond the brick veneering. By clinging to the brick, he could edge along that narrow ledge from the fire escape to Balboa's windows. It appeared that he had two means of access: a ladder from the parking lot or the granite block ledge. But where would he get a ladder? Would his cabbie friend have one? And would he let it be used for an office break-in? Probably not, if he was smart.

He returned to the entry lobby and went to the nearest tenant office. A receptionist glanced up as he entered. "*Habla inglés?*" he asked. She nodded. "Good. I'm moving some furniture into our space up on four this evening," he said. "Do you know when they lock the lobby doors?"

"Yes," she said. "You'll have to use your key after six p.m. to get in the building."

"Thank you." He went outside and hailed a cab.

He had the cab stop at a Sprago store on his way back to the hotel and bought a pair of sneakers, a black T-shirt, a length of clothesline rope, and a small flashlight.

Later, though, warmly torpid from dinner, his resolve began to ebb. He could fall and break a leg or something. Or get caught and arrested. Felonious entry was a crime down here, just like everywhere else. Jules used his computer to check Feinberg's file. Would he leave it booted up? Probably not, and he could never find his access code. But they must have paper files as well, for contracts, listing agreements, leases, whatever. Mike wondered about legal alternatives. Could he initiate a lawsuit against Feinberg and subpoena Balboa for the address? That would be legal and smarter, but expeditious? He doubted it. Feinberg's response to a lawsuit might be flight.

At 8:45, he ordered a cab. It was a ten-minute ride. The streets were not crowded in that area at night. The building's lobby lights were all on, and as he left the taxi, he noted many of the upper-floor offices were bright as well. Balboa's office, though, was dark.

He sauntered through the abutting parking lot to the rear of the building. There he tied a plastic bottle of soda, which he had brought from the hotel, to one end of his clothesline. On his second toss, the bottle and attached line slipped between the bottom two steps of the cantilevered stair section. He gave the line slack, letting the weight of the bottle bring that end of the line down to him. To that point he hadn't broken any law that he was aware of. His next move, though, would put him over the line. He looked up the alley for signs of activity. There were none.

The stairs complained with a terrible groaning as he pulled them downward. Lord, they could probably hear that in the next block. He hurried up the steps and climbed over the rail and out onto the two-inch ledge. The mortar for the brick veneering was inset a half inch, just enough to allow him to grip the bricks with his fingertips. Facing the wall and clinging to the bricks with death-grip determination, he began sidling along the narrow ledge.

His fingertips soon began to tingle from the pressure of his gripping. If the nerves went numb, he couldn't maintain his hold and would fall. He wondered about that. Twelve feet wasn't very far, but he could easily break something no matter how well he landed. He continued to scrape along till he reached the building's rear corner. With some difficulty, he negotiated around it to the building's side wall. The muscles in his forearm were fatiguing and beginning to tremble in little spasms. *Oh God, I'll lose my grip before I reach the window.* He imagined breaking both legs in the fall and lying unobserved in the parking lot. In the morning Luis would find him and ask what his banker said.

Light from the street cast a faint illumination on the wall on this side of the building, but fortunately there was not much foot traffic that might notice him. At last he edged up to the windows. Mike tried to remember which one he had unlocked. It was one of the middle two; he was certain of that much at least. He tried the first one. With his right hand gripping brick, he pushed up on the lower pane's sash piece with his left. If he pushed too hard, he could send himself off the wall. One hand wouldn't do it. He released his right hand from its clawing grip then leaned into the window well and pushed with both hands. It wouldn't budge. God, was it painted shut? He edged over to the next window.

Just as he got in position, a group of noisy revelers stopped out on the street by the front of the building. One of them headed into the narrow little parking lot, coming to where he could easily see Mike, frozen there on the wall. Then his buddies called something. He turned, answered, stood there for a moment, and then rejoined them and they wandered off.

Mike tried the second window. The muscles in his arms began to quiver from the strain; then finally it loosened and slid upward. Gasping for breath, he eased inside and collapsed, his heart pounding as if to escape from his chest.

There was enough light from the street and the hallway that he easily found his way to the file cabinets. There were five, each with four drawers. Shielding his flashlight as best he could, he scanned the drawer tags. "*Administración, impuestos, empleados…*Jesus, which one? I don't have time for all of them." Then he saw a cabinet tagged *archivos clientes.* That must be it. Feinberg's file was in the top drawer. He pulled it and moved back into a darker area of the office.

The second sheet gave Feinberg's address. He was living in a high-rise called the Azulaire Tower. It gave a street address on Avenida Italia. Mike returned to the cabinet and had just replaced Feinberg's file when the room suddenly blazed with light. His heart stopped.

One of the building's janitorial workers was pushing his service cart through the front door and saw Mike frozen by the file cabinets. He stammered for a moment. The janitor asked something in Spanish that Mike guessed was "What are you doing in here?"

"Oh…um…*dormido*." He thought he had said napping but wasn't sure. Then he looked at his watch. "Oh, look. Time to go. *Pronto*." He started toward the door. He knew he could never make it out the way he came in.

The janitor had his cell phone out and was punching up a number. He waved his hand, palm outward and took a carpenter's hammer from his cart, "*No, no. Alto!*" He kept his cart in position to block Mike's path and made a threatening gesture with the hammer.

"Okay, okay." Mike raised both hands in a gesture of surrender. "Okay. While we wait, I'll give you a hand with your cleanup here." He grabbed a wastebasket from alongside one of the sales desks while the janitor looked on, nonplussed. Mike set the basket on the receptionist's desk. "*Mira, amigo. Fuego.*" He then took his cigar lighter and struck flame to the basket's contents. In a second it flared up to a bright little blaze. "*Aquí.*" He tossed the basket to the janitor, who jumped back, away from his cart and the path to the door. The metal basket bounced on the tile floor and scattered bits of charred paper. Mike pushed the cart aside and bolted into the hall. He headed for the rear exit. In four clumsy leaps, he bounded down the stairs and reached ground level. He heard an intrusion alarm go off as he burst through the double doors and into the alleyway.

Halfway down the block, he looked back and saw the janitor standing there in the rear doorway. Mike kept running. He stopped at the end of the alley to catch his breath and wondered which way to head. There was little traffic in that area of town, auto or pedestrian. Out on the street, he'd be easily spotted by the police, and he realized they were probably on their way. He had to get a cab or get off the street immediately.

There were no cabs in sight and probably wouldn't be for some time. He jogged along for another block. There were signs of activity up at the next intersection, a few pedestrians and some auto traffic. When he reached it, he saw a Starbucks store halfway down the block to his left. They were still open, thank God. Out of breath, he got inside just as a police patrol car hurried by, its blue lights flashing.

He stood at the counter for several seconds with the barista watching as he labored to catch his breath and settle his nerves. "*Baño?*" he asked. She pointed to the rear. Mike rinsed his hands and used paper towels to dry the perspiration from his head. He wasn't in any hurry; he would give the police enough time to move on to their next call.

Finally, he returned to the counter and ordered a latte. The clerk, an attractive young woman, advised him, though, that their espresso machine was out of order. A maintenance man in coveralls was squatting on the floor, poking tools up into the guts of the espresso maker. "We are closing soon, anyway," she said. "But I can give you a brewed coffee."

"That would be fine. Before you close, could you order a taxi for me?"

She said she would.

Mike took his coffee to a seat in the rear of the store. As he got settled, a second police car drifted by.

Minutes later a zapping noise came from the broken espresso machine. The maintenance guy gave a frightened curse, and the room went dark. After a few moments of confusion, the barista found a flashlight and came around the counter to Mike's table. "Okay," she said in English. "I'm sorry, but you must leave."

"The taxi?"

"No, I can't do that now. Around the corner, you will see a hotel. You might find a taxi there."

"Well…"

"*Señor*, you cannot stay here now. It could be dangerous for you."

Mike felt there was more danger out on the street, at least for him personally. "Okay," he said. With a nervous pace, he headed for the hotel. As he came near, he noticed a taxi moving up the street quite slowly as if preparing to stop and drop a fare. Mike waved. The driver pulled up to the curb, and Mike gratefully jumped in. "Hotel Riande Granada, *por favor.*"

"*Sí.*" The driver nodded then keyed his cell phone. "*Hola,* Ramon," he said. Then in rapid Spanish, he passed a brief message. Probably his dispatcher.

For the first few minutes or so, Mike kept his eye out for police patrols. Oh hell, he thought finally, they were not going to start searching taxis. He began to relax, almost amused by his evening adventure. He smiled to himself; most tourists don't enjoy this kind of excitement. His hotel was about fifteen minutes away, but now he noticed they were moving through a tenement neighborhood. He hadn't come that way. "*Pardon. Habla inglés?*"

"Yes."

"Did you understand, I want the hotel Riande Granada? This doesn't seem to be the right way."

"Just a little different route, *señor.*"

"Oh." Mike didn't believe him. At first he thought the driver was running up the fare. Then he remembered they charged on the basis of zones. It didn't matter which route you took, or at least it wasn't supposed to. The neighborhood looked a little rough—graffiti scrolled on building walls, trash on the curb. The driver dropped his speed as if looking for an address. Mike wondered if he were lost. Then they pulled in to a short alleyway and stopped.

"What's the problem?"

"No problem, *señor.* Jus' get out of the cab."

"Not here, buddy. Back this wreck out of here and take me to my damn hotel."

"I don' wan' to tell you again. Out of the car."

Two men appeared from out of the shadows. One opened the door and pulled Mike from the taxi. The other stood back, holding a gun.

Mike put up his hands. "Okay, okay, guys, let's be cool here." He emptied the cash from his wallet and started to hand it to the guy who had pulled him from the cab. The guy with the gun said something.

The driver had climbed out now and was watching. "He wants the wallet also," he said.

"What? The wallet won't do him any good."

"Give him the wallet."

Mike sighed. "All right. I'll just take out my driver's license and stuff." He started to remove his credit cards as surreptitiously as possible. The gunman watched.

"Ramon," the cab driver said, "convince him."

The one called Ramon took a knife from his pocket, snapped it open. The blade glinted as it caught rays from the nearby streetlight. He put the tip of the blade against Mike's neck. Mike stepped back. The knife followed, with Ramon's leering face right behind it. The gunman stood and smiled as Ramon flicked his knife in threatening gestures and deftly took a nick out of Mike's left ear. Mike handed him the wallet and cards.

"Now the watch and ring," the cabbie said.

"Okay. The ring I don't care about. But the watch was the last present my poor mother gave me. It's just an inexpensive watch, but it means a lot to me. The only memento I have from her."

The cabbie said something to the gunman. The gunman shook his head and responded. The cabbie turned to Mike. "He don' care about memento. The watch...and your belt. Give them to him now, or he kills you and gets it all anyway."

Kill him? He probably already intended to do that anyway. Even in this poor light, he'd seen their faces. He slipped off his watch and handed it to Ramon. The ring fit tight and refused to come at first. In a week or so he wouldn't be wearing it anyway. Next he gave up his belt.

Ramon said something to the cabbie.

"He says he likes your shoes."

"My shoes?"

"They look new. He thinks they are about his size."

Mike removed his new sneakers. Now the bullet would come. He tried to steel himself for it. What an amazing irony. In one instant he was a multimillionaire. Then, because he planned to stiff Janet, he was duped by an attorney, mugged at Shilshole, accused of murder, and finally robbed and murdered in a Panama slum. And the worst part...he was sober.

As he watched Ramon try on his new shoes, a ploy he had seen in a movie came to him. It might work. Mike clutched his chest with both hands. He made a croaking noise, rolled his head in a crazed manner, and gasping for breath, stumbled toward Ramon as if he wanted him to help somehow. Ramon's eyes bugged out. Mike started to drool and stagger. The cabbie and gunman gawked. Mike groaned and fell to his knees. He let out one final gasp and collapsed. He hoped they thought he was dead.

The alley was silent for several seconds. Finally, Mike heard them mutter something. Then there was the sound of car doors closing and the cabbie starting his engine. He continued to lie there for several minutes to be sure that they all had left. As he wondered about getting up, he noticed he was lying in a muddy scum that had a foul smell. Then he felt a throbbing in his knee. This was just wonderful.

He teetered out of the alley, not sure if he was happy to be alive and wondering what the hell to do without money or credit cards. Hitchhike? He hadn't noticed the slow drip of blood coming from his ear. Farther down the street, he saw a few lights coming from what appeared to be tenement housing. Would anybody there help him? He doubted it. Maybe he could use their phone, though. Who would he call? The police? Would they come and take him to his hotel? They might.

The tenements along there were two- and three-story walkups built right to the edge of the sidewalk. The ground-level units, tacky little shops of questionable legitimacy, were mostly dark. He might have to go inside and upstairs to find a phone. Then he saw the fluttering blue glow of a TV shining through the ragged curtained window of a *lavandería*. He went to the door and knocked. There was no answer. He pounded louder; the door shook as if it would come loose from its hinges. Then it opened a crack. A voice said, "*Sí?*"

"Telephone, *por favor.*"

The door closed and he heard the lock click.

Toward the end of the block, a narrow entryway, a kind of a *porte cochere*, led into a small central court. Two levels of apartments formed a U around it. Mike went to the first one that showed lights. He heard a loud grumble from inside in response to his knock. Then a man carrying a can of beer came to the door. He looked familiar.

"Oh God…Ramon."

# CHAPTER 33

Mike froze. He was weary and too depressed to run. It wouldn't matter anyway. A younger man in shoes, his new Sprago sneakers, would catch him easily.

"Did you say Ramon?" the man asked, speaking reasonably clear English.

"Uh."

"Ramon is my brother. I am Roberto."

"Oh." Mike examined the man's face. "Yes, of course."

"You are a friend of Ramon?"

"Well, acquaintance would be more like it."

"So what do you want here? You looking for Ramon?"

"Uh...no." Mike shook his head. "He's not here, is he?"

"No."

"Huh. Well, he said you might let me use your telephone."

"He said that?"

"Sure."

"So Ramon's telling guys out there, even *gringos*, you want to call somebody, just go use my brother's phone. Seems pretty strange to me."

"Uh. Well, it's not quite like that. More in case of emergencies. You know, no other place to go, that kind of thing."

"Uh-huh. Local call?"

"Yes."

"Who you callin'?"

Why should he care? He had intended to call the police. But that didn't seem like a good idea right then. Roberto didn't look like the type who would appreciate police coming to his place. The whole damn neighborhood probably felt that way.

"I was thinking my girlfriend. Do you have a directory...a phonebook?"

"I think so." He wagged his head. "The phone is back this way." Roberto led Mike back to his kitchen and found the directory. Then, as if for the first time, he noticed Mike's appearance. "What happened to your shoes?" He didn't mention the dirty shirt and trousers.

"Uh...I took them off for a while, and then they were stolen."

Roberto squinted. "Drunk, huh?"

Mike shrugged. "Yeah."

"You should be more careful."

"That's good advice."

There were five Whites in the phonebook. Fortunately, Lorene had her own listing. Mike noted the number and hoped it was a local call, as he had said. She answered on the fourth ring.

"Lorene, it's Mike."

After a pause, she said, "Yes?"

Roberto was standing there listening; Mike gave him a smile. Then into the phone, he said, "I hate asking, but I am in a bit of a spot. Could you come to..." He turned to Roberto. "What's the address here?" Roberto said something that Mike didn't understand. "Could you come to *calle*...something." He turned to Roberto again.

"Tell her it's near the old bingo hall."

"Did you hear that? Roberto said it's near the old bingo hall. Oh, you heard. Good. Well?"

"What are you doing there?"

"Oh..." He gave a wan chuckle. "Just on an outing. Ended here, sort of by mistake, you might say."

She didn't understand that at all. "Well, why call me? I'm going to bed. Call a cab."

"Of course. I would if I were in a position to, but I'm not. You see, I was involved in a little accident, actually. But anyway, thanks to my friend Roberto, standing here, helping me out, letting me use his phone, I'm able to call you."

"Yeah?"

"Yeah." Then, with heavier emphasis, he added, "Let's just say that you are the only person in this city that can help me right now."

"Oh?"

She still hadn't said she'd come. "Uh-huh. I met a group of guys that were short of funds. So I helped them out."

Roberto frowned at hearing that.

Lorene seemed to catch on. "You were mugged."

"Right."

"All right. I'll be there in twenty minutes. Wait by the old bingo hall."

"Great." Mike cradled the phone. "Thanks, Roberto."

Roberto nodded with a skeptical look.

"And when you see Ramon next time, give him my regards."

Thirty minutes later, Lorene pulled up to the bingo hall. Mike was standing up against a doorway. He jumped in as soon as she stopped. On the way to his hotel, Mike gave Lorene a brief recap of his evening. He wasn't sure how candid he should be when describing the office break-in, or intrusion, actually. He didn't break anything, but he was a miscreant regardless. There were enough unsavory aspects and doubts in his recent past that Lorene was already aware of, and he didn't want to add to it if he could help it. So he loosely described his experience as an after-hours walk-in. Lorene didn't question it. He was quite forthcoming, though, regarding his adventure with the cab driver, Mr. Gun, and Ramon.

"So they took your things, but didn't rough you up?"

"Well, Ramon cut my ear, but yeah, they didn't do much else."

"How'd you get so dirty, then? Your shirt and pants?"

He told her about his fake heart attack ploy and went on to explain whose phone he used to call her.

"Ramon's brother?"

"Yeah. Isn't that a kick? Can't you just imagine their conversation, Ramon and Roberto, when they get together next time? Roberto tells him about this nut that came in without any shoes and used his phone." They both laughed at the thought.

Lorene glanced over at her sorry-looking passenger and changed her course. "I'm taking you to my place. Get you cleaned up. You look terrible. Dirt and blood all over your clothes. They probably wouldn't let you in the hotel."

Lorene's place was actually her parents' home. Her mother was up and waiting. She frowned when she saw Mike drag in behind her daughter. She hadn't expected that. It was easy to see she disapproved. Lorene ignored it. "Mother, this is Michael Collins. He is down here searching for a man that stole from him."

"Yes," she said, showing doubt.

"He was beaten and robbed tonight by a taxi driver and two compatriots."

"Oh, dear."

Lorene turned to Mike. "Michael, this is my mother, Estelle White."

Mike smiled. "I'm pleased to meet you, Señora White, and I apologize for even being here, especially in this condition. The robbers took everything—money, credit cards, watch, and even my shoes, as you see. Lorene is the only person I know in Panama and the only one I could call for help." He shrugged.

Estelle continued to assess his looks and didn't show any signs of sympathy.

Lorene explained that she would launder Mike's shirt and trousers the next morning and that Mike could spend the night in her brother's old room. Mike didn't expect that. Then, looking her mother straight in the eye, Lorene said, "Maybe he could borrow one of Dad's robes till his clothes are ready."

Estelle nodded.

Lorene applied some antiseptic to Mike's ear and gave him a towel for the shower.

After he had cleaned up, Estelle showed Mike to her son's old room. "This became our spare bedroom after he finished school and married," she said.

It was easy to see that Estelle was not pleased by any of this. Mike decided not to gush or overplay his gratitude. "You're very kind to let me stay," he said in a level voice.

"Sleep well," she said.

■□■

Mike awoke late; it was after nine. Agitated by the evening's activities, he had tossed and lain awake for several hours. At about four, he finally dropped off into a deep slumber. He awoke hungry and reasonably composed. He noticed things he had overlooked the previous night. The son's old room, where he had slept, had a three-quarter bed, a desk, a chair, and a bureau. The walls were bare except for two pictures: one of the Blessed Virgin and one of the Sacred Heart. Whatever posters or trivia the son had were gone, and aside from a picture on the bureau, a handsome man in a graduation gown, there was no sign that it had been his room.

Mike could see that Señora White was a fastidious housekeeper—everything in its place and no clutter. He found his shirt and trousers, cleaned, pressed, and folded on the desk chair. He dressed and made up the bed.

In the living room, two upholstered chairs had doilies pinned to the armrests and chair backs. A low, glass-topped table fronted a leather settee that was angled toward the television. A crucifix with a faded palm frond was hung above the doorway to the hall. Bold floral prints, framed behind glass, adorned the room's two larger walls.

Estelle was busying herself in the kitchen. "My," she said as he entered. "Such a sound sleeper."

"Yes, well, I guess I'm still on West Coast time." He looked at his wrist and remembered he no longer had a watch.

"We ate hours ago, but I saved some for you. Lorene has gone on an errand. She should be back for *comida*…lunch. Mr. White is outside in our little garden. After you eat, you can meet him."

Señora White worked in a narrow little kitchen, more like a hallway. The back porch, or *veranda*, had been screened in, though, and she had a nice-sized table for food prep out there. The room smelled of clove and basil.

Estelle joined him with a cup of coffee as he dug into a hearty breakfast.

"Lorene told me about your loss of the lottery prize." She spoke as if there was doubt regarding Mike's story.

"Yes?"

"Mmm. And if you don't recover it, what will you do?"

Mike shrugged. "Return to Seattle and notify the police up there that I had located the man that stole from me."

She nodded skeptically.

"You see, they would have charges against him for arson and conversion…maybe fraud regarding his boat insurance. I imagine they would attempt extradition."

"I see." She sipped her coffee. Mike went back to eating. "What do you do in Seattle? What kind of work?" she asked finally.

"Telephone company…technical staff."

"Oh." She watched him eat. "You have family up there…mother, father…wife?"

Mike smiled. Estelle was getting to it now. "Both my parents are dead. I'm not married." He thought that sounded better than "divorced."

The loss of his parents seemed to provoke a touch of sympathy. "It is hard losing a mother and father. That must be distressful for you. Were you very close?"

"My mother and I got on well. As much as sons and mothers usually do, I suppose."

Mike studied his coffee. "Not so with Dad, though."

"Oh? Why was that?"

Mike wondered why she should care or if he should even bother her with an explanation. Then he realized he wanted to get it out. He didn't expect sympathy. Understanding would be enough, and maybe sharing it with this woman, who was almost a stranger to him, would ease the hurt he still felt toward his dad. "I had a brother, Tim. He was two years older, stronger and smarter too. He was great at everything…sports, school. And he was good to me. We were best friends, a little competitive sometimes, but rarely disagreeable. Dad adored him. Tim was everything my dad wanted to be."

Estelle sat forward a little as if closeness expressed her interest, her sincerity.

Mike continued. "We were camping by a river. This was our last outing of the summer before Tim was to leave for college. Dad was taking a nap while Tim and I went fishing. Somehow Tim slipped and fell into the stream. The current carried him down through a stretch of rapids and into some snags that had caught on some large rocks in the middle of the river. At first I thought he would free himself and swim ashore. But he just hung there…not moving any…the cold water sweeping around him. I shouted. No response. I was plenty worried now. I went into the water upstream a bit and let the current carry me to him. When I hit the jammed up snags, some of them broke loose. Before I could grab Tim, the current swept me off. I was carried downstream a ways before I could finally work my way to the bank and get out. When I got back to the snag jam, Tim was gone."

Mike let his gaze settle on Estelle's eyes. Before she could respond he went on. "His body was never found. The river was searched all the way to the sea. Dad was crazy with grief. Sometimes, after he had been drinking, he would rant that Tim was alive…had amnesia…would recover and come home. He might have felt some guilt that he wasn't with us when Tim fell. But, if he did, he resolved it by shifting it onto me. It was my fault, he said. I abandoned my brother. I couldn't convince him otherwise. He never forgave me." Mike dropped his gaze, studied his nearly empty cup.

Estelle watched for a moment. She nodded slowly. "It's sad." She met Mike's eyes. "But all you can do now is forgive him."

"Yes…I think I have."

After Mike finished breakfast, he went out to the garden as Estelle had suggested. Mr. White was pruning roses. They shook hands. "Just call me Don," Mr. White said.

"And I'm Mike."

They chatted a bit, mostly about Mike's mugging.

"If it's not impolite to say so," Mike said finally, "I notice no trace of an accent in your speech."

"No, you shouldn't. I grew up in Idaho. After high school, I took a job with Peter Kiewit in heavy construction. We got a large contract down here in Panama that lasted two and a half years. I met Estelle, and when the job finished, I stayed."

■□■

Lorene returned at noon. "We will have a little lunch, and I will show you where I work and some of the city."

"Well, I've just had a nice brunch, but the tour sounds great." He guessed Feinberg would have to wait. As he considered that, Mike wondered at the casual way he was accepting diversions from his intended mission. "Could we go by my hotel first? There are a few things I need to do regarding my stolen cards."

"No problem."

■□■

At the hotel, Mike arranged a cash advance from the hotel cashier. Then he called Janet.

"Janet, it's Mike."

"Yeah." He could almost see the frown on her face. "You calling about the summons?"

"Summons? From who?"

"I can't remember their names. Some guy and his wife are complaining that you beat them up several weeks ago. They want a lot of money for the pain and permanent injury. A guy showed up here yesterday to serve the papers. I told him we were divorced and refused to sign anything."

Mike sighed.

"You just can't get enough trouble, can you?"

"The guy's an asshole. He was slapping hell out of his wife. I tried to stop him. He doesn't have a case; it's just a shakedown. Maybe he saw something about the lottery. I don't know, but that's not why I called. I got mugged and my credit cards were taken."

"You were drunk and just lost them, you mean."

"No, held up. A gun and everything."

"So why are you calling me?"

"Well, you are on these cards too, you know."

"So?"

"I need to call the card company and get them canceled. And I don't have the card numbers or anything." He began drumming his fingers on the desk.

"Don't you keep a record of those things?"

"Not down here."

"Not down where?"

"Panama City."

"Panama City? What are you doing down there?"

"On vacation."

The line was silent for a moment. "You're looking for Feinberg, aren't you?"

"Yes."

"You find him?"

"I'm close. Anyway, I need the numbers for Visa and MasterCard."

"How about Texaco and Macy's?"

"I'm not worried about them right now."

Janet's mind was working fast. "Okay. I'll get them and call you back. What's the number down there?"

"Can't you just get the cards out of your purse now? I can wait."

"No. It'll take me a few minutes. What's your number?" she asked again.

He gave it to her. "I'll wait here in my room." It occurred to him that what she really wanted was the name of his hotel. She would get it when the switchboard girl answered. But why? What good would that do her?

■□■

After Janet returned Mike's call and gave him the credit card info, she called her attorney, Sheldon Mains. "I just talked to Mike. He's in Panama City."

"Oh yeah?"

"He thinks Feinberg is down there."

"Why'd he call you?"

Janet explained the mugging and loss of credit cards.

"Well, well. I'd say that mugger did us a favor. I think we should hire a private detective down there. If Mike has a lead on Feinberg, we should be ready to step in. Do you agree?"

"Certainly."

"All right. The agency we use here should have an affiliate or a contact in Panama. If that doesn't work I'll send a local guy down."

# CHAPTER 34

Janet had been referred to a homeowner who had just received relocation orders. On Monday morning she obtained the listing, which she thought should sell quickly. She returned to the office in good spirits. She smiled as Larry came over to her desk.

"How about an early lunch?" he asked.

Mondays weren't their usual play days. "Well, okay."

He grimaced. "I'll tell you about it at lunch."

They met at the Safeway lot as usual. Larry asked if Chinese was okay; there was a Cantonese spot close by. Sure, she said. She could tell he was disturbed. Neither spoke until they reached the restaurant and were seated.

"You sold your house yet?" he asked.

"No. Had a few tours. No offers, though."

"Would you like a roommate?"

She wasn't sure how to answer. "Who'd you have in mind?"

"Me."

"Oh…Sure."

"I'm not serious, of course, but I am moving out of the house. Felicia's filing and is raising hell."

Janet gaped as if in surprise. "Well, if you need a place for the time being."

"Thanks. No. I've lined up an apartment." He shrugged. "Infidelity. She apparently found out about us."

215

"I thought we were pretty careful."

"I did too. I don't know what put her on to it. But she had us watched for a couple weeks."

"A detective?"

"Yeah."

"I never noticed anybody."

"I didn't either. But I guess he got pictures."

"Of what?" She winced, imagining flagrante delicto.

"Going in and out of the motel."

"Oh." She lowered her eyes, studying her tea in the little ceramic cup. "I'm sorry, Larry, sorry for you. It may have been wrong, but our affair has meant a lot to me." She reached across the table and touched his hand.

"Well...for me too," he said.

As they finished their lunch, in a coy, almost shy way, she asked, "Think it would be okay to stop at the motel?"

Larry was almost stunned by the question. "God, I don't know. You think we could? My spirits are kind of flat right now."

She gave him a sympathetic look. "I understand. You may be feeling some guilt, but you shouldn't give in to it. I think if our home lives had been better, we wouldn't have needed each other."

Larry nodded.

She touched his hand again, lightly stroking it.

He smiled.

Well, Felicia must have found the tube of lipstick.

# CHAPTER 35

Lorene maneuvered through the city traffic to Avenue de Los Martines then on across the Bridge of the Americas, which spans the Pacific entry to the canal. As they drove along, she explained that she had begun her work at San Jose de Malambo as a nursery attendant and assistant teacher. Since she now had her degree, she would intern under the staff psychologist, and in six months, she would replace the woman who was retiring.

"They have psychologists at the orphanage?" Mike asked.

"Oh, yes. We care for children from infancy to age eighteen. They come to us at various ages and from different backgrounds, and often with issues."

"That will be your life's work, then, at the orphanage?"

"Probably. The pay is modest, but that's not why I am there."

"Sounds noble."

"Perhaps not as much as you think. It's very rewarding working with the children. In a way, they give you more than you give them."

Mike nodded.

"Oh, after a few years, with more experience behind me, I could seek a position in the public sector or in private practice. Those are options, but not immediate ones."

At the orphanage, Mike was introduced to Sister Josita Panagua, the nun in charge. Lorene explained that Mike was here on a short visit but seemed interested in their work. Then she added, "Perhaps you could show him around while I finish a small item in my office."

They watched her hurry away down the hall.

"Such dedication," Sister Josita said, smiling.

Mike agreed. "She loves working here."

"Yes." The nun studied Mike's eyes. "Have you known Lorene very long?"

"No, just a few days, actually. Though we met briefly in Seattle."

"I see. And that's why you are in Panama now, to see Lorene?"

Mike made a soft smile. "You might think so. I wonder about it myself. But no, I came down on business."

"Mmm. Well, it's unusual for her to bring a friend here. You must have made a favorable impression."

"I'm glad if I did." He pursed his lips at the thought. "She certainly has made an impression on me."

Josita nodded, all the while watching his eyes as if she could see through them.

Mike went on. "She is a remarkable woman, beautiful in many ways. I'm surprised she is still single. You'd expect a fiancé, or boyfriend at least." Then he gave a slight chuckle. "Maybe she has one."

The nun looked away for a moment and then said, "Come on, I'll give you a tour."

San Jose de Malambo was actually more than an orphanage, much more. They housed abused and abandoned children, as well as those who had lost their parents. A special nursery unit cared for HIV babies, who sadly had a limited future, there or anywhere. In addition, needy, indigent children from the surrounding neighborhoods were brought there each day for a breakfast. Any child in need, no matter its circumstances, was welcome and loved at Malambo.

Several brightly painted buildings, about the size of dwellings, were set on ground that sloped down from the administration building toward the highway. They provided the living quarters for the resident children and staff. The grounds were attractively landscaped and maintained, which gave the setting a pleasant and inviting aspect.

As the tour ended, Lorene rejoined them outside the nursery building.

"Well, what do you think?" she asked.

"I'm very impressed. By the facilities, of course, but more so by the nuns and lay people that I have met here."

Sister Josita smiled. "Yes, we are blessed."

■□■

On the way back to Mike's hotel, Lorene took a short side trip to the Mira Flores locks. "I know you are anxious to contact Mr. Feinberg," she said, "but I thought you should see the locks before you leave."

Mike agreed. He bought them espressos, and they spent an hour touring the visitor center and watching ships transit the locks.

At 4:30, they pulled up to his hotel.

"I've had a wonderful day. I hate to see it end," he said.

"I'm glad you enjoyed it. I am proud of my city. Oh sure, we have problems we need to resolve, social issues, education, but we are making progress."

"I believe you are." They exchanged smiles. "You have probably had enough of me, possibly too much, considering last night. But I was hoping we could have dinner tonight."

Lorene hesitated for a moment. Then she said, "Well, I guess that would be okay."

"Good. I'm going to try Feinberg's. If he is there and lets me in, that might take an hour or more. Hard to say how he will respond to my demands. How about a table at eight? You pick the spot, something nice."

As Lorene pulled away, Mike hailed the first waiting cab and was on his way to the Azulaire. Traffic stretched the ride to twenty minutes. The Azulaire was one of the city's newer high-rise condominiums. Large glass double doors led into a spacious lobby. Upholstered chairs and settees were arranged to each side of the reception desk, which occupied the center of the room. The vaulted ceiling almost disappeared three stories up. Four elaborate chandeliers floated twelve feet above the lobby floor.

Mike noticed the opulence and muttered, "My money goes a long way down here."

The attendant looked up and smiled as Mike approached. "*Señor?*"

"Mr. Feinberg in ten twenty-five, *por favor.*"

"Mr. Feinberg is out," the lobby attendant told him in clear English. "Possibly until tomorrow. He left as I came on duty. Should I tell him you were here?"

"Yes. Michael Collins. Tell him I'll come back tomorrow."

Mike then thanked him and wondered if he was ever going to get to that guy.

■□■

Back in his room, Mike placed a call to Maxine. She answered on the fourth ring.

"Maxine, it's Mike."

"I've wondered about you. Any news?"

"Yes, I've found Norm."

"So I was right."

"Yes. He has a condo in Panama City. It's been a hassle tracking him down, though. At first I got an address in Boquete. Flew up there to find he had already moved."

"Just a sec. I'm building a drink." Mike heard the sound of ice cubes dropping into a glass. "Boquete, did you say?"

"Yeah. A small town up north."

"I can't see Norm in a small town."

"Me either. Anyway he's back here now. He was out today. I'm going to try again tomorrow. It's been a real adventure. You got a minute, I'll tell you about it."

■□■

Lorene reserved an eight o'clock table at Restaurante Angel. She phoned Mike to give him the timing. "How did your meeting with Feinberg go?" she asked. "Are we celebrating?"

"Didn't see him, I'm sorry to say. I'll try again tomorrow."

"Too bad. Well, you should enjoy dinner anyway. The restaurant has great seafood, and the dress is casual."

That was good news to him because he had no dress clothes with him.

Lorene picked him up at 7:45.

Restaurante Angel made a very positive initial impression: linen on the tables, waiters in black and white, high ceilings, and classic decor.

Mike would have liked to start with a martini, maybe two, something to mute the brooding regard he held for himself. "Would you like a cocktail?" he asked.

"Yes. A glass of wine would be nice."

"A glass of wine it is, then." He ordered two glasses of Pinot Grigio.

While they waited, he asked her about the orphans' school and what the prospects were for increased funding. She explained the limit on state funds and the need for private support, which had been somewhat inconsistent. "There are several things we need to do or would like to do. We are at capacity now, and yet the need continues to grow."

The wine came and Mike raised his glass. "To your health and your school's success."

Lorene smiled. "And to your success in Panama." They touched glasses.

Yes, success—whatever that would be.

Dinner conversation covered what they had seen and done that day. Over coffee, Mike paused, then said in a low voice, "I want you to know how much being with you has meant. For the last several weeks, it seems every turn in my life has been distressing. You've been the only bright spot."

Lorene smiled quietly.

"Yes." He nodded. "The only one. And I find it extraordinary that you have given me so much of your time."

"Well, it's been nice for me too, Mike."

"I'm glad, but I wonder if there's a boyfriend out there that isn't so happy right now."

Lorene studied her coffee. There was a long moment of silence, and Mike thought he might have overstepped propriety.

Lorene looked up finally. "Well, there was such a person for a while. We were engaged before I left to go to school. Summers I came home for a month and everything seemed fine between us...till last year. He said he had found someone else. I was stunned. Then later I learned he had been going with this girl for over a year." She watched Mike's eyes for a reaction.

"I'm sorry," he said.

"Yes, well that's in the past now, and I prefer to leave it there." Then to lighten the air, she asked, "Do you think Feinberg knows where Buddy's gone?"

Mike was still considering her last remarks and was slow to answer. Finally, he said, "Possibly. I'm hoping to see him tomorrow. I'll ask him. If Buddy got his cut, I'd like to know where he is. I doubt it's down here, though."

"No?"

"Probably doesn't have a passport, for one thing."

Lorene nodded. "Probably not. And Buddy seemed more of the Las Vegas type. He'd have a big time at the shows and gambling."

"Yes, if he got his million. But then, I don't know why he'd leave town if he didn't."

"Mmm."

"Well, anyway, that's the way I see it. That note about Ecuador was a ploy. Probably Norm's idea. I think they drove to Portland, then split. If Buddy went to Vegas, he may still be there, being the high roller. So I might find him just as his money runs out. It'd be my luck."

They finished their meal with coffee and chocolate truffles. As Mike settled the tab, he asked, "Would you like to go to a cabaret or someplace to dance?"

Lorene studied his eyes. "Um, maybe another time. I had an early start today while you slept."

Mike smiled. "Well, you are right about that. I nearly missed lunch." He held his smile. "Another time, then."

The short ride back to his hotel was brief and quiet; neither spoke. Mike contemplated the almost immediate affection that he was feeling for the young Panamanian woman and regretted that he would be leaving soon. As they came to a stop at the hotel entry, Mike released his seat belt and opened his door. He eased out of the car without a word then turned and leaned in a bit. "Thank you for everything, Lorene. You saved my life last night and gave me a wonderful day today, one I will never forget. It's probably too much to expect, but I find myself hoping to see you again."

Lorene smiled. "I was glad to do it. Today was fun for me too." Mike had started to close the door when she blurted, "If it works out for you tomorrow, with Feinberg that is, would you like to go to mass Sunday with my family?" As soon as the words left her mouth, she blushed as if she had been indiscreet, too presumptive. Obviously going to church with the family had implications in Panama.

"I would love to. That would be nice, very nice. Perhaps I will offer a prayer of thanks."

"For the success you will have had tomorrow?"

"Yes, and for meeting you."

# CHAPTER 36

Mike found a cab in front of the hotel and handed the driver Feinberg's address. Morning traffic was moderate, and they reached the condo complex in fifteen minutes. The driver pulled into the passenger load zone and asked if he should wait.

"No. I'm not sure how long I will be." Mike paid the fare and headed for the entrance. The lobby attendant looked up as Mike entered. He remembered him from the day before. "You are here for Señor Feinberg, is that right?"

"Yes. Norman Feinberg in ten twenty-five."

"Yes, and your name?"

"Michael Collins."

"I will phone his apartment." He keyed four digits into his operator set, probably Feinberg's unit number. After several seconds, he said, "I'm sorry. There is no answer."

"Is he out, do you know?"

"I don't know, but it is likely. You could try again later. But I believe it would be best to telephone Mr. Feinberg first."

"I would if I had his number. Could you tell me what it is?"

"No. I'm sorry. I can't do that."

"Oh." Mike wasn't surprised. "Guess I'll be back later, then." He was sorry he had dismissed his taxi. He thought to ask the attendant to call for one, then decided to see some of the city as a pedestrian.

■□■

Janet was just leaving for work when she heard the phone. She caught it on the third ring.

"Janet, it's Sheldon. Mike has located Feinberg."

"Oh! I guess I'm surprised. Feinberg must be in the book."

"No. His phone's unlisted. I don't know how Mike found him."

"Are the police involved, do you know?"

"I don't think so. I just got a call from Riley, the private detective I hired—we hired. Says Feinberg has a nice condo overlooking the bay. Mike went there this morning, but hasn't seen him yet."

"You think Feinberg got wise and skipped?"

"No. Riley checked with the lobby attendant, who says Feinberg's coming back later today."

"You think Feinberg will meet with Mike?"

"Pretty sure. He knows Mike will bring in the police if he doesn't."

"So what do we do now?"

"I should go down there, intervene on your behalf, and get your share."

"Can you practice there?"

"No. If we have to appear in court, I'll use a local attorney. I think I'll take one along for the confrontation anyway. Probably hire a policeman as well. Now here's the deal: If Feinberg refuses to deal, I'll notify Seattle police and have him arrested. No matter what terms he offers Mike, we shouldn't settle for less than four million. I think the presence of a local cop will scare him."

"Okay."

"Right. Now to do all this, my fee will be 25 percent."

"One million!"

"That's right, assuming we get the full four."

"A little high, don't you think?"

"No. I'm working on a contingency here. And 25 percent is not unusual for cases like this."

Janet wondered about that. "But you won't be doing a trial. It shouldn't involve that much work, should it?"

"It's hard to say. We may have to bring Feinberg back to Seattle, though I think he'd want to avoid that. Anyway, that's my deal, and honestly, I believe it's the only way you'll get anything."

He was probably right. "Okay. I guess it's a deal, then."

Mains had his secretary obtain a list of Panama City attorneys and book him on the next flight.

# CHAPTER 37

As he finished his dinner in the hotel coffee shop, Mike noticed the man at a table across the room. Something about him seemed familiar. He was tall and lanky, Mike could tell that even though the guy was slouched over his meal. His face resembled the man who played Lurch on *The Addams Family*. Then he remembered: he had seen him twice while he was meandering through town today. That was odd too, considering the route he had taken. After signing for his meal, he went over to the man's table. "Excuse me for interrupting, but you look familiar." The guy almost gagged on a mouthful of pudding. "Are you in the communication business?" Mike asked, certain that he wasn't.

"Uh…no. Must have me confused with someone else."

"Huh. Thought I saw you at a convention last year." Mike followed the guy's eyes as they darted about apprehensively. "You down here on business?"

"Family matters," the guy said.

"Um. Well, it's quite a city, isn't it?"

"Huh? Oh. Yes. Yes, it is." He started to look a bit uncomfortable.

"I'm from Seattle, myself, which is nice, but I must say Panama has impressed me. Didn't expect such a large, modern city. Where you from?"

"Uh, Kansas City."

"Missouri?"

"Yeah."

"That's quite a city too. Used to go there on business. My favorite restaurant was Berbiglia in the Hallmark Plaza. You know the one I mean? Great seafood."

"Right."

"Ever eat there?"

"Well, not lately."

"Uh-huh. Well, nice chatting. I'm Mike Collins, by the way."

"Nice meeting you, Mike."

Mike stood waiting.

"Oh. I'm Albert Riley. Friends call me Al."

"Enjoy the rest of your stay, Al. Maybe we'll bump into each other again."

"Yeah. You too." Riley gave Mike a nod.

Mike was sure that Riley had lied. Anyone who had ever lived in Kansas City knew Berbiglia was the largest and best liquor retailer in the state. You couldn't miss their ads, even if you weren't a drinker. Mike was sure: Riley had been following him. But who put him up to it? Must be Janet and her shark attorney.

Mike took the elevator to his floor, passed by his room, and proceeded to the service stairs. Before entering the stairwell, he looked back down the hall. "You back there, Riley?" he muttered. "Guess you're finishing your tapioca."

There were two exit doors at the first-floor landing, *Vestibulo* and *Empleados*. With the confidence of someone who belonged there, he nudged through the employees' door. Hurrying along a wide hallway, he passed the employees' restroom and hotel kitchen. The hall terminated in a freight receiving area. A set of double doors with panic bars led to the alley. He pushed through, to the surprise of two employees who were sneaking a smoke. "*Hola, señores,*" he said. They gawked.

In front of the hotel, he took the only waiting cab and headed to Feinberg's condo for his second attempted visit of the day. Traffic was light, and in fifteen minutes they were at the building's entrance.

There was a different man on duty. With a frozen face, he watched Mike enter the lobby and boldly step up to the reception desk.

"Señor Feinberg in ten twenty-five, *por favor.*"

"Your name, *señor?*"

"Michael Collins."

"Is he expecting you?"

"Possibly."

"Um." The attendant nodded and punched Feinberg's number into his com console.

Feinberg might ignore the call or, as he hoped, let him come up. Almost at once the lobby man was speaking in rapid Spanish. If that was Feinberg on the other end, he certainly became fluent quickly.

"*Sí,* Señor Collins," the attendant said to the phone. There was a brief pause then, with a nod, he said, "*Sí, bien.*" He cradled the handset and led Mike the few steps to the elevators. There he inserted a coded card into an electronic reader and, almost silently, the doors to the nearest car glided open. The attendant reached inside the car and pressed number ten on the button panel, then stepped back and motioned for Mike to enter.

On ten, the elevator opened to a vestibule that had been furnished with a mirror, two framed paintings, an umbrella stand, and a small table set against the wall below the mirror. An abstract bronze and onyx sculpture gleamed from its resting place on the table. There were four apartments on the floor. Mike noticed they were numbered 1005, 1015, 1025, and 1040. He went to 1025. Before he could knock or find a bell button, the door swung open. A very muscular, dark-complexioned man stood there, his cold eyes measuring Mike.

"I'm here to see Mr. Feinberg," Mike said.

"Step inside and raise your arms."

"Huh?"

"I said, step inside and raise your arms."

"Oh…sure."

The man frisked Mike for weapons and then said, "This way."

Mike followed. The man's shoes squeaked as he walked, as if made of plastic. From the entry foyer, a gallery hall led past a sunken living room, then a den or library. Indifferent framed prints, large floral still lifes, graced the walls. Mike thought of a Hollywood movie set. They came to the master suite and the man motioned him in.

The room was nearly dark. Heavy draperies were drawn across the windows. Mike noticed an ozone-like smell. As his eyes adjusted to the muted light, he saw that the room was indeed a master suite. The plush of the carpet swallowed the soles of his shoes. An upholstered chair, settee, low table, and giant TV were casually arranged in the area to the right. A wet sink and liquor cabinet sat near the TV. Two straight-back chairs and a Trenton pub table were over by the windows. Several steps into the room on the left wall, Norm had a double bureau, and beyond that, a wide entry led to the dressing area and bath. Across the room Mike saw a figure propped by pillows, recumbent on a queen-sized bed.

"Hello, Collins, you dumb bastard." It was Feinberg. His voice was scratchy and weak. Then he said, "Roy, would you brighten the room a bit?"

The bodyguard went to a wall-mounted rheostat and raised the lights. Norm looked awful. His eyes were reddened and weepy. He appeared to have lost weight, and his skin had a yellowish pallor. An oxygen tank and wheelchair sat next to the bed.

"Are you surprised to see me, Norm?" Mike's voice was firm, spiritless, indifferent.

"Yes. I guess I am. It doesn't bother me, though. Nothing does anymore." He let the words trail off in a submissive fade.

Mike waded up closer to the bed. "You don't look too good."

"No kidding. You really think so?"

"Yeah. If you don't feel better by tomorrow, maybe you should see a doctor."

Norm gave a weak chuckle. "I see we both have a perverse sense of humor."

"Something we share...not my Lotto money, though."

"More's the pity." Norm tried to adjust one of the pillows. "What did you expect out of coming here? Toss me out the window like you threatened in Seattle? Roy might not let you do that." Then, with a feeble gesture, he motioned to Roy, who came over and rearranged the pillows. "Yeah, that's better, thanks." Norm watched Mike as if he were waiting for a reply. "Or maybe just to watch me die. Is that it?"

"How long am I going to have to wait?"

The unemotional directness of the question prompted Norm to a colorless smile. "Three weeks, maybe four."

"That long, huh?"

"Yeah." Norm looked around the room and then turned to Roy. "Would you get one of those chairs over there for Collins here?" Roy nodded, grabbed one of the straight-backs and set it near the bed.

Mike thanked him and faced Feinberg. "What's killing you? Remorse?"

"You're a prick to suggest that. But the irony is that's part of it, the mental part. On the medical side, the doctors say it's nodular melanoma. First symptom appeared in Seattle. I didn't realize it, though. Then it really came on up in Boquete." A phlegm cough stopped his speech. He wheezed for a moment, wiped his mouth with a tissue, and then went on. "Did you go up there?"

"Yes."

"What'd you think of it?"

"Only place in the world without a Starbucks store."

Norm smiled weakly. "Almost. Nice climate, though."

"Big change in lifestyle."

"Yes. I realized that myself. There's an expat community there. They garden and play golf. I met a few."

"I didn't notice any. Oh, no, I did see one—your neighbor lady."

"The widow." Norm chuckled softly. "She ask you to take your pants off?"

Mike shook his head. "Gee, I would have too."

Norm smiled at that. Their conversation was taking a more normal, unaffected tone now. Not quite so bitter. They both were too weary to maintain a corrosive level of enmity.

"So you came back to the city for better medical care?"

"Yeah."

"Nothing they can do?"

"Too advanced. I get morphine and some anti-nausea pills. I go to a clinic for radiotherapy, but it's a wasted effort. "

Mike eased his lips into a thin, dry smile. "Do you find it ironic that of all people you ever knew, I'm the only one seeing you now?"

"I suppose. But you didn't come here to keep me company. So don't start feeling noble."

"Don't worry about that. Your dying is not my immediate concern."

"I wouldn't expect it to be." Norm made a slight cough again and sipped some liquid from a glass by the bed. "How'd you find me?"

"Maxine saw the fee for your health statement. That started it."

"Christ. I thought that was off the books. Paid cash." He sniffed and barely shook his head. "Then it went from there, huh?"

"Yeah. She had a computer guy go through your PC. If it wasn't for the doctor's statement, though, you and your man here"—Mike wagged his head toward Roy—"would be all to yourselves right now."

Norm lowered his lids.

Mike continued. "Everybody, including the police, thought you were dead. I've been their lead suspect for murder."

"Yeah, I planned it that way. Had to hang it on somebody. You were the best candidate; the only one, in fact. Bought a Mariner's hat to wear and left your pen in the dinghy."

"My pen? How'd you get that?"

"It fell out of your pocket when we scuffled in my office. After you left with the police I saw it on the floor."

"The police felt that was their best piece of evidence."

"That's what I expected."

Mike slowly shook his head at Feinberg's iniquity. "You could have put me in prison." He expected a reaction, maybe a weak apology, but there wasn't any. Norm's face was a torpid mask. He was unmoved by any concern for Collins. "The money alone wasn't quite enough, huh?"

"I didn't want you or anyone else looking for me."

"It almost worked out that way."

Norm shrugged.

"That reminds me, how about Buddy? You know where he is?"

Norm closed his eyes for several seconds. Mike thought he might be falling asleep.

Then he said, "Well, more or less, but not exactly."

"Where then…more or less?"

"Puget Sound."

Mike blinked. "He went down with the boat?"

"Yeah." Norm's eyes glazed with fluid.

Mike watched quietly.

"Yeah, he went down with the boat, but I see him all the time."

Mike waited for him to go on.

Norm turned a little to face Mike straight on. "I find myself marveling at this meeting that we're having. You seemed to have lost some of your anger, and I am actually glad that you're here. Yes. Glad. Can you imagine that? The guy I conned out of eight mil and set up for murder, and here we are chatting like indifferent acquaintances." He waited to see if Mike would agree, but he remained mute.

Norm continued. "I'm going to tell you about Buddy. Maybe it'll help me sleep. Go to confession like a remorseful Catholic." The corners of his mouth pulled up a little at the irony. "Isn't that a kick? But who better to unload on than you?"

He explained how he had bought a used car and gave it to Buddy, but not for the reason that Buddy thought. "His car was my transportation. Allowed me to leave mine at the marina." He went on to describe the celebration dinner at Ray's. "I got Buddy drunk." He paused. His gaze passed through Mike then and focused on the wall behind him, as if he saw someone there. "Then I had to change my plan a bit."

Mike waited as Norm seemed to consider his last remark.

"We went to the boat and motored out a mile or so. I gave him a bottle of bourbon to work on while I set things up for the explosion and fire. Before I finished, he passed out, his homely little head lying in a puddle of bourbon on the dinette table. Now this is the part that I see over and over, sometimes all night long. I have to get drunk or drugged up to get away from it."

Mike was amazed to be hearing this.

"Anyway…" Norm closed his eyes. Then, in a soft voice, he said, "Oh God."

"You okay?"

"Yeah, I'm okay. I want to finish telling you this." He took another sip of water. "I launched the dinghy. Tied it off on a stern cleat. Went back inside and took the bourbon bottle, poured myself a stiff shot, and then emptied the rest on Buddy. Soaked his clothes with Jack

Daniel's. This is happening, and now I can't believe that it is me doing it." His eyes widened as the scene played through his mind. "Then I opened the valve on a tank of propane. A candle set up in the forward V would touch off the gas when it reached that level. I had opened the sea cocks down in the engine room to be sure the boat would go down no matter what. Then I got in the dinghy and cast off. The damn motor wouldn't start, and I forgot the oars. So in a panic, I hand paddled to get away from *Jezebel*. I thought I might go up with the boat when it blew. I got far enough off, though.

"In seconds after the explosion, the boat was blazing. I saw Buddy stagger out to the rear cockpit. He was all aflame." Norm paused and took a labored swallow of water from his glass. "It was ghastly. He had his arms spread out like Christ on the cross, flames curling around his head. He saw me, sitting there in the damn dinghy. In a voice, croaking like a demon from hell, he called my name. I don't know if he understood what I had done. He may have expected me to help him, or he may have been giving me a curse. I'd feel better if I knew it was a curse."

Mike looked off, vacantly gazing about the room and uneasily considering his indirect guilt in Toops's terrible death. "It seems the Lotto ticket became a curse for all three of us," he said in a barely audible voice.

Silence settled in the room, as if mutual guilt had taken away their voices. Roy sat stiffly erect in a straight-back chair by the bedroom door, his face blank and nonjudgmental. Norm lay deathly still, his eyes closed, as if pondering Mike's last remark. "Yes, it turned out that way," he said finally. "I'd be dying anyway, in Seattle, though, and without Buddy's ghost."

"If you weren't going to give Buddy his slice, why didn't you just take off and leave him?"

Norm sighed. "I had intended to. We had one hundred thousand dollars wired to his bank. That was supposed to be the convincer that I was playing straight with him. I told him if he kept quiet about my part, he would get the rest of his share. He seemed to buy that. He knew, or thought from what I had said, that I didn't want my wife to know about the money."

Mike winced at hearing that.

Norm went on. "His secrecy was important to me. Originally I planned to get him drunk and send him home in a cab. Then after blowing the boat, I'd use his car to get to the bus terminal. I had the spare ignition key. I'd leave it on some side street with a few empty beer bottles laying on the floor. Buddy would think it had been stolen for a joy ride by some teens."

"He wouldn't suspect you?"

Norm turned away and gazed emptily at the ceiling. Mike's patience began to fray, and he was about to repeat the question when Norm turned toward him again. "I didn't think so. Like everybody else, he'd think I went down with the boat. Then he would probably start scrambling to find the rest of the money. That's what I thought, anyway. But that night, just as we started on our first drink at Ray's, he pops off saying he knows about the money going offshore. Said he guessed I was going to take off and cut him out of the nine hundred thousand and the story about my wife was bullshit."

"How'd he figure that?"

"He went to the bank. Took a look at the wire transfer order. Saw the money was going to Antigua."

"He could have told the bank to cancel it."

"Yeah. He was smarter than I thought, though. Said he figured there was more to this scheme than what I had told him, more than just keeping money from my wife. I tried to convince him that the money was going offshore to be sure it was secure. He said, 'Secure from who? Your wife? She doesn't even know about it.' Then he came on real strong, the little punk. I didn't know he had it in him."

Norm reached for his glass on the nightstand, lifted it, noticed it was down to melting ice, and set it back. "He said if I didn't level with him, he was going to the bank first thing in the morning, before the wires go out, and cancel the order. I was a little surprised he hadn't already done it. He looked me in the eye and said he thought we should consider a change in our deal. Christ, I knew he meant a bigger piece for him. I got a little panicky. So I told him the truth, or at least a version of it." Then he paused for a moment.

Roy came over to the bed. "Want anything?"

"Yeah." He pointed to his water glass. "Put some gin and ice in that."

"Gin?"

"Yeah…don't worry about it."

Roy took the glass and left the room.

"Where was I?" He asked Mike.

"You were opening up to Buddy."

Norm nodded. "Anyway, I told him the ticket was stolen from you, told him about the ruckus in my office, and said we had to keep the money out of your reach. That shook him a bit. I said you didn't have any proof of ownership, but there could be a trial. He didn't like my story."

"I don't blame him. Didn't he think it odd that we were meeting on your boat?"

"Yeah, he did. But I'll get to that." He wrinkled his brow. "So, anyway, he's sitting there, studying his drink, then tells me we have a new plan. He realizes now that neither one of us can stick around and hope to hold you off. I agreed with him. So we are fifty-fifty partners now—that's what he said. I couldn't think of what to do."

Roy returned with Norm's drink and set it on the bedside table.

Norm nodded his thanks and took a pull. "Ahh, I needed that." He looked over at Mike. "You want anything?"

Mike thought some gin would be nice, but he said no. Then as an afterthought, he asked, "Got any beer?"

"Yeah, we do," Roy said, and he left to get it.

Norm took another taste of his drink. "I could see I had a problem, one I didn't expect. If I left Buddy behind now, you'd find him and he would rat me out. I could take him with me, but that involved too many problems. Faking my death was key to my plan. I knew that I'd lose everything if you or the police found me. So I said okay, I guess four million would be plenty for me anyway. That brightened him up. Then I gave him a little more of the story. Explained that I'd invited you to a meeting at Shilshole as a ploy. Set you up for destroying the boat and my murder. His eyes popped nearly out of his head. He said he didn't think I was that diabolical."

He paused to gather his breath. "Then I explained that we couldn't leave a trail. We'd both have to appear to have gone down with the boat. I told him I'd call my wife from the restaurant and tell her that I was taking him along as a backup when I met with you, in case it got rough again. He seemed to buy that. We shook hands, and I ordered another round. Doubles. Then I went to the lobby and pretended to make the call." Norm took another pull on his gin.

"So Buddy was a little too smart for his own good."

"Yeah. You could look at it that way. Doesn't help me much, though."

"I had intended to attempt some sort of bargain with you," Mike said. "We'd split the money, you'd give me some evidence you were alive to clear the murder rap, and in return I would leave and keep quiet about your whereabouts."

"Why should I believe that?"

"So what if you don't? I know the whole story, and you're gonna die anyway."

Norm's rheumy eyes half closed then widened a bit. After a few seconds, he said, "You have a different plan now, though."

"Yes." Mike couldn't tell if Norm was interested or just stringing him on. "Oh, and I intend to give eight hundred thousand to Maxine."

Norm blinked at that. He considered what Mike had just said. "You been balling my wife?"

"Yes. But what do you care?"

"Maybe I should."

"I can see it's breaking your heart. You dumped her in a hole. She can't do anything. Your practice, the life insurance, house, car—everything sits as is until you're declared dead. And I doubt you intended to send her a notice. No, it's not because we had a romp in the hay. I'm giving her a share because she is the one that got the lead on you, and she shared it with me."

Norm closed his eyes again.

"You victimized both of us, Norm. It seemed it was only fair to share whatever I get here."

Norm lifted his lids to a squint and studied Mike's face as if he might see some sign of dissembling.

"But now, Norm, I'm going to suggest something that might help settle your mind." Mike's voice was emotionless, almost deflated.

"Oh my. What could that possibly be?"

"Redemption. Maybe for me too."

Mike was waiting for Norm to laugh or curse or even order him to leave. But he didn't. He lay there lazily focused on the ceiling. "Redemption, huh? You're not just dumb, Collins, you're crazy."

"You're probably right. Unless we agree, though, when I return to Seattle, your name will be shit. It'll be worse than that."

"Do you think I care?"

"I think you do. You're not a rich gringo in PC anymore. You're a rotting, dying cheat. The only thing you have left to be concerned about is your name." Mike raised the level of his voice. "You want to piss that away too?"

Roy jumped up from his chair and studied Mike, waiting for another outburst.

Norm let his lids droop, composing his answer. "Look, Collins, the cat's out of the bag now. When you get back to clear the murder charge, what I did will be front page."

"Some of it, I suppose. But not Toops."

"You'd be quiet about that?"

"Yes. Can't see any point in mentioning it. You've already been given your death sentence." Mike studied Norm's eyes. "And if we agree here, I don't think I'll go back anyway."

Norm turned his head toward Roy. "Roy, I think I'm ready for a hit."

Roy went into the master bath, fiddled with something, and returned with a syringe. He pulled the sheet back from Norm's hip and plunged the needle into the flaccid flesh. After a minute of silence, Norm pulled in a deep breath and let it out slowly.

"Yeah, thanks."

Roy nodded and returned the syringe to the bathroom. Mike could hear him in there, readying for the next shot, maybe taking one himself.

"Okay, so what's your deal?"

"Can we talk alone?"

"Why? I don't keep secrets from Roy."

"I'll bet you do."

Norm studied Mike's cold, emotionless face. "Okay. Uh, Roy, would you excuse us for a few minutes?"

Roy frowned as if he didn't like that idea, but he didn't object. "Sure." He stole out and closed the door behind himself.

Mike waited a moment. "What did you do with the cash? Convert it?"

"Yes, bearer bonds."

"I didn't know they issued them anymore."

"In Europe. There's no trail when you move them around."

"So what happens to them three weeks from now?"

"I can't decide."

"You gonna give them to Roy?"

"He might think so, but no." Norm looked toward the door to see if it was still shut.

"But you're going to leave him something."

"Yes. I was thinking forty, fifty grand. That's a lot of cash down here. Especially for a few months' work."

"And the rest?"

Norm was tiring. "I just told you; I don't know."

"All right."

Norm turned away, his eyelids lowered.

Mike thought he might be drifting off. "Norm, pay attention now, God damn it. This isn't what you would have expected. Not from me, anyway. It amazes me that I'm even suggesting it."

# CHAPTER 38

Sunday morning, Lorene pulled in to the hotel lot at 8:10. Mike had been waiting in the lobby and bounced right out when he saw her car. He smiled as he climbed aboard.

She was wearing a white cotton sundress that was scooped low, exposing the top third of her breasts. As a compromise to modesty, and probably to placate her mother, she had a gossamer shawl over her shoulders that tempted more than it concealed. She noticed Mike's interest. "Like my dress?"

"Indeed. You're a beautiful woman, Lorene—beautiful no matter what you wear."

She smiled. "Thank you." She saw that Mike had a carnation. "For me?"

"Your mother," he said. "A little thanks for her hospitality."

The corners of her mouth drew back in a wry smile.

"You seem in a good mood," she said. "Did you see Mr. Feinberg yesterday?"

"Yes, I did. It went very well. There's a lot I want to tell you. Perhaps after church we could stop for a coffee or something. Oh, yes, and I will be needing your help this week."

"My help? Well, if you don't have other plans, how about a visit to Casco Viejo? Quite a lot to see. We could have lunch there, and you can tell me all about it."

■□■

They met her parents in the church vestibule. Mrs. White was polite, but cool. She graciously accepted the carnation and said it was her favorite flower. Mike already knew that.

After mass, they loitered at the church entry for a moment; then Estelle, rather uneasily, suggested a noon meal at their home.

"That would be nice, Mother, but I'm taking Michael to Casco Viejo." Mother and daughter traded sidelong glances.

Mike was pleased at the prospect of another day with Lorene, but was surprised she was willing to spend so much of her free time with him. Estelle held her cool look as they bade good-bye. Lorene assured her that she would be home early. On the way to her car, Lorene smiled and said, "Mother doesn't interfere, but she remains protective."

"A sign of love."

"Yes. It can be seen as distrust sometimes. I hope you don't feel offended by her impassive way."

"Not at all. She has her doubts about me, and I don't blame her. Here's a troublemaker ne'er-do-well, imposing on her daughter. I'd feel the same."

As they drove into the San Felipe district, Lorene explained that Henry Morgan and his pirates destroyed the original city in 1671. "What's left of the ruins is called Panama de Viejo, or ancient Panama. Then in 1673, they began rebuilding in this area, which is called Casco Viejo, or old central city. Since Panama was the transit point for travel and shipping across the isthmus, the city grew. As it expanded and newer neighborhoods developed, this area fell into decline. The exceptions, of course, were the government buildings and the cathedrals, which were well kept, as you can see."

It pleased Mike to have Lorene telling him all this. The history was interesting, of course, but he felt she must trust that he respected her for more than just looks. "Well, the church and the government always do seem to take care of themselves," he said.

She smiled. "Yes, they do. And while they managed, Casco Viejo became almost a slum. Now, though, as you see, it is undergoing renewal. Restored houses stand next to dilapidated ones, which eventually will be restored also."

Mike noticed that the condition of some of the structures was so bad that restoration didn't seem practical. Yet there they were, propped with scaffoldings and foundation jacks. "In the States, we'd tear these down and build new. I'm sure they could replicate the architecture. It would be much less expense."

"Yes, it seems they wish to preserve as much of the original as possible, though. And you are right about the expense. As these old places are restored, the current tenants can no longer afford them, only the well-to-do."

She found a parking spot near Simon Bolivar Plaza. The air was still and quite warm under the late-morning sun. Lorene removed her shawl. "I thought we'd visit the International Museum, Santa Maria Cathedral, the Presidential Palace, and Las Bovedas."

"Whoa."

"Oh, there's more, if we have time, and if we don't, perhaps that will give you a reason to return to Panama."

"I already have one."

As they hurried along, Lorene offered a commentary that gave the history of each place, with some fascinating vignettes tossed in to add flavor. Other tourists started to follow them. "You could be a tour guide here," Mike said.

At 1:30 she suggested a restaurant near the French Embassy. The menu promised a memorable meal. They ordered a Muscadet to start, and Mike began describing his meeting with Feinberg. "I expected a confrontation, but it didn't happen. He's dying, and was surprisingly amenable to my proposal."

"Death does that. Takes the fight right out you."

"Yes." He smiled at her bon mot. "It's cancer. He says he'll be gone in three or four weeks. The illness, and what occurred in Seattle, changed him. I guess you would expect that."

Lorene nodded and sipped her wine.

"I've also found since being down here, though it's been just a few days, that I have changed some myself."

"For the better?"

"Yes, I think so. I can't say I've become a better person, but I seem to have a more earnest sense of things now." He smiled. "As if that means anything."

Lorene returned his smile. "I would think it does."

"I've spent my life being too casual about things—school, my job, whatever—and I should have been more strenuously involved in a lot of it. That sound too maudlin?"

She wrinkled her brow. "I don't know."

"Anyway, I seem to feel more interested in others now. In their welfare, that sort of thing." He focused on her eyes for a second. Then, with a facetious smile, he said, "Hopefully it won't last. I'd hate to think I have matured or reformed."

"Well, if not matured, more venturesome certainly."

Mike didn't know what she meant.

"Did you see the Saturday paper? Oh, no, you wouldn't since it's in Spanish."

"What did I miss?"

"A brief article on page two about this daring burglar that broke in to a real estate office. He came in through a second-story window. Then when accosted by a janitor, he set fire to a trash basket, brazenly hurled it at the man, and made a dashing escape. The janitor said, luckily, he wasn't injured. He added that the assailant was an Anglo." Lorene smiled broadly. "What do you think of that?"

"I toast the burglar's quick thinking." Mike lifted his glass in a salute.

"Yes, I was thinking that myself." She smiled. "Do you suppose the janitor noticed your newly softened heart?" Her grin widened and they both began laughing.

"Okay," she said as they were finishing their entrées. "How is it I am to help you?"

Mike leaned forward. "Feinberg has the money in bearer bonds. Keeps them in a bank vault. His man is picking them up Tuesday morning."

"The entire eight million?"

"Yes. Well, aside what he has spent."

Lorene blinked. Mike went on to explain his agreement with Feinberg and how she could help. She was dumbfounded.

As they left the restaurant, Mike noticed Riley standing behind a parked car across the street.

# CHAPTER 39

Mike was back at the hotel a little after four. He immediately tried calling Janet. There was no answer. Then he remembered she often worked on Sunday and it was 2:15 in Seattle. He decided to try again later. The TV in his room carried three English-speaking channels: CNN, ESPN, and the BBC. He skipped around among them but was too hyped to center his attention on anything. At seven he gave up and ambled up the block to Via Veneto. As he crossed Morales, headed for the Las Vegas Hotel, he thought he spied Riley slogging along about forty yards back. Maybe he should let Riley catch up and invite him to join him. But when he looked back, Riley had disappeared.

The Las Vegas had a wine bar restaurant that, in addition to an extensive wine list, offered a nice selection of dinner entrées. Mike ordered a glass of Sangiovese and a pasta salad.

■□■

At nine he tried Janet's number again. She picked up on the third ring.

"Well, did you get your credit cards canceled?" she asked.

"That's why I'm calling. The Visa number was wrong. I might have made a mistake jotting it down."

"I can believe that. That's all you do, make mistakes."

"Janet, you're so sweet to say that. I'm getting diabetes just listening." He paused, waiting for a reply. "Could you just give me the damn account number?"

"Sure, but why did you wait two days to call once you learned it was incorrect?"

"I've been on a religious retreat."

"Drunk, you mean."

"Yes, that too."

Janet found her Visa card and read the numbers to him. Mike pretended to copy them, repeating each one as she read it.

"So how much longer do you expect to be in Panama?"

"I'm not sure. I know where Feinberg lives now. He has been away for a few days, so I haven't seen him. But he's coming back, and I'll see him Tuesday afternoon."

"You talked to him?"

"Telephone."

"And he agreed to see you?" Janet was amazed.

"Yeah. He seems to regret what he did, stealing my ticket."

The line was silent for a moment while Janet considered that surprising development. "So then, what do you plan to do after you see him?"

"Let's just say that's my little secret. But I don't think I will be returning to Seattle."

Janet found Sheldon's home number in the directory. His wife answered and said he was staying at the Granada. She didn't have the telephone number. Janet went on the net and found the hotel's Web site. Mains had just returned to his room from dinner when her call came through.

"I just talked to Mike," she said.

"Yeah." Mains sounded edgy.

"Something wrong?"

Mains sighed. "Not that it matters, but I hate air travel. It took twenty hours to get here. Two stops on the way. I think we flew over most of the United States. Sitting that much constipates me. I'm drinking magnesium citrate, and I hate that too."

"Oh."

"Yes, and I'm immediately sorry that I just shared that with you."

Janet was going to suggest an enema, but then thought better of it. "Well anyway, he called about the credit cards again."

"Uh-huh."

"And he said he was meeting with Feinberg Tuesday afternoon."

"He said that?" Mains perked up. "Why would he tell you that?"

"I don't know. He said he had talked to him over the phone and Feinberg agreed to a meeting. He said Feinberg regretted what he did."

"Well, we know he hasn't seen Feinberg yet. Apparently he's been in a clinic or something for a couple days."

"How do you know that?"

"Riley, our detective, bribed the condo attendant. I don't think Mike knows I'm down here, but that story he gave you may be a ruse to put us off. Doesn't matter; we're keeping our eye on him. We'll be there no matter when he has his meeting. I'll have a local attorney and a policeman with me. Put some heat on 'em. If Feinberg refuses our terms, I'll notify Seattle police and have him extradited. The local attorney will have a court order freezing the money. I'm not sure how well that works, but I don't expect it to go that far."

Janet hoped he was right. "You think Feinberg·will just surrender the money?"

"Unless he's a fool. The money won't do him any good in jail. I think he's smart enough to give us your share and then quibble with Mike over the rest."

"Mike said he plans to take off once he gets the money. Said he wasn't coming back to Seattle."

"I'm not surprised. But we'll have your share before he gets anything."

"You suppose Feinberg has the money in his apartment?"

"I doubt it. He'll have it in a bank, maybe invested in a brokerage account someplace. It will probably take a few days to liquidate the four million."

■□■

Tuesday, trusting that Riley was somewhere watching, Mike spent half the morning in the hotel café, drinking coffee and reading the *Herald Tribune*. Then he strolled over to Via España and browsed the shops. At Tres Monedas he bought a ten-dollar watch, a Timex knockoff. Finally, at 2:30, he slid into one of the waiting taxis outside the hotel.

At the Azulaire, the lobby attendant told Mike as he came up to the reception desk that Mr. Feinberg was expecting him. "Go right up," he said.

Roy met him at the door, wearing a rather cheerless look. "They're in the living room."

Feinberg looked better today. He was erect in his wheelchair, wearing a fine dressing gown that hid his frail arms. His hair had been brushed, and he was freshly shaved. Feinberg turned his head toward the other guest, who stood as Mike entered the room. "This is Michael Collins, Don Belasco. He is my unlikely partner in today's affair."

Belasco extended his hand. As they shook, Feinberg continued. "And this is Don Miguel de Belasco, Michael. Don Belasco is a provincial judge here in Panama City and a member of the board at Malambo."

"The pleasure is mine," Belasco said. "You can't imagine how much your help will mean to the orphanage." Then he pointed to a file folder on the coffee table. "Perhaps we should get right to our paperwork. Señor Feinberg said we may have visitors here very soon to contest the disposition of the funds."

"Yes. I told my wife about this meeting and that Feinberg would be surrendering the money. A detective, I believe hired by her attorney, has been watching me, so they know I'm here. I feel certain that they will have someone come to intervene. Her attorney might even be here himself."

"We could have met and executed these papers covertly. I don't understand why you induced them to interfere."

Mike nodded. "Yes, that might have been easier, avoid the confrontation. But I want the matter settled here and now. I don't want Janet's attorney or private investigators hounding me or Feinberg, looking for money. I want them to know, as certainly as we can convey it to them, that the money is gone. We don't have it."

Belasco looked over toward Feinberg, who nodded his agreement. Then Feinberg turned to Roy. "Roy, would you call the lobby and instruct the attendant that I expect additional guests, but to check with you before sending them up."

Roy nodded and left to make the call.

■□■

Earlier, while Riley kept watch on Mike, Mains was at the office of the attorney he had retained as local counsel. They had just secured the employment of an off-duty policeman. Riley's call came through as they were finalizing the arrangement.

"He just left in a taxi."

"Okay. We'll meet you at Feinberg's place. We have to pick up our muscle. Be about thirty minutes."

Twenty-five minutes later, their taxi pulled up to Azulaire's dramatic entry.

"Mr. Feinberg is expecting you," the lobby attendant said. "I will tell him you are here."

Mains blinked at hearing they were expected.

A man was standing in the doorway as the elevator door opened. "Here," he said almost as a command.

As they ambled over, Mains maneuvered to the front.

"Who speaks for this group?" the man asked.

"I do, and who are you?" Mains blurted.

The man glared into Mains's eyes for a second. "I am Señor Feinberg's *mayordomo*, Roy. You may introduce your party to Mr. Feinberg and his guests."

Mains didn't say anything, and they quietly followed Roy down the hall.

As they came to the living room archway, Mains stopped to glance into the room, assessing its occupants. His little entourage—Riley, the young Panamanian attorney, and the uniformed policeman—all halted abruptly behind him.

Feinberg made a wan smile. "Mr. Mains? I am Norman Feinberg."

"Yes. Sheldon Mains." Puffed up with confidence, Mains stepped into the room and over to Feinberg, sitting in a wheelchair. They shared a limp handshake. Mains studied Don Belasco and ignored Mike.

Feinberg noticed. "Permit me to introduce Don Miguel de Belasco. Don Belasco is a provincial judge here in Panama."

Mains was momentarily surprised and wondered what role the judge might play in their little tête-à-tête. They shook hands. Then Mains gestured toward his support group. "Permit me to introduce my associates." He beckoned them forward. As they stepped into the room, the policeman, dazzled by its grandeur, missed the shallow step and pitched forward and sprawled onto the carpet. Mains could have shit, and he wouldn't need citrate. His grand entrance had become a farce. His smile was tight as the cop got back up, and then he forged on with the introductions. They all shook hands. Mains gave Mike a cursory nod.

Riley found a comfortable chair, and the policeman went to the window to admire the view and remove himself from Mains's glare.

"Well, Sheldon," Mike said. "Down here on your hourly rate or, more likely, for a contingent cut?"

"I don't see that my terms with your wife—ex-wife—should be of any concern to you, Mr. Collins." Mains scowled. "But enough of that. I shall come right to the point." He turned toward Feinberg and Belasco and, in his somewhat stentorian voice, he announced, "I am here representing Janet Collins. Janet was Michael Collins's wife at the time he purchased the winning Lotto ticket. Accordingly, under the community property laws of the state of Washington, she is legally entitled to one-half of the lottery proceeds." He directed most of his speech to Belasco, who Mains expected should appreciate the significance of law and agree with his demands.

No one responded to his opening remarks, so he continued. "We understand the Lotto check may have been negotiated contrary to Mr. Collins's instructions, but that is not an issue we intend to address. As I believe the funds are in your possession, Mr. Feinberg, I have a court order, obtained today, that enjoins you from the use or disposition of those funds until a hearing can be scheduled here in Panama."

He thought that would unnerve Feinberg. He waited for a response, yet no one spoke. He continued. "Now, that will be an inconvenience, to say the least. And since the outcome of the hearing is hardly in doubt, to save time and expense for all parties, I am prepared to set this injunction aside upon receipt of four point three million dollars, which is Mrs. Collins's rightful share." He looked at Feinberg, who seemed entirely undisturbed. "You and Mr. Collins can settle the remainder however you wish."

He pulled the injunction order from his briefcase and held it toward Feinberg as if it possessed a destructive power. The room remained silent. Mains felt victorious. It was easier than he had expected.

Judge Belasco stood. "You may serve that order if you wish, Mr. Mains, but it will have no effect. Mr. Feinberg and Mr. Collins have reached and executed an agreement. The lottery proceeds have been surrendered by Mr. Feinberg and, pursuant to the agreement, have been directly delivered to an irrevocable charitable trust. In addition, under the terms of their agreement, Mr. Collins waives any and all claims or action under law against Mr. Feinberg. And neither of them have the privilege of those funds any longer." Belasco then handed a copy of the trust to Mains.

Mains gave it a glance. "This trust may be properly drawn, Don Belasco, but Mr. Collins's assignment to it was a fraudulent transfer and we contest it."

"How so? Under Panamanian law, the husband is the manager of the marital estate and has the explicit authority to make such a bequest. Your challenge has no standing here and, I would expect, not in Washington State either."

Mains huddled with the local attorney, who kept shaking his head. Riley seemed to be enjoying Mains's frustration. The hired cop, bored by the unintelligible English babble, remained by the windows.

"Well, we're not done with Mr. Collins. You can expect judgments from our court that will invalidate his bequest. Now then, wouldn't it be reasonable to dismantle your so-called trust, settle Mrs. Collins's legitimate claim, and close this matter without further expense and anxiety?"

Belasco regarded Mains's increasing agitation. "I think I have given you our answer, Mr. Mains. But I will add, for your information, that Panama recognizes your federal courts only. State and county judgments from the United States are not considered here."

Mains winced. He knew that was correct and that federal courts rarely handled domestic issues. For several seconds, he struggled for control. He turned to Mike. "You worthless sot! How can you live with yourself? Thanks to your God-damned greed…" His mind skipped off the track for a second. "Can't you do the decent thing for once? Janet deserves her share; give it to her. You can donate the rest any way you like." He shook his head as if he couldn't believe any of it. "Look at the mess you've made for everybody." As he finished his castigation, he began to shiver as if Mike's evil ways put a chill in the room.

"You're not far off the mark, Sheldon. It was greed, and I regret it—more than you can imagine—but not because it deprived Janet. The money has brought out the worst in several of us, ironically probably you and Janet as well. So it's been given away, given to where it will do some good. I don't think any of us really deserve to have it. In a sense, Janet is getting her share. She is getting the same as me." Mike paused.

Mains stood wide-eyed, his face flushed with anger.

Mike went on. "Perhaps it is odd, but Norm and I have reached a kind of reconciliation. Not that we like each other suddenly or can forget the past…I think it's recognizing that continued enmity eats away your soul. You become the victim of your own bitterness."

Mains continued to shake his head in disbelief.

"Now I am not naive enough to think that you or Janet will ever feel that way. I don't care. You can hate me and make yourselves miserable. I will feel sorry for both of you." Then Mike smiled and slowly wagged his head, "I can't believe I just said that."

"Oh, spare me your pious bullshit, Collins. You made more sense when you were drunk."

"Probably."

Mains swept up his papers. "Well, we are not through with you. We have no intention of walking away from four million dollars that you seem so happy to just piss away." He turned toward Riley, still comfortable in his chair. "Are you going to just sit there? We're leaving, you dumb ape."

Before he left Norm's apartment, Mike said he would call Maxine to let her know how things had settled. "I'll explain that her eight hundred thousand dollars will come from the trust."

Norm showed fatigue. He nodded, but made no reply.

"I've told her about your cancer."

"Oh."

"Would you like to see her? I could suggest she come down."

Norm's rheumy eyes floated their gaze about the room. Then he said, in a soft, resigned voice, "No. No, I don't think she should come. I wouldn't want her clemency. And it will be better for her to feel completely estranged. No sympathies or maudlin reminiscence to complicate another relationship, which I hope she finds with someone."

Mike made his first call to the orphanage.

"Miss White is in a counseling session," the receptionist said. "Can I take a message?"

"Yes, tell her Mike Collins called. I'll try again later."

"Oh, Mr. Collins, I am certain she will want to take your call. Please hold for a moment."

When Lorene came on the line, Mike described the meeting. "You could say it all went as planned."

Lorene was ecstatic. "You can't imagine the reaction here," she said. "You are a celebrity. The nuns are planning a banquet. Can you stay a few days longer for it?"

Mike smiled at the irony. He was a celeb now. "That won't be a problem. I'm not leaving."

"You'll be here for a while, then?" she asked tenuously.

"Permanently."

"Oh." She hesitated. "Too many bad memories in Seattle?"

"No. I have one perfect reason to stay here."

Lorene understood the implication. "I think you will be very happy here."

■□■

Maxine was sorting through the mail when Mike's call came in. She was quite surprised by the turn of events in Panama. "So you gave it all to an orphanage, then?"

"Yes."

"Why the hell would you do that?"

"Right now I feel it was the right thing to do. Don't ask me a month from now, though."

"My, my. You go to Panama and get religion. Is it the heat down there…or the sight of a dying man?"

"Neither. Though drying out might have been part of it."

"Drying out?"

"Yeah. My heavy boozing days are over. I'm a social drinker now."

"Jesus, Mike, you're losing all your character. You'll fade away like a mist in the sun."

"I wonder about that myself." He paused for a moment. "Anyway, I wanted you to know your eight hundred thou will be coming from the trust. They agreed to that. You'll also get copies of the death certificate. Won't be long, he's fading fast."

"Well, I'll be getting the life insurance money then, even if I won't get the boat insurance payoff, since the Coast Guard proved Norm sank the boat on purpose. And I'll be able to sell the house. So I'll be okay. I could share the eight with you."

"No. None of the trust proceeds can come to me."

"Who would know?"

"Janet's attorney might find out somehow. He's relentless."

"Some news from my end—Bernard has given me a ring."

"Bernard?"

"Bernard Levine, Norm's partner...or ex-partner."

"Well, congratulations."

"Yeah. We couldn't set any kind of date, of course, till the business with Norm is settled."

"Looks like you can now."

"Yes...I guess so." Maxine pondered what Mike had told her. "I feel it's unfair. I get my share and you end up with nothing."

"I'll be okay. Norm deeded his Boquete place to me. I plan to sell it and use the money for a little business down here."

"A business down there? Now I know you're crazy. You're staying in Panama?"

"Yes."

"Addled by the heat, huh?"

"No, by a woman."

"Oh."

"Yes."